Marry Me Again

A Billionaire Second Chance Romance

Nicole Snow

Content copyright © Nicole Snow. All rights reserved.
Published in the United States of America.
First published in November, 2016.

Disclaimer: The following book is a work of fiction. Any resemblance characters in this story may have to real people is only coincidental.

Please respect this author's hard work! No section of this book may be reproduced or copied without permission. Exception for brief quotations used in reviews or promotions. This book is licensed for your personal enjoyment only. Thanks!

Cover Design – Kevin McGrath – Kevin Does Art.
Photo by Allan Spiers Photography.
Formatting –Polgarus Studio

Description

HE CAN BUY ANYTHING EXCEPT A SECOND CHANCE WITH ME...

KARA

Once, when I was young and stupid, I had *that* boy. The charmer, the Adonis, the one who torched every woman's panties in our small town. He was my brother's best friend, practically part of the family. When he proposed, he promised me forever.

Then the bastard disappeared without a word.

It's taken five years to get over Ryan. I drowned myself crying a thousand times over. I moved on.

I'm finally remembering what it's like to smile when *guess who* shows up. Everything about him is different. For one, he's become a freakin' billionaire. He walks like he's Mr. Tall, Dark, and Alpha incarnate. I know there's no justice in the world because his body matches his *huge* ego.

Worse, he wants me to play Cinderella again. I can't. I won't.

I don't believe in second chances. I'll never forget what he did.

And if he's stupid enough to try kissing me with those unforgettable lips, he's going to feel my teeth.

RYAN

I did a terrible thing. No, I'm not talking about the filthy secret that wrecked everything.

Leaving Kara killed me. I didn't have a choice. No amount of money, success, or bedding any woman I want whenever I flash my patented smirk makes up for losing her.

She was the one. Hell, she still is.

Time to remind her why. Whatever it takes to put my ring on her hand for good.

I'm ready for the curses, the screams, the burn of her palm against my cheek. I'll taste her lips again, even if she bites.

Just one catch – she can't find out what happened the night I left. There are no second chances if my past ruins us.

I: Love at First Tease (Kara)

The first time I see him – drinking him in with my puppy love eyes – he makes me bleed.

"Ow!" Pulling my finger up from the staples I'd been pulling in daddy's office, I survey the damage.

Two neat little pinpricks. A worthwhile flesh wound for the long, secret peek I snuck through the tiny window leading out to the garage, where the hottest boy alive is working on a Mustang from the seventies, raised with its metal underbelly sticking out.

It's a one way spy job.

He hasn't spotted me in here. Even if he had, why would he take a second glance?

There's barely time to suck my finger before daddy bursts in, his booming voice ringing out behind me. "Peanut, I need you to finish up in here, get home for dinner, and get cracking on your homework. I'll pay you for the extra half hour you're missing on the clock, so don't worry."

Swiveling around in his office chair, I smile with a quirk on my lips, quickly folding my arms to hide my injured finger. "I finished everything for school this morning before I came in. What's happening out there that makes you want to kick me out early?"

Daddy opens his mouth, but before he gets in a word, the loudest F-bomb I've ever heard shakes the whole building.

For a second, he's frozen, turning red and glaring through his open door. It's Mickey, one of his thirty-something full timers. He's sitting on a crate, massaging his knee, grinning up at his co-worker Jack, who just belted him in the arm.

"What the hell's the matter with you?" We hear him blubber.

"Man, I'm just doing you a favor. Worrying about the pain in your arm's gonna take your mind off that bum knee."

With a heavy grunt of disapproval, daddy kicks his door shut behind him. We both share a look.

I put my hands out, lifting my eyebrows. "Don't worry about it. Really. I've heard worse in the halls at school and –"

"Kara, no. I promised your ma I'd bring you here to work, not learn to cuss like a sailor. You're only fourteen, for Christ's sake. Hey, what happened to your hand?"

I can't hide anything from him. Daddy grabs my wounded hand, holds it in between his thick calloused palms, and takes a good long look.

"Poked myself pulling staples. Nothing serious."

"How did that happen?" His eyes search mine, as if they can't believe I'm less than perfect.

I shrug, refusing to tell him anything. Because that would involve confessing my crush on his newest, hottest employee. The boy who rarely smiles, and always makes up for it with a body that looks like it's been put on Earth to make every girl in a hundred miles break out their fans.

Daddy pushes past me, reaching into the cabinet overhead. He holds out a small Band-Aide and ruffles my hair a second later. "Put that on before you head out. I ought to make you cover your ears, too, but now I'm more worried about catching hell at home because I let you let you get hurt."

"Please. It was my fault. I wasn't paying attention." I roll my eyes. "Daddy, you worry too much. I'm not a –"

"You're my little girl, peanut, and that's the way it's gonna stay. Now go. Save me a spot at the table for dinner."

Defeated, I smile. There's no arguing with him, even if he can be as overprotective as a mother hen sometimes. "You know I will."

Turning, I make my way out the office, fixing the little bandage to my hand. I take a second outside before I head for the back exit, listening to the banter between Jack and Mickey. They're still ribbing each other with a dozen expletives packed into half as many sentences.

Then I look past them, and see him. He's reaching up underneath the Mustang, a wrench in his hand, his jaw clenched tight as he goes to work, flexing muscles no boy under twenty should have.

What the hell did this town do to deserve Ryan Caspian?

Easily Split Harbor High's hottest eligible bachelor. The

boy *every* girl in every class swoons over.

The walking question mark who showed up in town without a history. The one who aces every test and put the Greenthorne gang in their place his first day at school.

That's right. Everybody still talks about how Devon Greenthorne, the senior ringleader with the mohawk, got in Ryan's face and backed him into a corner with his goons. It lasted all of sixty seconds before Devon hit the ground, nursing a broken nose.

The bullies brought their heavy, sloppy strength to fight a lion. I only have to stop and stare to see Ryan's refined strength.

His oil spattered shirt clings tight while he's standing underneath the Mustang, his arms high over his head, biceps bulging like he's been lifting since he hit puberty. Only, no one at school has ever seen him in the weight room.

The very edge of his shirt rides up, exposing his abs. Until Ryan, I never knew what *washboard* meant.

Now, I understand. I see it in every rolling crease of his six pack, every time his skin ripples while he grunts, turning a bolt on the underside of the car, muscles bristling from head to toe. He's working, lost in his own world, completely oblivious to the older, rowdier men cursing and laughing like chimpanzees around him.

God. Eyeballing him too long starts to burn, no different than gazing at the sun. *I have to get home before he sees me.*

I'm about to move, when Ryan's wrench slips, and he brings it down against his thigh with a resounding slap. His face tilts toward me as he steadies himself. Then our eyes lock, and my heart forgets how to beat.

Eek. Holding my squeak in, I try to hide my blush and head for the exit, just as his voice rings out – deeper than it should be for a young man.

"Hold up, there's crap all over the –"

Too late. I'm practically running when I hit the oil slick. The world turns into black ice beneath my sneakers. I slide at least five feet before I hit the wall, spin around, and crash elbows first on the hard concrete.

As luck would have it, elbows first into the edge of the same grimy slick that took me down. The shame hits before I realize I'm already screaming.

The men around me aren't screwing around anymore. My voice echoes through Bart's Auto, alone and scared. Everything goes quiet in the garage except for Zeppelin banging away on the radio. Somebody grabs me under my arms, pulls me up, and tips my beet red face to theirs.

It's Ryan. I think I'm about to die on the spot.

Too many chemicals explode simultaneously in my brain to drink him in, up close and personal. I can't appreciate his eyes, as royal blue as Lake Superior's shores, or the little wave in his thick, dark hair. Not even the perfect dusting of stubble across his jawline – the kind that would surely make any girl lucky enough to kiss him burn for more.

I can't take in our resident Adonis because I'm too busy shaking, the hot, prickly shame overwhelming me in waves.

"Are you okay?" he asks, digging his fingers into my shoulders reassuringly.

"Okay?" It's a whine.

Are you kidding? That's what I think, but I can't form words, much less fire sarcasm his way.

It doesn't matter. Before I can say anything, he's got his arm around me, leading us to the little work bench in the back where the boys keep towels and rags to clean themselves up.

I'm still speechless when he starts cleaning me, very gently, slowly soaking up the oil splattered on my arms. I don't know whether to shut down or say thanks.

He probably thinks there's something wrong with me because I haven't said a word since I all but tumbled into his arms. There's just that worn towel in his hands gliding across my skin, him stealing concerned glances every time he brushes the grime away.

It's almost a brotherly look. *Ugh.*

The last look in the world I want from our local hottie. It's a cheap one, too. I can get big brother eyes anytime from Matt, when he isn't getting after me for taking too much time in the bathroom we share at home.

"What the hell's happening out here?" Daddy's booming voice rings out above us, and my anxious haze breaks.

"I fell," I tell him, my eyes on the floor while heat lashes my cheeks. I'm about three seconds from going up in a puff of smoke once the shame hits combustion level. "I wasn't looking, and there was oil on the floor."

"It's my fault, sir." Ryan stands, stepping in front of me, almost like he's offering protection. "We should've had a sign up. I saw her at the last second, and yelled out a few seconds too late. There's no excuse. It's company policy to have the warning signs up, and I didn't do my job. Never thought anybody else would be walking through here on a Sunday."

Daddy and me are just staring, listening to him talk.

Has he lost his mind? He's standing there, straight as a soldier, telling my crazy-eyed father that he's the reason his little peanut nearly broke her back.

For a second, daddy glares at him. I'm expecting his huge ex-Navy hands to reach out and wrap around Ryan's muscular throat.

"Kara, cover your ears," he says, voice as deep as thunder.

I oblige, but I press so lightly I can still hear everything through it.

"Kid, you fucked up," daddy says, stepping up to Ryan until there's barely an inch of space between them. "You put a co-worker in danger, and not just any worker, but my daughter. That said, you do good work. *Damned* good work for a sixteen year old. You don't complain, you punch the clock when you should, and you're more mature than you ought to be for somebody who's had it rough, going through who knows how many foster homes before you wound up here. If you want, you've got a bright future doing cars or just about anything else. That's why I'm going to cut you some slack, just this once."

"It won't happen again," Ryan says, bowing his head. "It's my mistake, and I own it. All I can do now is learn."

"You're right," daddy snaps, stabbing a finger into his chest. "You're also straight with me, I'll give you that. But I don't care if you're Honest Abe's long lost grandson, and you've got a magic ability to build me a Viper from the wheels up. We don't skimp on safety in this shop. Screw up again, cause anybody else to fall down on their ass, and you are fucking gone."

"Got it," Ryan says, holding his ground while daddy pulls his hand away.

He gives me a look over Ryan's shoulder that says it's okay to bring my hands down.

"You weren't the only one with no focus today. I'm having a talk with Jack and Mickey next. You've only been working for me six weeks. They've been here for twelve years, and they ought to know better. Here, do me a favor." He pauses, reaches into his pocket, and pulls out his keys. There's no warning before they're airborne, landing in Ryan's hand. "Drive my daughter home. It's only a couple miles, and she knows the way."

I don't know who's more surprised – me, or Ryan.

Guess he wants to prove there's no hard feelings. But Ryan's had his license for about six months. Sure, it's such a small town, daddy's other employees do little favors like this all the time.

Still, my father's trusting him with me. Alone.

"No problem," he says slowly." I'll have her home, and be back here with your truck in five or ten."

Daddy nods briskly, walking away without another word. I'm standing, but I'm barely processing the fact that

Ryan freaking Caspian is taking me home.

It's going to be the longest two mile drive I've ever had in my life.

* * * *

"You don't say much," he tells me, as soon as he starts the engine, checking to make sure I'm buckled in.

"I'm just as surprised as you," I say, eyeballing that unreadable expression on his face. It's so good at hiding whatever he's really thinking. "Why did he give you the keys after chewing you out?"

"Your old man believes in second chances. I screwed up, and owned up. Besides showing me there's no hard feelings, he saw how I jumped to help clean you up after the spill."

His eyes flick over while we're stopped at a light. He's either gawking at the total mess I've become, or noticing the notebook sticking out the top of my backpack's broken zipper, clutched tightly in my hand for stability.

"What's in there? List of all your crushes?"

My head turns slowly. I'm tired, I'm dirty, and I'm mortified that the only crush I've ever had is driving me home like the world's handsomest babysitter. Worse, if he digs too far into crushes, it won't take much for him to realize there's only *one* on my non-existent list.

"It's math homework, Ryan. Miss Harper's Geometry class."

"Oh, geometry. I did that like three years ago."

I turn my head back toward the window, flicking my hair angrily. Like he has to remind me how incredibly smart and gifted he is. By now, everybody in school knows he's a freak.

The Samson body has a brain attached, and it's brilliant. He's been skipped so far ahead in math and science, he's taking advanced classes at the local community college. He only shows up at our school half-days for English, social studies, and a few other electives.

"Didn't mean anything about the list. Just giving you crap," he says quietly, when we're just a couple streets away from mine. "Guess your parents don't let you date. It's cool, Kara, you're only a freshmen."

Only? This ride home from hell isn't getting any better.

Then he looks at me, a mischievous smirk pulling at his lips. "I'm not here to pry. Just meant to say you're going to have your pick when you're old enough to make it count."

"My pick? What're you talking about?"

He punches the accelerator, and we fly past the last few houses, before I motion to the little blue one on the right. He shifts the truck into park, pulling along the curb.

"Let's just see." Before I can stop him, he reaches for my bag, pulling the notebook out and flipping through it.

"Hey!"

Ryan whistles to himself, sifting through my equations and formulas. If he's looking for boy talk, he won't find it there. My friends and me have perfected our system, passing secret notes back and forth.

Too bad I forgot about the drawings. He hits the back of the notebook, stops, and turns it around on its end. I've drawn the world's derpiest looking caribou on the page, practicing a sketch for last week's art project.

I don't know what I was thinking. I let my mind drag my hand across the page with the charcoal, giving my poor animal antlers bigger than his body. Deciding to roll with it, I drew his eyes squinted with his tongue sticking out, like he's struggling under his own weight, trying to hold up the branches growing out of his head.

He starts laughing. Then, he can't stop.

I'm officially mortified. "What's so damned funny?"

"Quite the little artist, aren't you, Kara-bou?" he says, shaking his head as he pushes the notebook back into my hands. "That's the funniest thing I've seen in weeks. Why'd you leave his tongue sticking out? And those horns!"

"Because he's mocking jerks like you!" I sputter, angrily unzipping my bag to stuff the shameful secret away. As soon as the final version is done, I'm going to burn my stupid caribou drawing in the nearest fire pit.

"Hey, hold on, I didn't mean any damage." He reaches for my face.

The kid has the nerve to put his hand on my cheek, if only for a moment, stemming the flow of hot, angry tears fighting their way out. "I'm starting to see why everybody keeps their distance," I tell him, clutching my bag. "You're a dick."

Ryan's grin fades to a sly smile. It's like he has to think about the insult. I'm mad because that means it hasn't fazed him at all.

"You're cute– even if you're a little clumsy. Give it another year or two. You'll have guys falling all over themselves to take you out. You're gonna leave every boy in your class with their tongues hanging out." He's looking at me intently, honestly, but I won't let my eyes meet his. I don't dare. "Take it easy, Kara. Watch what's in front of you next time we meet."

I'm stuck. Fumbling for my seatbelt, I decide to overlook his last condescending, trademark Ryan Caspian remark and focus on the fact that he just called me – Kara Lilydale – cute.

His hand crosses the space between us, brushes mine, and pops the button for me. The belt rolls over my shoulder and snaps against the side. I'm halfway out the door, more relieved than I've ever been, before I stop myself and finally look back.

"Thanks for the ride home, Ryan. Keep staying on daddy's good side."

I run toward the house, hoping I can make it past mom and Matt without any side questions about the dark oil residue drying on my shirt and skin. Sometime between my shower and pre-dinner nap, I decide Ryan's playing an elaborate game.

I don't know why. There's no other reason he'd compliment my looks...right?

Sure, I can see myself changing in the mirror. I'm growing up, heading for womanhood, doing my best not to screw it up.

But no one's called me cute. Ever.

Maybe daddy has something to do with the shyer boys keeping away. Everybody knows his take-no-prisoners reputation. His shop hands out some of the best paying jobs in town to the kids who are the least bit mechanically inclined.

That doesn't explain why Mister Mysterious, Untouchable, and Perfect thinks I'm something special, and has the guts to say it.

Whatever's happening, it won't be a one off. He's rattled my head, and left his mark. There are only a couple hundred kids at our school.

I can't walk away from what happened today. I can't pretend it's nothing.

It's a guarantee I'm going to see him again. *Next time* – he said it himself.

That night, I lay awake beneath the covers, pulling about a thousand imaginary daisy petals. It's not a question of whether he loves me, or loves me not.

I'm frustrated, trying to figure him out, and I have an ugly feeling it's hopeless. I'm going to either kill this boy or kiss him before he graduates.

* * * *

Two Years Later

No matter how many times I sit down to dinner with him at our table, I feel like hyperventilating.

Ryan looks up when I come downstairs to take the seat across from him. My older brother, Matt, is blabbing on about his latest antics in some shooter game.

"Dude, I flamed his ass hard," my brother says with a grin. "He came at me as soon as he got a second chance, and I blasted him again."

They're the same age, but the maturity level gap between them could fill the sky. I don't know why they're friends, being such opposites. I guess even Ryan needs to lighten up on the broody, aloof act sometimes.

Part of me hopes he does.

"Kara-bou." He says my name and smiles, capturing my eyes in his stare, stark blue and deep as oceans. "Where you been hiding yourself all week? About time you showed up to join us."

"Dance recital," I say smartly, wondering why I have to spend my night off with homework and Ryan's barbs. It's like he expects the world to fall neatly to his feet, even when he's a guest in our house.

"Don't mind her," Matt says, brushing me aside with the wave of his hand. "She's too good for us now, hanging out all the time with her *boring* ass friends. Kara-bou used to be fun back when she drew those silly pictures, but the herd's got its hooks in her now."

The worst part about that pet name Ryan gave me a couple years ago? Everybody's using it.

My friends, my teachers, my dance coach. It's even turned up on daddy's lips a few times, as if it's a perfectly acceptable replacement for 'peanut' now that I'm getting older.

I give Matt a dirty look, but I don't reach across the table and push his soda into his lap, like I've done a few times before when he gives me crap. I don't want to catch hell from mom.

Besides, he isn't the one I want to punch. The boy who

deserves it is next to him, staring smugly across the table at me with his freakishly handsome face.

Two years have only added to his good looks, like a master sculptor putting on the final touches. Ryan's filled out. His muscles are bigger, harder, and more natural looking after years of hard work in daddy's garage.

He's still killing it at school, too, and he's probably going to graduate Valedictorian in a few months. That *really* irks the smart kids who got their 4.0s outside the college courses. While they're busy living high school drama full time, with all the rules, Ryan's bringing headphones to the lab and doing advanced work in math and programming.

Of course, all this means is that his head's about the size of a hot air balloon. To think he laughed at my stupid caribou drawing years ago for being way too top heavy.

Mom comes in just then, pauses next to the table holding our bread basket, and smiles. "Glad you could join us for dinner again, Ryan. How're Greg and Sally?" Her face softens as she sets down our piping hot slices of bread with a bowl of honey butter, completing the delicious feast laid out in front of us.

Ryan's smirk disappears. "They're okay. Busy as usual. I like eating here better. Dinner smells delicious as usual, Mrs. Lilydale."

Mom beams, but it doesn't completely erase the quiet concern on her face. We've heard the whispers.

Ryan's foster parents are the reason he's started coming around for dinner three, sometimes four times a week. They've been unemployed for awhile, several months after he moved in. Last year, CPS paid them a visit when too many teachers noticed him going empty handed at lunch, and Ryan slept over in Matt's room for the better part of a week.

Daddy calls them deadbeats. Losers. People hiding behind charity to enrich themselves, taking in older kids every so many years so they can use the extra stipend from the government to feed their drinking habits.

"You clean up so well, Ryan," mom says, sliding a chair out to join us. "If only Bart could freshen up as fast after work. We wouldn't be sitting here with our stomachs growling up a storm."

She taps her fingers impatiently on the table. Fortunately, we hear daddy's footsteps coming a second later. He walks into the kitchen and smiles, stopping to kiss my mother before he takes his seat at the head of the table.

Ryan might have brains, good looks, and an ego too big for our little town, but I feel like I'm the lucky one, watching him across the table while Matt whispers some crude joke in his ear. He cracks a smile, but it's different than the one he wore when he greeted me. It hasn't been the same on his beautiful face since mom asked about his folks.

I'm fortunate to have such a loving family. That's something Ryan's never had, if everything we know about him is right.

Of course, he always deflects. He never dwells on his problems, his past, or admits he has any issues. Nobody dares to tease him about his background after he established his willingness to throw fists at bullies asking for it. And my parent's questions about his family quickly fall away whenever he starts talking about school, or the latest haul he caught out on Lake Superior, fishing with Jack and Mickey.

I listen to the small talk after we've served ourselves, munching on garlic potatoes, asparagus, and meatloaf. A few minutes in, after we've given him our one-line answers about our day, daddy turns to Ryan.

"So, you got a better idea about how you're going to put those brains to use outside my garage?" he asks, a friendly interrogation that's been happening about once a month at our table since Ryan started his last semester at Split Harbor High.

"I've got a few big ideas, Mr. Lilydale. It'll take a lot more practice coding in my off hours when I'm not busy in your garage this summer. Hoping I can pick up another class or two in Marquette this summer to fill in the gaps in my knowledge."

Daddy's fork slips and clatters on the plate. "What happened to Ann Arbor?"

I pull on my skirt nervously under the table. Everybody knows he was offered *several* full ride scholarships to the best schools in the state earlier this year.

Ryan looks up, and glances at me, before looking daddy in the eye. "Degrees don't get a man anywhere with what I'm trying to do."

"Bull –" Ever the gentleman when mom's around, my father catches himself. "Son, you've got three tracks in life when you live in Split Harbor. Go to school, join the service, or get stuck here forever."

Matt nods across the table, silently agreeing. He's been talking to a recruiter with the Marines, eager for bootcamp later this year.

"You left out the fourth option. The one the Draytons did, and they've been riding high ever since."

My father smiles, shaking his head. "Things change a lot in a hundred years. Nobody's becoming a railroad and mining baron in this town or anywhere else in the U.P. You're a century too late."

He isn't wrong. Everybody knows the name of the most charitable, wealthy, and respected family in Split Harbor several counties over. Nelson Drayton, the seventy-something year old patriarch, just finished his last term as mayor. They're loved because they stay here and help us when they don't really need to.

The Draytons could move anywhere, taking vital money away from our town. They're the whole reason we aren't losing more people and hemorrhaging extra jobs. Sometimes, it feels like we're hanging by a thread tied to one family and a whole lot of history.

"It's never too late to see potential, just like they did a hundred years ago. Split Harbor needs jobs and new industries," Ryan says firmly. "This town can't lean on fishing and mining forever. We need to innovate. If I can invent something new, create our own little tech boom here in the U.P., we'll do something incredible."

I snort, unable to resist cutting in. "The Upper

Peninsula isn't Silicon Valley, and you know it."

My eyes turn away from a very surprised Ryan to daddy, who I expect to see looking on with approval. Instead, he looks sad, subdued, like he's too disappointed by what Ryan said to argue back.

He knows it's wishful thinking of the worst kind. We all do.

"Look, we can't keep leaning on the same old industries, or the decline is going to become a crash," Ryan says matter-of-factly, before he turns to my father again. "I know you don't agree, Mr. Lilydale. I'm old enough to respect a difference of opinion without getting mad about it. But I'm not giving in without trying."

"I just want you to have a good career, son. You've got a better chance at that than most, and it's a shame to throw it away without turning all those college credits you've already got into a proper degree. You're the only kid I've ever wanted to take off payroll for the right reasons."

"Come on, guys. My man's going to prove us all wrong." Matt cracks a smile, holding out a fist to his best friend. "He'll be making robots for me to chase down bad guys overseas in a couple years. Isn't that right?"

I roll my eyes. I'm scared my brother's played too many games to take the military seriously, and he's going to get himself killed hamming it up.

"Not in Split Harbor," I say. "This town doesn't have the skill to run a factory with robots, much less make them."

Ryan looks at me while he bangs my brother's hand with his. "If you're not going to scamper off after dessert, Kara-bou, I'd be more than happy to sit here and talk all about local economics."

He's challenging me to a debate. I want to stick my tongue out, but I'm supposed to be older and better by now. Immune to his teasing.

"Sorry, Ryan. I need to brush up on French before I turn in. Big test tomorrow."

There's been plenty of teasing lately, too. Little remarks behind the garage when I come out for some fresh air, finding him back there on his break. He doesn't smoke like the older men, just leans against the wall, playing with his phone, studying lines of code that look as impenetrable as Egyptian hieroglyphics.

Nobody knows it except the two of us, but we walked into dinner with tension guaranteed after what happened the last time I saw him.

It's just my luck that everybody thinks I'm the second smartest person in our school after the boy genius. His very presence doesn't make me flush anymore like a the sad little freshmen I used to be. I'll tolerate him, up to a point, but I'll never be *comfortable.*

Last week, we got into it over the school's funding for extracurriculars. I held my own.

He said the levies they passed last year, giving them a funding hike, were supposed to go directly to classrooms. I told him what happens after school is just as important. We need to fund sports and art programs, giving us a chance to round ourselves out before we hit college.

Ryan said I had a point, if only it was distributed equally, and the dance team had more chances to flash their short skirts in front of half the boys at school.

Like yours, Kara-bou. I remember how the bastard said it. *Especially yours.*

I hadn't blushed so hard since the day he dropped me off, savaged my dumb sketch, and called me cute.

Almost two years ago. Where does the time go? And what will another two bring?

"You know, dear, Ryan isn't the only one whose future should be under the microscope," mom says, spreading butter on another piece of her awesome artisan bread.

"Shit, ma, you want to hear about boot camp again?" Matt's face lightens up, gloriously oblivious to the glare daddy aims his way for cussing at the table.

"Not just yet," mom says sweetly. She reaches over and pats his hand, turning her attention to me. "I'm talking about our Kara-bou."

My freshly eaten food gurgles in my stomach when she says Ryan's nickname. "What, the immersion school?"

"You're going straight there if they let you in, and I don't care how much it costs," daddy says, looking happier than he has all evening. He's proud of something that hasn't even happened.

"Immersion school?" It's Ryan's turn to look glum. His baby blue eyes darken a shade as he looks at me, catching the light from an odd angle. "You mean you're leaving Split Harbor?"

This isn't his usual tone. His words are sharper, angrier, almost…betrayed.

I blink, surprised. "I haven't decided *anything* yet, honestly. It's not like it's official."

"You're being modest." Mom wags her finger. "If you want it, the letter last week practically said you're a shoe-in. Somebody at this table is going to Ann Arbor."

I sigh, picking at the last of my mashed potatoes. I wonder why the bar is always so much higher for me than Matt, not that he's letting anyone down by serving his country. It's almost like being sent away to study something intense and respectable has been in the stars since day one.

But ever since I applied on a whim and took their assessment, thinking maybe I could wind up a teacher or translator, my parents have been waiting with baited breath.

They don't get it. Yes, I want a good education. I'm just not sure I want to jump on the first ticket to Paris and a fast track Masters I'm offered.

"Well, I'm going to follow up next week, if that makes you feel better," I tell my parents, still glancing at Ryan. He's staring at his plate, quietly clearing the food, refusing to even look at me.

What's the deal? Did I say something wrong?

"Always had a feeling you'd graduate early," mom says, a constant smile on her lips now. "If you do this, Kara, you'll be out in another year. Right on the heels of our boys."

Ryan finally looks up and manages a smile. I think the way she says our boys, plural, really touches him somewhere beneath that mysterious, handsome mask he calls a face.

"Speaking of French, I really need to run. Can I be

excused from cleanup tonight?" I ask hopefully, plastering on my biggest fake smile.

Daddy frowns disapprovingly. No matter how well I do, he isn't one to soften up, or grant any special privileges.

"I'll take over clean up tonight. Let her study," Ryan says, sitting up extra straight. "It's the least I can do to say thanks for another home cooked meal."

My father lets out a low growl, buckling to the pressure. I narrow my eyes, staring at Ryan, knowing he's just made an offer my perfectly polite parents won't refuse.

What I don't know is why. He's always done favors before, but he knows full well what the usual expectations are. He never gets between daddy and me.

"Thank you, son. Very kind. Matthew, go help your buddy," daddy says, reaching for the rest of his beer in the bottle next to him. "Kara!"

I'm standing, halfway to the stairs, before I freeze, wondering what I missed. "Say thank you to our guest. He's taking your chores tonight, after all."

I turn, one hand on the banister, and try my best to imitate Ryan's mysterious smirk. It must work, at least a little bit, because his gorgeous eyes widen a second later.

"Thanks for the dishes, Ryan. I owe you one."

I turn around in a hurry as soon as the last part is out, racing upstairs. I'm not giving him a chance to wave it away like it's no big deal, especially when he's acting so strange.

Besides, if there's one thing I've learned when this boy is in the house, it's to avoid feeding his huge ego.

* * * *

I wake up with my French book slumped over my chest. It's the third time this week I crashed out early, my sleepy teenage brain getting the better of my over-study habits.

About a minute passes before I hear the noise. It's dark in my room, and someone is gently knocking. Except it isn't coming from the door – it's my window.

I slide out of bed, pad across the room, and pop the window open. "Ryan?"

He lifts himself up, swinging his legs over the sill, crossing into my room. Why is he here? He should have left after hanging out with Matt hours ago.

"Why didn't you tell me about the immersion school, Kara?" he asks.

Kara. Not Kara-Bou. His face is flat and serious beneath the dim shadows in my room.

I'm more surprised that he cares so much, rather than the fact that he's standing here when he shouldn't be, just after midnight.

"Why do you think it's any of your damned business?" Crossing my arms, I glare at him.

I'm tired of the guessing games. I'm also blushing because I'm standing in front of him in my nightgown. It's a silky princess pink, a little more revealing than I'd like near the top.

Ryan reaches out, grabs my hand, and brings it to his chest. "Because I don't want to lose you, Kara. You're practically family. You and Matt are the only true friends

I've got in this town, and your old man took me under his wing like one of his own."

I'm stunned. The man who never likes to reveal anything actually has a heart.

Deep down, maybe I'm also a little annoyed that he doesn't see me as anything except a surrogate little sister.

"Who knows," I say, letting him twine his fingers through mine. "None of this is set in stone. There's a good chance I'm going to wiggle out of it. I don't know if I want to graduate early, miss my senior year, go away to Ann Arbor, and then the other side of the world. I –"

"Be serious. Your dad's right. Opportunity like this doesn't just fall into your lap every day. Not for people like us, here in these little towns nobody remembers except when it's time to go on a summer drive."

"Well, it's *my* decision. Frankly, I'm getting a little tired of the pressure coming from everyone." I pull my hand away and turn, leaning into the fresh air spilling through the open window.

He's behind me, and I know his eyes are all over me. I've been disappointed too many times to think he might be studying my curves, looking at me differently, like more than his best friend's tag along.

The trouble with treating him like family means I'm just the annoying little sister. Never anything more.

"Kara-bou," he whispers.

Why won't he let this go?

His hand lands on my shoulder, and squeezes hard. "You're going to do great, whatever you wind up doing.

You're as smart as I am. You've got your shit together. I have big plans I'm going to chase – won't be able to live with myself if I don't – but there's no guarantee they'll go anywhere. You don't have to take my questionable risks to live a great life, and I'm happy for you."

I do a slow turn. My jaw practically hangs open. He's never been known for modesty when it comes to his genius. His hand stays on me, and when we're face-to-face again, I realize how close he is. Just inches apart.

"Thanks. Means a lot coming from Mister Perfect." I'm trying to sound sarcastic, but I actually mean it. "I wondered why you were acting so weird over dinner. You never cut in like that to cover for me."

"You needed the break. Things keep changing for everyone, and they're exciting. I'm on your side, Kara-bou. I know you're tired of everybody else breathing down your neck, telling you what to do. Never doubt it."

"Uh, I never did. Even before you came through my window." Remembering how he got here reminds me to keep my voice down to a low whisper.

We live in a modest house. Matt's room is next to mine, and my parent's isn't much further down the hall. If daddy catches him here, in the middle of the night, I don't want to imagine the consequences.

"There's something else," he says, loosening his grip, pulling his hand away.

It's back a second later. Both of them.

Heat spikes through my blood as his arms go around me. For a second, I'm wrapped in his muscle, bathed in his beautiful eyes. Anxious for what's coming next, even though I've never felt safer in my entire life.

"Fuck it. Kara-bou, I'm just going to come out and say it, because I'd be kicking myself if I let you jet off to Paris next year without telling the truth. I love Matt, your ma, and your dad more than I do my own family. You, though…you're more than that. You're all I think about after I've wrapped up for the day and I lay down on that crappy couch they give me to sleep on."

"Ryan…"

This is either a terrible idea, or the best thing that's ever happened. I'm scared to find out which. Fireworks are blooming in my young brain, and it seems like every sense has been heightened, like there's a steady current humming through my skin.

"No, don't say anything," he tells me, gently bringing one hand to my face. "Let me take you out. We missed prom a couple months ago. We've got the whole summer ahead, and I'm cashing in my savings for a car soon. I want you by my side. We'll go wherever you want, see if this works, or if it's just in my head."

Scared or not, I'm smiling. It's even cuter that he's doubting himself because I haven't said anything yet.

"As long as you have a plan to keep yourself from getting killed when daddy and Matt find out, I'm game. They're going to know what's going on as soon as I'm asking permission to hang out. I like you, too, Ryan, by the way." I bat my eyes, a giddy warmth spreading through my veins.

He grins. "We don't need to worry about them."

"Huh?" Panic shoots through my chest for about the dozenth time that night.

"I spoke to your family after dinner. Told them my intentions, and assured them I'd be the best boyfriend you ever had. They made it clear I'd be a dead man walking if I ever let you down – and I'd expect nothing less – but they gave me the nod."

I can't believe it. I'm lost for words, too, so I just wrap my hands around his broad neck and bring myself in closer, laying my forehead on his.

"You remember the day I called you cute? First time we really met, and I took you home, after you tumbled in that oil slick?"

"Yeah," I whisper. Like I could ever forget.

"I've been biting my tongue the last two years so it doesn't happen again. Holding in all the things I want to say. Hell, let's be honest, you're not cute anymore, Karabou." He pauses, moves his fingertips gently into my skin, tipping my face to his, forcing me to look at him. "You're beautiful. And you'd better believe I'm going to treat your beauty, your brains, and ever other part of you like gold."

There's about one second to prepare for my first kiss before his lips are on mine. It's rainbows, lightning, and crackling fire racing through my blood. My heart goes mad, pounding in my chest like a drum the whole ten seconds our lips are locked, exploring each other for the very first time.

When he pulls away, I've learned what *swooning* means.

"I have to get out of here before we get really crazy," he

says, brushing his lips against mine one more time. "We're going to be dynamite. Try be patient, Kara. I know, it's not easy – you've been wanting a piece of this for years, every time I see you give me that look across the table."

"Look?" *What look is he talking about?*

"Did not!" Smiling, I push him, trying not to laugh, knowing full well I'm lying through my teeth.

"I'll call tomorrow. Let's figure out where we want to go for our first date. I hear they're starting the summer tours at the Armitage Lighthouse next week. Awesome view up there. Perfect for a couple of history nerds."

"Yeah, perfect for you." I stick my tongue out. He laughs, and I blush, knowing I can't hide anything. "I'd love to check it out, Ryan. We'll talk after school."

We share one more smile, and he's gone, crawling out my window. I hear him bounce into the bushes, and run off into the night. I always feel bad when he leaves, knowing he has to go back to his disgusting, lazy foster parents for the night.

Tonight, there's extra guilt, because he deserves better. I hope he finds it sometime in the next year, whatever happens with us, especially now that he's turning eighteen and he can finally move out.

I'm going to make him happy, any way I can.

It's the least I can do. He's just made me the happiest girl in Split Harbor High, and I'm excited to see what it's like when a dream comes true.

II: Happily Never After (Ryan)

Eighteen Months Later

It's her eighteenth birthday, and we're heading to our favorite spot. Where the hell has the last year gone, anyway?

I can't stop thinking about it as we drive, the roads flanked by beauty, like entering a real life oil painting.

The trees have become a fiery band of red, orange, and yellow between Marquette, Split Harbor, and the surrounding counties. The hues near the Armitage Lighthouse are so beautiful they're almost blinding. It's late August, and autumn has come early to Michigan's Upper Peninsula. Almost like nature decided to give my girl her finest before she leaves for college next week.

Too bad they've got nothing on the hottest woman alive in the seat next to me, clutching the leather purse I worked my ass off to get her close to her chest. It's hunter green – her favorite color – a forest shade that fits her eyes.

"Why doesn't this get old, Ryan?" she whispers, laying her head against my shoulder. "How many times have we been here this year? About a dozen?"

"Not enough," I say, reaching for her hand while I pull into a parking space at the little park attached to the historic site. "The summer flew by. Think we only came here once between work and graduation."

She smiles knowingly. "I'm glad I slowed things down. I would've missed a lot leaving for Ann Arbor too soon."

"Yeah, you would've missed the hell out of hanging with your boyfriend." I give her the smirk that always makes her cheeks turn red, the same with a magic power to drench her panties. "And I would've hauled my ass down to your college every other week, just to put anybody stupid enough to come sniffing around you in his place."

"Nice save." She smiles, just as I cut the engine on my old Ford LTD. I got the car last year on a bargain after her dad helped me fix it up, and it's served me well ever since. "Better do something about the jealous tick. You're going to have to get used to me living on my own."

"We talked about this already," I remind her, a low growl rising in my throat. "I'll live with it, I'll support everything you do, but I don't have to like it. You're making room for me in that little dorm whenever I come down."

She nods, still wearing that kissable smile, squeezing my hand. "Let's go! I want to see the upper deck before the rain blows in."

Kara isn't kidding. Perfect sun beams highlight the glorious foliage on the way in. They won't last forever, judging by the dark clouds on the horizon. We've got thirty or forty minutes before it leaves Superior and hits the shore, if we're lucky.

Plenty of time for what I've got planned.

She hugs my arm like she always does while I lead her up the narrow metal steps, high into the lighthouse. This place is a hundred years old. It'd be derelict and falling apart without the Drayton's charity, preserving the piece of history that put our town on the map before the railroads and mining left their mark.

"Just beautiful." She releases a long, wistful breath as soon as we're at the top of the stairs on the observation deck.

The old light at the top was gutted a long time ago, leaving visitors more space to walk around and look out to sea. It's a quiet day, just like I expect. Most families are distracted, rushing their kids to school, changing gear for the seasons, too busy to take one last trip to the lighthouse before they return in a few weeks for peak fall colors.

"It always is," I tell her, leading us to the huge glass window overlooking Superior. "We're coming back every time there's a few days to spare. Don't think either of us can live too long without these familiar waters."

She smiles and nods. I'm dead serious about seeing her as much as I can, bringing her home on weekends. I'll drive all seven hours a thousand times if it means making the spark we've lit the last two years burn brighter.

I'm still at Bart's Auto. Earning about two extra bucks an hour than I did when I started. It's a living, enough to afford the one bedroom apartment in the duplex I'm renting on the edge of town.

Half the time, I'm too damned tired to hit my coding as hard I should when I get home after work and the gym. It's a dangerous rut, threatening to spoil my dreams, one lazy evening at a time.

No, I haven't given up. I never will until I've had my day in the sun, and accomplish something great, but I've learned to pace myself. There's another reason wild riches and success don't mean as much anymore, and she's standing right next to me.

"How does it feel to be eighteen, Kara-bou?" I turn, taking her hands and staring into her big green eyes.

The sun hangs lower in the sky, slowly creeping toward the rainy horizon, casting its fragmented light all over us. Perfection, your name is Kara Lilydale. Couldn't be more obvious than it is today.

Sure, she's always beautiful, but right now, in this light, she's fucking radiant.

"It's strange. I've seen you, Matt, and so many of my friends reach the magic number. I always thought I'd be ready. Thought I'd do something special to mark it. Instead, I'm just happy to be here, living in the moment, doing the same things we always do."

Smirking, I pull her into my arms, holding her close, running my hand slowly down her back. My fingers pass through her long blond locks. They're like silk spun gold in the Michigan sun, as vibrant and alive as the sun beams flickering out on the lake.

She doesn't have a clue what I have planned. Hell, I'm trying to believe it myself, wishing my balls would magically double in size so I can get it out.

I've never been so nervous in my life. Of course, I don't

show a damned sign of it. Nothing's ruing the surprise.

"You're just excited for your presents, birthday girl," I tease, holding her face with my hand. "Your old man's been bringing in a lot of extra business for the big day. Probably gonna buy you a new car packed to the brim with i-Everything."

"No iPad. He's probably trying to pay for my dorm alone. Ann Arbor isn't cheap. The scholarships and loans will help a little, but there's a lot left for them to cover." She looks at me slowly, her eyes narrowing a little. "You're the one who should be excited for tonight. It's *finally* happening, Ryan. Remember?"

My cock twitches hard in my jeans. Yeah, fuck, I'd have to be dead to forget.

I've been counting down the days until she became legal, crushing her beneath me during every make out session we've had the last few months. I had to keep myself on a tight leash every time she dropped another hint. Every raging instinct I have wanted me to take her then and there, but I promised to save this for today, the day I'm going to have her for all the right reasons.

"It's going to be incredible, baby," I whisper, my hand sinking low, grazing her ass. I lean in closer, pushing my teeth against her earlobe. "You've been waiting for your birthday promise, Kara-bou, so here it is: tonight, I'm going to make you *scream.*"

She squirms underneath me. My woman knows I don't make empty promises, and that goes double for sex. Plus she wants it just as bad as I do, aching to seal the love we've built the most primal way possible.

After sundown, I'm taking her cherry. What starts with a kiss is going to end with me balls deep inside her, claiming her the way I've wanted since we locked lips in her bedroom years ago.

"Can we check into our room early?" she purrs, wondering about the little place I've made reservations for, just on the other end of Marquette, a short drive down the shore. "I don't know how much longer I can wait, Ryan. Seriously."

Normally, I'd be all over that. But there's one more thing I have to do before I bring her to bed, strip her naked, and watch every beautiful inch of her moving, rippling, fucking beneath me.

I see it all. Every filthy, incredible movement I've imagined since I started bringing myself off to her several years ago.

Every dirty word. Every vicious kiss. Every moan leaving her throat, every grunt leaving mine, just before she wrings the come straight from my balls.

Fuck. If I graze her nipples now, I know they'll be hard, begging to be sucked soft.

"There's something else," I say, fighting to control the volcanic hormones raging in my veins for just a few more minutes. "I didn't just bring you up here for a birthday sendoff, Kara."

Her eyes go big, wondering, especially when I use her name without the pet part tacked on the end. I grab her hands, hold them in mine, so tight it almost hurt.

"Don't care if you go off to college, or Paris, or the

friggin' moon. I can't live without you, babe, and I'd be a fool not to do everything I can to show you I'm serious."

"Oh my God…" Her voice dies as I sink to my knees.

Thankfully, it only takes a second to reach into my pocket, picking out the carefully concealed box I've been carrying all day. It's taken me the entire summer to save up for the modifications with the jeweler, getting it re-sized and inscribed like I want.. As for the ring itself, I had a little help.

My thumb flicks the top open, and holds it out to her. "It's your grandmom's ring. Bart gave it to me this morning, after I told him I was going to marry you, and I wanted his permission first."

I owe her dad big time, it's true. Especially when he's been like a father to me for years, long before he's becoming my father-in-law.

Those beautiful breasts I can't wait to pillage bob on her chest as her breathing quickens. For a second, I'm afraid I've made a huge mistake, and she's going to say no.

Grabbing her hand, I grip it in mine, bringing it closer to the ring. "Look, I know we're young. I know this is sudden. Most people our age are focused on school, or figuring out what club they're going to hit the next night, and who their next fling is going to be. I don't care about any of that. The day I met you, Kara-bou, I knew you were mine. We're young, and people will bitch, but I don't care what they think. Fuck the crowd. I'm spending my life with you, love, every single day I can. By this time next year, I want to be planning our wedding, assuming you say you'll marry me." I'm rattling on like a fool, so I shut up and look at her, lacing my fingers tighter in hers. "Will you, baby?"

She answers me by falling down on her knees so hard the bang of bone on metal echoes through the lighthouse. I've seen her speechless before a hundred times, but she always gives me an answer.

This time, it's the best wordless reply I've ever heard. She jumps me, snatching at the ring with her free hand, bringing her hot little mouth to mine.

We kiss for eons, rolling around in the lighthouse, lost in each other for so long it's dark and raining by the time we finally stop for air. If it wasn't for the risk of retirees or oddball travelers popping in, interrupting our privacy, I'd take her here on the floor, having our first time overlooking the cool, choppy waves below.

"I love you, Ryan Caspian. I can't wait to be your wife."

Shit. She's serious.

The prettiest girl in town just said *yes*. It's the first time one of my crazy plans worked. Means so much I don't care if it ever happens again.

It's my turn to be speechless. She's just told me the best thing a man can hear. I'm only twenty, not even old enough to drink, but I know it's true. Know it every time my heart beats a little harder, staring at my new fiancee, imagining how hot she's going to look dressed up in white, coming toward me at the altar.

"Love you, Kara-bou, and it's getting stronger every day. I'm never letting go. Don't care if the sky breaks open and spills everything it's got on our heads. We're meant to be together," I say, my voice deepening an octave, pulling her closer in my arms. "A lot can happen when you get married as young as us. I'm ready, and I know you are too. Long as we remember everything we said here today, everything we promised, we'll make it. No doubt. I promise, babe, you're mine forever."

"I promise, too." It's the last little sound she makes before I wipe away the tears rolling down her cheeks with my lips.

"Turn it over. Look inside," I say, clasping the ring in her hand with mine, bringing it up to our faces.

Always, my love. Always, always, always.

I agonized over the text for weeks. Then I realized there was only one word fit for telling her how I really feel, one that won't ever change, no matter what the universe throws our way.

Overwhelmed, she leans in, kissing me again. Her mouth tastes hot, wet, desperate. I love it, every single brush of her lips on mine, our oneness overflowing in every sticky fusion.

My fingers cup her face, pulling her into me, dancing across the tiny scar she has from a gym class mishap a year ago. They were playing golf, and her friend, Zoe, wound up her swing too much. One blow to the face later, she's marked forever. I remember Bart bringing his little girl home from the emergency room, while Matt and I scrambled to help with ice.

I held the pack against her face while the stitches set. Many months later, it's healed nicely. The kind of perfectly imperfect scar that gives a man one more thing to fall in love with.

We kiss for another five minutes, her on my lap, the sun peeking out one more time through the rain to salute us. Then we're heading downstairs, walking through the cold, wet bullets to my car.

Hand-in-hand, we're engaged. And we're about to make this official at our hotel, loving each other in ways far more exciting than gold and diamonds will ever be.

* * * *

Two hours later, she's laid out on top of the sheets. Naked as the day she was born, and goddamned beautiful.

My cock doesn't need more than a second to turn into granite. Never does when her hands or mouth are anywhere near it, really. Except today, a charging bull couldn't knock down the hard-on pulsing between my legs.

I let her undress me before she laid down. Her little hands rolled up my shirt, undid my belt, and pushed down my jeans.

She gasped when she saw the new tattoos lining my shoulders, falling down my back like flaming swords. It's ink I've been slowly expanding whenever I have a little extra money. I love the fire because it reminds me to keep everything I've worked for burning bright on the tinder of my past.

I smiled at her knowingly, told her she could kiss it, scratch it, drag her tongue across the fire any way she liked.

My tattoos mean I don't look back. Not at the abuse

that sticks in my head some long, dark nights from my real parents – both of them junkies who left me alone most days in a ratty Detroit apartment. Not at the three sets of assholes who couldn't be bothered to make up for it, three bad foster families who starved me, kicked my ass, and used me as a government ticket to more booze. Not at the orphanage, or the system that failed me, because I turned out pretty good in spite of it.

Greg and Sally did the best, lazy drunks that they are. At least they weren't violent, and that isn't saying much. The last set of boozers to put a roof over my head left me on my own as long as I cleaned their dirty house. They did me a solid by bringing me to Split Harbor, though, because without their shit I wouldn't be standing here today, looking at the most beautiful sight I've ever seen, my cock in my hand.

I'm ready to claim the only woman I've ever loved – only one ever I will.

I move onto the bed and grab her legs, throwing them over my shoulders. She moans softly, closing her eyes. Doesn't take much to get her going today. Nothing except the faintest touch.

It's normally like that with the little things we've done before, yeah, but this is something special. She's shaking. She can't believe it, and neither can I, but the only cure is to fuck right through until it's real.

Nothing will stop me now. Her soft, silky skin feels so fucking hot.

I kiss her skin, inhaling long and hard, filling my lungs

with her scent. My eyes shift down to the sweet swollen pussy I'm about to own.

She smells incredible. My tongue burns, instinctively telling me she's going to taste even sweeter.

It'll be my first time sucking her supple little cunt, fucking her with my tongue. Can't hold in the smile when I think how she's going to jerk and scream once I get her going.

"Ryan…please!" she whimpers, her legs shaking gently in my hands, trying to pull apart.

Yes, please, baby girl. Her desperation makes my dick throb harder, and I feel a pearly drop of pre-come oozing out, landing on her thigh.

"What if I want to hear you beg a little longer?" I tease, knowing full well I'm playing with fire. If I don't do something soon, I'm going to shoot off on the bed like a fucking rookie.

My worst nightmare, something I've done everything I can to prevent with all the porn I've watched, my hand, and two girls I had before we met.

They're nothing compared to her. She's immaculate, sexy, her hips and tits calling me like sirens in the soft light.

"Keep your legs open," I order, grabbing her thighs with my hands, pulling them wider.

She whimpers when my fingers dig in. It's a prelude to the places where my lips land, falling across her sleek inner thighs.

Up, up, heading straight for her wetness, the cherry pink center between that's drawing my tongue like a magnet.

I kiss her pussy once. The sound she makes – a little half-whimper, half-moan – pours kerosene on the fire in my balls.

I need to eat this girl.

I need to fuck her.

One fine day, I *really* need to put my seed inside her, empty myself deep in her hot, wet cunt. Imagining how she'll look someday with her breasts and belly swollen from my kid sends a jolt down my spine.

Everything inside me turns rough and primal, ready to hijack every single inch of her.

No more teasing. I push my face hard against her steaming center, tasting the sweetness I've been thinking about all night.

"Ryan!' My name comes out like a curse and a prayer on her lips.

Doesn't she know it only makes me want to take her harder? I'm smiling when her whimpers get harsher, louder, turning into screams.

I lick up and down, toying with her virgin cherry, taking her apart with my tongue. My mouth tells me she's insanely tight. My pulse hammers in my cock twice as fast while I lick, suck, and bring my tongue against her clit, painting it with pleasure.

It takes maybe ten strokes there before she comes. My Kara tenses like a spring.

Every fucking muscle in her beautiful body goes taut before she grinds against my face, trembles, and loses herself in my tongue.

Three words hit my ears while I'm growling against her

convulsing pussy, licking her as fast and hard as humanly possible. I can't stop. I want to eat her until I'm all that's on her mind; morning, noon, and night.

Her head flips back, and she screams.

"Ryan!"

"Fuck!"

"Yes!"

Those words threaten to blister my ears. My lips and tongue are so busy against her clit I can't smile anymore. Inwardly, I'm glowing. I just heard the last three sounds I want to remember on my deathbed.

Her thighs keep trying to close with the pleasure overwhelming her. I hold them open, digging my fingers harder into her skin, keeping her apart so my tongue can bring her off as long and hard as her body allows.

There's no mercy here. No sweetness.

Not tonight, when I'm about to fuck my lovely wife-to-be for the very first time. Not when it seems like the entire universe is singing our song, from the furious rhythm in our hearts to the fire roaring in our veins.

I don't let up on her delectable cunt until she's breathless, literally gasping for air. Then I have to break myself away, or I'm going to die between her legs, and that would be a tragedy without having my cock there first.

I'm looking down, admiring her while I lick the last of her sweetness from my lips. Kara's eyes are lidded, and her tits roll on her chest, rising and falling in shallow waves as she tries to catch her breath. Reaching down, I cup her chin, bringing my lips to hers.

She tastes so good I want her to share it. Lord knows she's done the same for me many times after sucking me off with those perfect lips – our favorite past time, up until now.

"You come beautiful, babe. Don't know if it's because you're more turned on tonight, or if it's because you're about to be my wife." I whisper softly in her ear, the first of many sexy, sweet praises I'm going to be singing her until the universe itself goes cold. "I love you, Kara-bou. Are you ready?"

Her green eyes open, their energy returning. It's not really a question. The next word out of her mouth better be *yes,* or I'm going to stroke myself off and spill my come all over her.

I can't wait to have her pussy wrapped around me anymore.

I can't. Can't. *Just fucking can't.*

"Yes…" She says the magic word, reaching up to brush my face with her fingertips.

I always try to keep a faint shadow of stubble on my face. She loves it when it brushes her skin.

"Ryan," she purrs, slowly opening her legs while I reach for the box of condoms on the nightstand. "I've imagined this a thousand times. You don't have a clue."

I'm smiling because she's flat-out wrong about that. If she's dreamed about sex a thousand times, then I've stroked myself at least double, always thinking about how she'll feel wrapped around me when I blow.

"Yeah? And how's it holding up?" I ask, unsure if I really

care about the answer as I tear the foil with my teeth, then roll the latex down my throbbing shaft.

"Fantasies were never this good." Her eyes go wider, and she looks at me intently, forming her mouth into a seductive little O. There's something wicked coming over her, and I think I like it. "Fuck me, Ryan. Show me what it means to wear your ring."

Oh, hell.

She doesn't know what she's asking with those words. That look. That perfectly sexy set of lips that doesn't ever need to ask.

"We'll go slow, baby," I say. My skin tingles when I hear her moan, pressing the full, thick length of my dick against her opening.

She's as ready for me as she'll ever be. I remember to ease her into it, fighting my baser instincts to give her all of me, hard and fast.

She's never done this before. I've only done it a few times. Every woman, including her, tells me I'm *big*. Judging by how the jealous pricks at Split Harbor High used to stare at me in the locker room after gym, I know it's true.

I take some pride in my size, but nothing boosts my ego more than staring into her eyes, knowing I'm claiming a woman who deserves every inch.

The swollen tip of my cock rubs her slit. I suck her bottom lip between my teeth, savoring the moment before I'm in her. I brush her cheek with one hand, grazing the little scar from her golfing accident.

"Please, Ryan. *Please!*" She's whimpering now, laying her legs over mine, running her feet down my calves.

Our eyes click. I swear we can see the electricity charting the space between us.

My hips roll forward. I'm pushing in her, one furious inch at a time, and fuck it feels good.

She cries out, locking her legs around me, pulling me deeper. Something gives way around my cock, and I see her scrunch her face up. Uncomfortable, but urging me on.

We don't let hell itself stop us now. Her incredible pussy hugs me so tight I can feel it through the condom, constricting around my cock every second I push just a little deeper.

"Good?" I stop to kiss her again before I let her answer.

I know it has to hurt, stretching around me like this. But the way she's panting, the way her nipple softens when I roll it between my fingertips, tells me there's pleasure waiting for us, and it's going to be like *nothing* we've had before.

"Don't. Stop." Two little words leave her mouth, all she can manage, and she hugs me with her legs harder. "Fuck me, Ryan."

She never swears, except when we're alone. Hearing her curse feeds the inferno in my blood. This side of her is mine.

Mine alone, and hell, do I love it.

My hips go wild, crashing into her like waves. Love and lust collide like a mad scientist's cocktail in my blood, and I'm thrusting into her good and deep, setting a rhythm that's going to carry us to ecstasy. I only pause to put my lips on hers, steal the pleasure from her lungs, and growl while my tongue sweeps hers.

Soon, we've found our pace. We're fucking so good, just like we were always meant to. I won't last long at this rate, fire welling up in my balls.

Kara can't either. Her nails find the flames on my shoulders, using them as targets, sinking into my skin as her pleasure boils over.

Her eyes flutter open just enough for me to see them roll. My woman, my wife, my baby comes on my dick, so hard her pussy squeezes me. The world's softest flesh pulls at my cock, begging me to join her in release.

Who am I to say no? What red blooded man in his right mind *would*?

I drive down deep, slamming into her with everything I've got, slapping her little ass with my balls. The flames inked on my shoulders come alive, sending energy straight down my back, igniting every nerve.

Pure magma churns at the base of my cock, before erupting a second later. "Kara!"

"Ryan!"

Her name is all I can manage. There's nothing but thunder in my throat the whole time as I spill myself into her, coming in the woman I'm going to marry for the first time, the first and only love of my life.

Everything goes white, the sound of our groans fading from my ears, and there's nothing except my cock heaving fire to the *thud-thud-thud* of our hearts. I'm coming a hundred times harder than I ever have with my hand. Harder than I ever did with the other chicks I messed with before.

Hell, none of them are in the same universe as *this*.

Yeah, I'm man enough to admit the touchy-feely shit adds something amazing to the storm. If this sex is mind blowing because my heart bangs my ribs a hundred miles an hour every time I look at her under me, because every voice inside me is howling to claim this girl from the inside out, tonight and forever, then I don't want a damned thing to do with heartless fucking ever again.

I stay in her while I'm coming down from the high, listening to her breathe, subtly matching her tempo. It takes more than a minute before I soften, caressing and kissing her the whole time. I pull out, carefully unroll the condom, and throw it in the little waste bin across the room.

"Well?" she says, propped up on one elbow, bringing her free hand to my chest to draw circles. "Was it everything you expected?"

Just my luck, the little minx has remembered how to speak faster than me. I give her a slow, smiling glance. "No."

Her eyes go wide, full of horror. I wrap an arm around her, drag her lips to mine, and lay down a kiss before I rest my forehead on hers.

"It was more, Kara-Bou. So much fucking more." I watch the relieved smile spread across her face. "Best part is, we've got all night to explore."

"And then the rest of our lives," she adds, making me grin like a fool.

It only takes me about a hundred seconds to get hard again. Moving my hand to her ass, I cup one cheek and squeeze, pulling her on top of me.

Despite being as young and horny as I should be, I'm grateful for the two minute rest. It's plenty of time to imagine the better days to come.

The day when she says, "I do."

The day when she's coming home with a degree in her hands, and we take one more anniversary trip to the Armitage Lighthouse, before we leave Split Harbor for her immersion school in France. By then, I'll have the money and success to live like a king with her in Paris, God willing.

Then there's the day when we're coming home, buying a big house on the shore outside Marquette, the first of many kids quickening inside her.

I want it all. I'm going to have the whole package after the hell I've suffered. Family means more to me than the average twenty year old because I've never seen it up close and personal until the Lilydales brought me into their lives. They've given me a taste of what a normal, loving family should be.

It's ambrosia to a starving man, and I'm grabbing life by the balls as soon as she's off to Ann Arbor so I can drink my fill.

I'll die before I let her down, or abandon everything I've worked for. It's been leading up to this moment since the day she slid in the oil at Bart's Auto.

No more games. No delays. No reminders.

Every day, every night, every single second she's wearing my ring and sharing my bed, I see what's ahead. I know what I need to do to make it happen.

When I tangle her blond locks in my fingers again and

take her lips with mine, I'm seeing through time and space, straight through our very souls. And damn, I like what I see.

Starting tonight, our future couldn't be more perfect.

* * * *

One Week Later

It's Labor Day, roughly a week later, and I'm working overtime for a VIP. Well, the closet thing we have to a Very Important Person at the only auto shop in this podunk town. Nelson Drayton brought his custom Porsche in for a rush job, buffing out a few scratches.

The sun is shining, and I'm alone with the big door open, Cold Play pipes through our sound system, spilling their rich melodies into the garage. It's an awesome contrast to the chill beginning to fill the air, the infamous lake effect blowing in, as it always does the instant the calendar flips to September.

Yesterday, I finished helping load Kara's things into a big white moving truck. She took off with her old man, heading for college, dreams spilling out every inch of her sweet smile. Some of them were mine, the dreams we shared, and they caused me to grin like a goddamned fool.

Her and Bart got a late start on the road. Two days later than they should've thanks to us celebrating our engagement.

Nobody minded the delay. Hearing her parents hammer us with thanks and throw sample wedding plans at us like rocks brought out the truth in the promise we'd made to each other.

This is really happening. I'm about to be the happiest man on God's green Earth because I'm marrying *her*.

Once we set a wedding date, happiness is in reach. Permanently.

I'll do my damnedest to move down to Ann Arbor while she finishes school, finding work at another shop if my business doesn't spike by then.

I'm buffing the rough lines out of the Porsche when I hear footsteps behind me. "This is taking all day, kid. Are you almost finished, or should I call Bart to do a man's job?"

How this asshole got by for decades in local politics by being a total prick, I have no clue.

He'd been out back alone for the past hour. Smoking his imported cigars like a fucking chimney since the second he rolled up, he threw me his keys, and told me to "hurry the hell up." For a man in his seventies, freshly retired from public life, there's no humility.

Seems like he's missing sympathy, empathy, and mercy, too.

Nelson Drayton walks, talks, and breathes like he's been chewing the silver spoon his entire life. He's also bitter about something, and ready to take it out on anyone who doesn't drop to their knees to make his worries disappear.

I do a slow turn, forcing my lips to form a smile so it doesn't look like I'm baring my teeth. "Five or ten more minutes, Mr. Drayton. That's all I need. I'll have her good as new in no time, we're just wrapping up now."

He wrinkles his nose. His weathered face sticks out of his suit, making him look ten years older than he truly is.

Or maybe it just makes him look like he's been marinated in a high end whiskey barrel for several years and then run over by the pretentious car I'm working my ass off for.

"If we're going to waste the entire evening, why don't you clean my interior too?" he says. It isn't really a question.

I nod politely, anger churning in my guts when I see him put another big stogie between his lips and fish out his gold plated lighter. "Absolutely, sir. My pleasure. We have a rule about smoking in the garages," I tell him, motioning to the safety sign on the wall, several feet from where he's standing.

He doesn't say a word. Just looks at me, narrows his eyes, and brings a flame to his cigar, drawing in a long pull of rich tobacco before he turns.

"I'll be back in an hour. You better be done with this shit by then."

I bite my tongue, grateful he's going for a walk. Last thing I need is the town's most entitled prick eyeballing me while I give his baby the sweetest skin she's had since the day she rolled off the lot.

I'm serious. Bart wouldn't have called me in today over Mickey, Jack, and the other guys if I weren't the best. I put my pride, sweat, and soul into this because it's given me everything.

No, I won't be a mechanic forever. It's good, honest work that's given me a whole hell of a lot, brought me my woman and introduced me to the Lilydales, the only folks who say they're family, and mean it.

I grit my teeth while I lean over the car, moving my hands across its sleek body with precision. I'm going to be as rich as Nelson someday, and I'll never be a prick about it. I'll have earned it, and I'll be grateful, too happy and fulfilled to stomp around with the sour scowl permanently plastered to his face.

It takes a little longer than I told him to finish the body work. Then I grab a vacuum and some polish for the leather seats, eager to wrap up this job.

I want to get out of here, maybe lay down some code at home this evening for a few hours before Kara calls to tell me how she's settling into her dorm. Lately, I've been studying auto components, searching for opportunities in the only field I know.

One minute, working on his car, the future seems like it can't get any brighter.

In the years ahead, I'll wish like hell I never opened the Porsche's door, reached under the driver's seat, and ruined my life.

Sweet, merciful Christ. If only I'd *known* what would happen as soon as I climbed in that car, I would have dropped my tools and ran, as far from this crazy town as my boots could carry me.

If I hadn't found that bastard's dirty little secret, I never would've blown my life to shit.

III: Red on White (Kara)

Ryan doesn't answer when I call him that night. He isn't responding to my texts either. He said daddy needed him for a special job today. It must be stressful, so I figure he's working late.

No big deal. I'm busy setting everything up in my dorm room, making new friends with my roommates, eagerly prepping for my first week of classes.

French V: Pre-Immersion is going to be my first official college class, bright and early in the morning. I've heard the professor likes to grill her students for fluency before she even passes out the syllabus. *Joy.*

It's a beautiful evening, my first full one in town. After a few hours walking the little college bars and stores around campus, Split Harbor seems like it's a million miles away.

I'm thankful for the last present Ryan gave me before we kissed for the last time and I climbed into the moving truck with daddy. The little silver locket clings to my neck, tucked neatly between my breasts, his tiny smiling photo nestled inside.

Every time something around school reminds me of

him, I laugh and play with the necklace, gently warming it my palm. It's like he's right here with me. I'm grateful for that, knowing I'll get through anything the professors throw my way as long as I have a loving fiance to come home to.

The next morning, before I head to class, I check my phone and see…nothing.

Okay, things are getting a little weird. It's odd that he hasn't texted me yet.

I go to class and survive my first real test from the French Professor.

I'm not worried until I check the Split Harbor news site over lunch. Hell, I don't need to dig deep, because there's articles from my hometown media lighting up my college Facebook feed.

Nelson Drayton Dead! Michigan Mourns Historic Industrialist, Mayor, and Philanthropist.

The headline hits me between the eyes. It's shocking enough to know a living piece of history is gone, but the bigger jolt comes when my eyes search the details.

My heart skips several beats. I try to remember what Ryan said about what he was doing yesterday.

Didn't he say he was working on Nelson's car? *Jesus.*

No, it's got to be a twisted coincidence. My stomach drops into an open pit when I scan through the articles, forcing myself to read the ugly truth. Every word makes me pull angrily on the little locket, twining the chain around my fingers.

Violent murder. Foul play. One suspect.

Three nightmare phrases so strange and out of place for

Split Harbor they don't seem real. Neither do the next few sentences I read, the ones that make my hands shake so bad they cause me to drop my phone. A few students across from me lounging in the commons look up when it bangs on tile. I smile uneasily, reaching to pick it up.

It's either smile at this point, or fall down to the ground and vomit.

I don't want to read it a second time. But I need to take another look, just to make sure this isn't a fever dream.

Bart's Auto is closed indefinitely while police examine the scene, the piece reads. *No suspects have been publicly identified at this time, though Sheriff Dixon says this could change quickly. Another press conference will be held as soon as local law enforcement have finished investigating their only lead.*

Only lead. Fuck, *only.*

Ryan, where are you?

I want to curl up and die. There's no way he's responsible for this. *None.*

Worse, I finally get why I haven't heard from him, my parents, or anybody else in town. Knowing the truth hurts.

The urge to call them and scream, demanding answers, forces the phone to my ear. I try to ring Ryan about four times. It goes straight to his voice mail. My parents won't pick up either, no matter what number I try. I don't dare ring the auto shop while it's under lockdown.

My evening classes are just a blur. The next time I check my phone, anxiously eating Ritz crackers with Sprite to ease the queasiness in my stomach, I see a message from Matt.

Call me whenever you get this. It's serious.

I'm grateful he's able to talk to me. He's in the middle of tactical training at some base in Pakistan, away from the combat zone he's normally stationed at near Kandahar. But seeing him write *serious* turns every vertebrae in my spine to ice cubes.

I wait until I'm back in my dorm, done for the day, before I call. He picks up instantly, breathing heavily on the end of the line.

"Kara?"

"Thank God. Matt, what's going on? I saw the news."

"Then you know about Drayton and dad's garage." He pauses, a brutal second so long it feels like it's going to make me suffocate. "Everybody's fine with them. I heard from mom this morning. Dad was just coming home from dropping you off when he got the call. Police told him to come to the shop right away. He's been with them all day, filling out forms and talking to investigators."

"Jesus." My heart dives, relieved my parents are okay. It pulls back in my throat when I come to my next question. "What about Ryan?"

"Kara…" This time, the pregnant pause after my name lasts so long it has triplets.

There's bad news coming. I'm about to throw up all over my desk, but only after I realize how pissed I am.

Enraged, actually, because I know he's hiding something. I'm won't stand being patronized.

"Matt, just tell me what happened. Where *is he*? Is he okay?"

"Kara…he's gone."

Gone? Just…gone?

What the hell does that mean? I'm having visions of a serial killer storming into the garage, murdering Nelson Drayton with a chainsaw, and then coming after Ryan.

"Don't tell me," I whisper, the terror in my throat so thick and hot I can barely speak. "He's dead, isn't he?"

"No. Not exactly," Matt growls, pauses, and lets out a sigh. "Look, you had to hear it from somebody, and I'm the best one to deliver the news. Nobody's seen him since he left his apartment to go to work yesterday morning. A big storm blew in from the lake last night, flooded everything, and a couple boats disappeared. Right around the time they think Nelson was killed. They found one washed up near Marquette. The other's still missing."

"Wait!" I close my eyes, wishing I could will this insanity away. "Wait, wait, wait, wait, wait. You're saying he *stole* a boat and skipped town? Just vanished the same day Drayton dies? Matt, I –"

"Fuck. Sis, I'm not gonna pretend I know what you're feeling," he says, anger and sympathy mingling in his tone. "You're a smart girl. You can put two and two together. You don't need me to tell you what everybody believes, word by word…right?"

There's about five seconds before the time bomb inside me explodes. The full horror hits me, the sick realization I'm engaged to a man they think is a killer, and a thief.

I'm gutted. My brain can't process why they're turning on Ryan like this, going along with the first insane possibility that explains what happened – the one I'll never believe in a million years.

I'm on my feet, shaking and screaming into the speaker.

"How can you even *think* that's what happened? Christ, how can mom or dad? He's your best friend, Matt." I have to remember to breathe, or I'm going to pass out. "I don't know what happened, but Ryan isn't a fucking murderer!"

"I don't know what he is anymore," Matt says coldly. "Let's leave this to the experts. Shit, maybe I can take an emergency leave to come home for awhile, or something, if my CO allows it. I'm sorry you're starting school like this, sis. We were all wrong about him, *so* fucking wrong. Maybe it's been building up for years from whatever happened to him in those orphanages and foster homes. It's a goddamned shame, I get it. I just heard about the engagement yesterday."

I don't care what he's heard. I've had enough.

My finger barely taps the key to end the call before I throw the phone on the floor. My roommate, Courtney, is an absolute angel when she comes home, and finds me curled up and rocking myself on the bottom bunk, face down in the pillow. She offers about a million things, trying to help. All I'll accept is time alone – and I think she's glad because I'm really creeping her out.

I could care less about anyone's sympathy. I refuse to pity myself.

I want Ryan to come home. I want this fixed. And I want to go back to the happy, hopeful future I left behind in Split Harbor, before what's left of my heart pulverizes into dust.

* * * *

Six Months Later

I can't believe I'm home, instead of Paris.

Can't believe I told mom to take my locket several weeks ago and hide it, destroy it, just get it away from me. My fingers still reach for the tiny piece of him that's no longer there.

It's the same with grandmom's ring. It's back in her drawer, slowly collecting dust, buried like my dying heart.

I never believed I could learn to hate a man I used to love – but I have.

I'm sulking around the office, back in daddy's shop, feeling more like a failure than ever today. It isn't like there's much else to do. Business hasn't been great since we turned into the place where a hometown hero died under mysterious circumstances.

"Pack it in for the evening, peanut." I don't even hear my father come in until he speaks. His reassuring hand comes down on my shoulder. "The boys went home early, and we'd might as well follow them. Not a lot of work going on with a winter this mild."

"Don't call me peanut. How many times do I have to ask?" I spin around in my chair, giving him a savage look.

Of course, I'm instantly reminded what a bitch I am when I see the smile on his face melt away. I'll never understand how he can be so positive after we've lost so much.

It isn't the mild winter that's reduced our usual lineup of body work, oil changes, and frozen starters. It's people's willingness to drive the extra twenty miles into Marquette. They'd rather have their vehicles towed there than deal with the outcasts running this tomb. They act like Nelson's ghost is going to come through the walls and howl in their faces for patronizing the place where he died.

"No rush, Kara," daddy says softly. "Take as much time as you need. I'll be out front, warming up the truck."

I drag my feet, sitting at the greasy computer, trying not to cry. It's taken hours to organize the week's meager receipts – work I used to fly through just a couple years ago.

I'm trying not to cry. It's never done me any good, and more tears aren't going to make my issues disappear now.

Outside, through the open door, I hear him coughing. Daddy's been trying to shake a nasty cold or something for the better part of the month, one more thing our family doesn't need after karma went scorched Earth on us.

It's times like this when I wish Ryan could see us, wherever he is. I want him to see what he's done to our business, to daddy, to *me*. I can't remember the last time I rolled over the possibilities in my mind, thinking he's innocent, imagining the terrible ways he could've gotten himself mixed up in killing Nelson Drayton without actually pulling the trigger.

Was there even a trigger to pull? I don't know. Nobody says how he died, and I don't want to know.

There aren't many public details at all about what went down that night.

Matt knows more than me, supposedly, but he's the last person I'd ask. We haven't been on speaking terms since he called me three months ago, trying to give me a pep talk. I wasn't in the mood, packing my stuff away at the dorm to come home. Constantly reminded of the fatal Fs bombing my GPA into the stone age.

My big brother is one more casualty of Ryan's stupid, selfish disappearing act. I can't trust anyone, not even myself. The uncertainty disgusts me more than anything.

By the time I drag myself out of the office, wrapping my coat tight against the winter chill, I notice daddy left the garage open. His truck is running, but he's not inside.

What now?

I race outside, pouncing into the messy snow piled up about three feet away, where I find him half-buried, struggling to get on his feet.

"What is it? What's wrong?" I start banging my fist on his back while I wrap the other arm around his waist, struggling to pull him up. He's making sounds like he's choking. For a second, I'm afraid there's something caught in his throat, but it doesn't make any sense.

He's a man of habit. He wouldn't be chewing anything large enough to spoil dinner when we'll be eating in a couple hours.

It takes forever to wrestle him backwards, drag his huge body to the truck, where he has just enough leverage to grab onto the flat bed for support.

I don't know who's shaking worse – him or me.

Christ, just seeing him rattling around like he's about to fall injects more fear into my veins than I've felt since the day I found out Ryan was gone.

"Daddy?" I'm reaching for my phone, wondering if I should call 9-1-1. There's something *very* wrong, and I know he'll give me crap about it if I'm overreacting.

"Help me, Kara. I'm sick."

My heart drops another five feet. If he isn't downplaying what's happening, then it's worse than I imagined.

Just like the night I lost the love of my life, I dial emergency, and let the next twenty minutes blur by in a daze.

I tell them my father is suffering some kind of attack. No, I don't know why.

Then I stand with him, my hand gently on his back, doing my damnedest not to cry, even when the ambulance pulls up with an ear bursting shriek.

I help him into the ambulance and ride to the hospital. Mom is already there in the waiting room shortly after we arrive. I watch them strip daddy away from me, lay him in a stretcher, and wheel him full speed ahead through the imposing metal doors. It's like I'm looking at a whale's mouth, eager to swallow up another piece of my world.

Mom and I sit outside and wait. Not very patiently. We don't say much.

Her nervous hand brushes mine several times. I take it, holding on like I haven't since I was a little girl.

For once, the worry in her eyes for me is absent, replaced by fear for daddy instead.

Matt calls later that night, as soon as his commander relays the news. Mom does the talking, which isn't much relief. My stomach tightens when I think about the forced, cold way we'll have to pull together as a family for my father's sake.

I can't forgive my brother for being the messenger, but I'm going to have to try. It's his voice that stole Ryan away from me forever, plunging me into this hell that's grown a few degrees hotter tonight.

I know it isn't right. I want to forgive him, to pick myself up and "just move on," live the three simple words my brother said during our last argument.

Mom is just finishing her update on the phone when Doctor Hanson appears through the door. I get up slowly, shuffling over to the spot where he's motioning us. The look on his face tells me whatever comes out of his mouth won't be pleasant.

"Bets. Kara." He says our names softly, as if it will help soften the blow. "I'm afraid there's bad news."

I hold my breath, waiting for it to hit me in the face. Mom looks like she's about to faint.

"He's stable, but we're going to have to get him to Marquette in the morning for surgery. We did several scans with the best equipment here. Each one confirms everything I wish I didn't have to pass along. There's a mass growing in Bart's lower right lung. It's a big one."

His lips keep moving. He's filling us in on the technical details about daddy's probable cancer, slowly dropping medical jargon, staring intently to make sure we're following along.

I stopped trying about thirty seconds ago.

Outside, the wind has picked up. I hear it banging

against the huge sheet of glass behind him, loose in its frame, like Jack Frost himself pounding his fists, trying to work his way inside.

There's nothing left for the cold to take. I wish I had something more than hot, empty tears for my poor father, but Ryan stole my sorrows, my joys, my capacity to give more than the smallest fuck at my world caving in a little deeper.

Losing daddy now – and deep down, I know I will – rubs salt in the wounds the sickening killer who stole my heart tore open half a year ago.

He played me then. Hell, he played us all, pretending to be a good, upstanding, loving young man who meant the very best for me. I'll never understand why he murdered Nelson. Frankly, I don't care.

All the imaginary excuses in the world aren't changing this train wreck.

The fact that he did, that's enough. An innocent man who loved me wouldn't run. Wouldn't abandon me while I flunked out of school and came home to this hopeless little town. Wouldn't have stayed gone while our family business died. Or when I'm going to lose my father.

I have to hand it to mom – she's the one who keeps talking to Doctor Hanson. Nodding like she understands every time he runs through what's next. She tells him how strong daddy is, that he's going to pull through, and it doesn't matter how grim the outlook might be in Marquette, where they can do a lot more for him than here.

Me? I'm not in earshot anymore. I've limped back to my

seat, my hands over my face. My head throbs, preparing to explode. Anyone looking at me would guess it's meant to cover the angry tears seeding my eyes.

They don't know I'm cursing Ryan Caspian for the thousandth time. I can't stop seeing red and white every time I remember his despicable face.

If I ever see him in this town again, I'm going to be Split Harbor's second fugitive wanted for murder.

IV: Celebration (Ryan)

Three Years Later

"Two million *fucking* dollars in one week!" Leonard slaps me on the back, his big off white grin taking over his mouth. "Tanner, my man, we have arrived."

I don't know what my small team gathered at the table in this Seattle coffee shop expect. A grand speech, maybe. Or else they're expecting me to jump up and start doing cartwheels like a madman, letting out the emotion that's been building like lightning over the past two manic years since I started working on Punch Corp night and day.

They don't have a clue that name – Tanner – still seems alien. Doesn't matter how many times I hear it.

Tanner reminds me I'm living a lie, even if it's a very profitable one. Makes me think about everything I left behind, especially the girl I lost. I don't care how many millions I make, I'd trade every red cent to hold her in my arms again.

I sit up, calmly taking a sip off my *venti* mocha. "We're just getting started, boys. Put that excitement to good use.

I want new interviews next week, checking every candidate until we've got top notch accounting. We'll need them to handle the new revenue coming in. Remember – this is seed money. You'll get your bonuses at the end of the month, but everything we don't need to live a little is going right back in the ground to grow some more."

"We're going to need a better lawyer," Leonard says, always getting ahead of himself. "I'm worried about the language in the license. We're big league now, Tanner. If we don't have this thing iron-fucking-clad, the giants are sure to walk all over us. If somebody gets the bright idea to rip off our patent – Jesus!"

"They wouldn't dare," I tell him, folding my hands and looking into his anxious brown eyes. "They know how valuable our product is. More of them are jumping on board every week. We're giving them what they need to get across the finish line and put self-driving cars on the streets. It won't be long before we add Ford, Chevy, Tesla, and whoever the hell else wants a piece of the future to our executive services."

Everybody laughs. *A piece of the future* is the corporate slogan I came up with one sleepless night.

Today proves it isn't just empty talk anymore. Not with our first big order from an honest-to-God national manufacturer, licensing our patented sensors for their first line of driverless prototypes, about to serve several large cities.

For a second, I let myself think back to Bart's Auto. Would I be here today, an overnight multi-millionaire, if I hadn't gotten my hands dirty under the best boss I ever had? If I hadn't seen the damage a sheet of Michigan black ice can do to a beautiful new car?

If I hadn't confronted that asshole after I found the dirty secret in his Porsche? If I hadn't ran? If I hadn't lost her?

"Ryan's on it," Leonard says, making me blink a little quicker than I'd like.

Of course, he means Ryan Hayes, the smart thirty year old at the other end of the table. He gives me a smile and jokingly salutes.

Yes, *that* Ryan. Not Caspian, who died on Lake Superior three years ago. I pushed him out of my head the second I found a man who could give me a new name and social security number.

Ryan Caspian was the second death that night. If he'd lived, Tanner wouldn't be sitting here staring at the greatest success of his life, managing men older and more experienced, who look at me like I'm some kind of freak who's going to lead them to billions.

Maybe I am.

"Take the night off to celebrate, people," I say, picking up the manila folder in front of me and tossing it over my shoulder. "Then I want your asses back here tomorrow, in your seats, making the calls that are going to grow this company. This week, we're two million dollars richer. There's a lot more where that came from, and we're going to get every dollar for Punch Corp."

They cheer. They grin. They slap each other on the backs. I think I see a few genuine tears threatening to roll down Becky's cheeks, our lead in customer service. Until next week, our only receptionist. We're going to need a lot more like her to field calls where we're going.

"Jesus, we're going to need more units," Leonard says, pushing tense fingers through his dark slicked hair. "Should I start making inquiries around SeaTac about who's willing to work on manufacturing until we can get a real factory?"

I shake my head. "Forget it. If revenue keeps rolling in the way I think it will this month, I have somewhere else in mind. Much lower costs of production."

Leonard cocks his head. I'm not going to ruin the occasion by dropping the surprise that we're going to be looking at Michigan for facilities in another year. Half the people here are Washington born and raised. I know they'll think Superior is a poor substitute for the Pacific, and the area around Marquette is a cultural wasteland.

"We'll meet on Monday again, and I'll have more suggestions then," I say, getting out of my chair. "It's been too damned great a week not to get out and unwind. Go crazy, everybody. You've worked for it."

I turn around and head for the door, making my usual exit. Tonight, they aren't going to let me go home by myself. There must be three sets of hands pulling on my arms, jerking me backward, attached to the mouths yelling invitations into my ears.

I start laughing. I can't help it. It's a strange sound, one I only mimic once in a blue moon to pretend I'm still human.

It's a beautiful moment. Tanner should smile and laugh

along with his employees tonight. For once, I won't hold the lying bastard back.

Deep down, I don't deserve it. Every day that goes by after walking out on my fiancee, abandoning my adopted family, after doing what I did in Michigan is one where I ought to be burn, instead of celebrating.

Nobody needs to know I'm indulging a privilege I don't deserve until I can make things right.

I'm only human. Turning around, I flash a rare smile to their happy faces. "Okay, okay! Give me a minute to get everything together, and I'll meet you at the usual spot along the pier."

"Hell yeah you will, boss. It wouldn't be a celebration without you." Leonard claps me hard on the shoulder. Reaching up, I squeeze his hand before I step out into the main part of the coffee shop. Bystanders are staring at us, wondering about the commotion back in our meeting spot. The cash we give the manager will probably be our last payment, now that we can afford a proper office.

Forget about Split Harbor tonight.
Forget the dead asshole.
Forget about her.

I turn the phrases over and over in my mind while I order a black cold brew for the road. It's the same shit I've told myself every single day since I took the new name, staring into the mirror and seeing the reflection that's still Ryan's.

It's an incredible day, but it doesn't matter. The words I've burned into my brain aren't going to magically start working, even if I wake up tomorrow a billionaire.

Talk is cheap. I need action if I ever want to make myself whole again, and this is just one more mile on the long, crushing odyssey home.

* * * *

Once everybody around me is good and drunk, I pull out my phone. I've been nursing the same scotch all night, pecking at a platter of shrimp and oysters.

I can't pretend to be happy here tonight without at least checking the news. It's the lone ritual I allow myself when work is done for the day, always around the same time, when I have a few hours left before crashing into sleep's merciful unconsciousness.

There isn't much new in the Harbor Herald. Hell, there never is.

Same old weather forecast for spring: gloomy with a chance for early thaw.

I scroll down the main page, and see a few local ads for Pepe's Garage, the new chain that's filled the hole left by Bart's Auto closing down. My fist tightens, and I clench my jaw.

"What's the word, boss? We brought you out of hiding, and you're still spending the evening alone?" Leonard slides onto the empty stool next to me, his hair a little messier above the drunken glow taking over his face.

"Just relaxing," I say. It wouldn't be another night as Tanner if I didn't lie about something, after all.

"Bullshit. You're working," he says, wagging a finger my

way. "Put that thing down and take in the scenery."

He elbows me gently. I give him a dirty look and lift my head, following his line of sight across the bar.

There's a woman waiting for me to flash her my ocean blue eyes. My gaze locks on hers, long enough to turn her cheeks red and send her eyes to the green margarita in front of her.

She likes what she sees, of course. They always do.

Gorgeous looks got me further than they should've back in Michigan. Today, they get any woman I want wet, ready to follow me to bed like they've been waiting their entire lives for the chance.

I've filled out. Changed. Gained a few more tattoos and one choice piercing. I've become a man who only resembles the sad, broken kid I used to see in the mirror.

Maybe it has something to do with the hours I put in at the gym, or running through every corner of this dark seaside city. I never miss a day, not even when it's pouring rain. When I break down and take a chick to bed for one night, giving into urges no man can neglect forever, I barely recognize the body fucking her.

It's huge. Inked like a storm criss-crossing the sky. Angry.

Would Kara recognize any piece of me?

Catching myself thinking about her, I realize I'm evil-eyeing the broad across the bar, giving me *come hither* eyes. Unfortunately for her, I'm in control tonight, which means I'm not in the mood for another anonymous fuck that has about as much meaning as blowing my nose.

Yes, as a matter of fact, I am a complete bastard when I get my rocks off. I never do it twice with the same chick. Drain my balls, and then move on.

No exceptions. Doesn't matter how good they moan for me when I'm fisting their hair, pushing every inch against their tongues, letting a bitter roar slip through my teeth when I blow, overflowing their lips.

After Kara, sex is mechanical. It has to be.

Falling for anybody else – really, truly *moving on* – is the equivalent of burying her alive, shoveling dirt on her face with my own bare hands. No, I can't have her, I can't even speak to her again if I want to remain a free man, but I'll be damned if I'm going to let go and accept this new life as a liar.

I don't give the stranger a second glance. Next to me, Leonard shakes his head, sadness and amusement warring in his smile. "Really, boss? You're going to pass her up?"

He can't believe it. Some nights, neither can I, but only the ones where I forget who I really am for a few empty hours. My right-hand man at Punch doesn't have my gift, but it's hard for me to fathom why a smart, well dressed guy isn't as on his game as I am.

"She's yours, boy," I whisper, turning to him with a sly smile. Nervous sweat instantly forms on his brow, and he pushes up his glasses. "Go over there, buy her another of those sugary green things, and tell her she has beautiful eyes."

"Boss…you're a hell of a guy, but sometimes I think you're fucking crazy." He looks past me, his face heating from alcohol and approach anxiety when he sizes up the woman I'm ordering him to chase.

"Don't make me put you back on the clock, Len. You want to see crazy? I'll make your bonus dependent on bringing me her panties in the morning."

Leonard's jaw drops. Reaching up, I slap him on the back, giving his drunken ass a little help up off the stool.

"Now, go. It'll be good for your confidence, and great for her to have a millionaire in the making. I don't want to see you again tonight unless you're back early to tell me how good it was."

He doesn't say another word. I knock down the rest of my scotch, watching his slow, somewhat awkward approach. Five minutes in, I know he's said a few things right, because the woman is turned toward him with a smile on her face, her heel bobbing like a cat's tail while she laughs at his jokes.

Smiling, I stare at my cup, empty except for the melting ice. There's no sane reason watching Leonard warm his dick up should feel more satisfying than the fact that we're bringing in over ten million dollars this month, but hell, it does.

I turn back to my phone, finishing my scan of the latest news from Split Harbor. There's a few words about twenty-something Reginald Drayton, Nelson's great nephew, holding a major fundraiser to help keep the Armitage lighthouse open.

I almost slam my phone on the counter then and there. Sure, the town deserves its history, but that place is always going to mean broken promises. My vow to marry her, make her happy, all destroyed that cold, stormy night I left forever.

Armitage isn't a happy place anymore. Every time I see the lighthouse's name, I hope the fucking thing burns to the ground.

Rage surges in my veins. I'm glad everybody else seems to have taken off, or else they're so lost in their own conversations they've forgotten all about me. I'll be calling an Uber soon.

But not before I stab at my phone with my thumb, flipping through a few more screens. The news about the local sports doesn't interest me. By now, the little brothers of the kids who feared me in high school are having their day on the field, living it up like any kid should, each one ready to roll the dice for his chance at a Happy Ending after graduation.

There's no happiness on the last page I scroll through, anyway. I barely read the obituaries, but today something forces me to go down the list. All five of the deceased names, quite a busy weak for the reaper in such a little town.

When I get to the end, I see it. The name hits me like a dagger in the guts. I'm motioning the bartender for another scotch, before I let my eyes roll over the ugly details.

BART E. LILYDALE, 56

Husband. Father. *Former* business owner. Lost his valiant battle with cancer last week.

Survived by his wife, Bets; one son, Matt; and a daughter. Kara.

I close my eyes, trying to summon the strength to walk out of here without turning the whole fucking bar upside down. It's like her pain reaches me across time and a couple thousand miles. Reaches down my throat, throttles my heart, and reminds me what a complete cowardly jackass I am for running, when she should've been my wife.

Leaving her to get lonelier, when she ought to have my hands, my lips, my smile in her eyes for comfort. My drink goes down in one gulp, and I stand, dumping a pile of cash on the table that's probably the biggest tip this bartender has ever seen.

I don't care. I need to get some fresh air, before my stomach turns over and half the crew sees me vomit hateful bile in the little urn holding the palm tree by the door.

I barely manage a few words to my driver as I climb in the black Lincoln taking me home. A cool Pacific rain pelts the car as it inches up the steep hills down by the waterfront. I'm on the other side of the country from Split Harbor, but rain is constant on the sea.

A rare, crisp lightning bolt cuts across the downtown sky as my ride rolls on. Too much like the night I had to leave, the darkness that would have swallowed me whole if it hadn't been for Bart.

"Go, son. Leave the rest to me. You have to get on that ship and go now. *It's your only chance. Remember – and it's going to be an absolute bitch – you can't come back. You can't call her. You can't write, phone, email, or send a note by fucking pigeon to anyone here. Because if you do, and they realize where you are…"*

Even after all these years, I remember his words perfectly. They still have a scary power to make my balls pull up inside me, like someone just dumped a bucket full of ice over my head. I never let my girl's old man finish before I got in his truck. He drove me to the boat, threw off the ropes, and made sure I steered it out into the screaming night.

Scariest storm I ever saw, much less sailed into. Yet, I survived. It's the only reason I'm in this car, with several million to my name on paper, and a whole lot more coming.

If it wasn't for Bart finding me, pulling me up in my zombie state, rinsing me off with a hose, and marching me down to the docks, I'd be rotting in a small town prison cell.

Shit, maybe that's where I deserve to be. At least then I'd be close to her, even though she'd probably spit in my face the second she found out the truth.

If only she knew I didn't have a choice. Not that it matters. No court in the world – certainly not in the U.P. – would hear any excuses for why their dearly beloved hero was slain in cold blood.

Halfway through my trip, I have the driver change destinations. He drops me at a twenty-four hour gym about three blocks from my place. I need to get this poison out of my system, and doing it by running myself ragged on the treadmill sounds more productive than boozing my brain into the next century.

The run only helps so much. My shirt and tie are off, hung over the chair next to the treadmill. I'm running like a maniac, alone except for the lights and the top of the Space Needle peeking through the window, abandoned to the brute regret that always comes.

It's on steroids tonight. Just a savage hulk trying to choke the life out of me, making me re-live the night everything went to hell over and over and over.

Fuck, I miss you.

Kara-bou. I'm sorry.

Apologies won't do me any good. They're a bad reflex, and they frustrate me a hundred times more when I catch myself turning them over in my head. If I could rip the fucking thing off, and be done with it all, I would.

It's not just regret with its teeth locked onto me, tossing me around the room like a ragdoll in a Rottweiler's mouth. It's the memories, and they come faster and harder than the sweat pouring off me, louder than my beat up heart banging thunder into my blood.

I remember her kiss. How hot, how sweet, how perfect she tasted the day she said yes to that simple little ring I'd worked like a dog to buy.

I remember her eyes, green and beautiful, deeper than the peaceful forests ringing our little town. Her hair, like soft gold, worth trading everything I'd earned before and after the engagement.

All gone.

Gone forever. Stolen by a freak accident.

Running isn't enough tonight. I step off the treadmill and dry myself with a towel. My legs are about to explode, but my upper body has some fight. I drag myself over to the punching bag, where I slip on the gloves to protect my knuckles, and lay into hell.

Yes, hell. That's what's spilling out of me every time my punches land. Thank God I'm alone because several minutes in, I fucking *scream.*

Over-dramatic? Insane? The sound of my own heart coming through my ribs in pieces?

Yes, yes, and yes it is. I don't give a single shit.

I can't. Because if I become a modern day Midas, richer than every billionaire who's ever turned grit to gold in this city, and there have been a lot of them, it changes nothing. Even if I out earn Ty Sterner and his huge local empire, the whiz kid billionaire who married his own step-sister, I'm the same hollowed out shell.

It won't take away what happened. It won't bring her back. And if it wasn't for trying to enrich my friends, my employees, nursing the dreams I'm clinging to for sanity, I'd hang it all up and turn myself in just for a chance to look into her eyes one more time.

I'm not an idiot, though. Bart would never forgive me if I gave up, lost it, and did something that insane. Now that he's dead, it seems like I should double down on honoring his memory, the second chance he gave me to make this life matter.

I owe him. I can't screw this up. And I damned sure can't bring his little girl more pain, even if every selfish bone in my body aches like mad for one more chance to make this right.

I'm a realist, the older I've gotten. It's done me a lot of

good. I wouldn't have gotten anywhere in a multi-billion dollar business without it.

When I collapse on the floor, drenched in a second wave of sweat, unable to put my exhausted fists over my head, I lean on that cold, rational side of me to put the leash around my throat. That's the part that keeps me in line, prevents me from doing something stupid.

And there's no possible way injecting myself into the ruins of Kara's life again wouldn't be. I'll leave her to grieve, and mourn us as long as I need to.

Come Monday, everybody in Punch Corp is going to know we're making plans for Michigan, even if it'll be years before we're manufacturing there. I'm coming home in six months as Tanner Brooks.

There's a chance we'll cross paths again, me and Kara, if I spend more than a week setting up the factory. If it happens, then there's a greater chance she'll still recognize me beneath the hurt, the muscles, the tips of the dark tattoos that sometimes bow up around my collar, or out the edges of my sleeves.

What then? What can I possibly say?

"I'll do what I need to," I mutter to myself, bowing my aching head. Serious as a monk before raw, divine power. "I won't hurt her again."

Except, that's one more lie. There's one thing I should do if I ever see my woman again – turn my back and walk away. It's the only option I've got to keep the big lie going, everything Bart spelled out crystal clear the night I lost it all.

Fuck prison.

Losing my freedom, going to jail, that isn't what worries me. It's reminding her of what we once had, and seeing the pain in her eyes as it's ripped away a second time.

V: Vicious Cycle (Kara)

Two years later

The asshole is going to be late for our engagement party. I'm already sick and tired of these pretentious toasts and tight black heels threatening to strangle my feet.

That isn't saying anything about being back *here*, in the Armitage lighthouse, the same place a man asked me to marry him for the first time ages ago.

Of course, I never told Reg about that. I think I've only mentioned the name Ryan Caspian once in the eighteen months we've been together.

He knows what happened, and so do I. We don't need to dwell on it. Everybody says we're a beautiful couple. Two families in town struck by the same tragedy, about to come together as one.

Don't get me wrong. I wouldn't be at this engagement party at all if Reg didn't sweep me off my feet.

It's been a whirlwind romance, a rollercoaster of highs and lows. I can't believe it was less than two years ago when he started to frequent my new cafe, Grounded. My little bakery and coffeehouse was deserted then, too new and too fresh to have any regulars, except for one.

Reginald Drayton. The man who didn't care that I chewed him out the first time we met over his answer to chalk board trivia for a ten cent discount. He just kept coming back for more of my stuff, smiling across the counter with his lean, civilized looks and wisp of a brown beard.

He's handsome, in his own way. He'll never be built like Ryan – but I'm over that.

He's wealthy. He's intelligent. He's logical, and it only makes him an asshat once in awhile, which means he's easy to fall for.

"Kara! Where's Reggie? We're about to fire up the speakers in less than an hour." I whirl around to face the voice, and see Patricia in her usual tall grey heels, a fresh perm, and a dress that must cost five figures.

"I've been trying to get in touch with him," I say, reaching for my phone. "He's probably taking the scenic route here. It's a beautiful evening out there."

She smiles, nods, and looks past me at the bright red sunset splashed across the horizon. I've known my future mother-in-law for more than a year, but I'm still outclassed. I'm standing here in an ivory evening dress he bought me a month ago, the one our wedding planner recommended. It looks like I'm wearing a potato sack against her jungle green flourishes with the gold trim and spacious neckline to show off her 24-karat necklace.

"He'd better not embarrass us again." She clucks her

tongue, her smile disappearing, facing me seriously.

I put my hands up, remembering how she blew up a month ago, when Reg picked me up late and we rushed to her charity art gala in Marquette. Naturally, we missed her opening act, where she aggressively reminded everyone they were there to raise as much as they could, buying paintings and statues worth more than most luxury cars.

"He won't, Patricia. It's our engagement, after all. He'll be here." An uneasy smile tugs at my lips. "Reg is very excited. He's been talking about it all week. I could try him again if you'd like?"

"No, forget it. There's no need to bother him unless Mr. Williams is doing the intro." She turns, like she's about to walk away, but then she stops mid-step and gives me one more hawk-eyed glance. "I'm not angry with you, Kara. I hope you know that. Creating more stress when you're trying to right the ship with my son is the last thing I'd ever want."

I don't say anything as she stomps away, heading toward a gaggle of attendants still shuffling a few last chairs into place for our guests, ready to micro-manage them to perfection.

My stomach sinks into itself. I hate that she knows the truth.

We've tried to hide our recent issues from everybody. Told ourselves we'll play the happy couple everybody expects, and we'll keep doing therapy until we get it right.

We love each other, and we aren't giving up before we've even begun.

It's *way* too early for that. Still, it's times like this I'm amazed how I can feel so distant from the man I fell in love with last year.

We were so good in the beginning. Almost like me and Ryan. Reg was the ultimate gentlemen, taking me out for long drives and evenings at the best restaurants. He never flinched when I snapped – and there was a lot of that. Just smiled his warm, smart grin with an uncanny ability to make me feel more comfortable than anyone had since I lost the other two men in my life.

Wait, two? What the hell is wrong with me?

Daddy's the one who really mattered. I catch myself thinking about the asshole who's ancient history by now, and I hate it.

Ryan should be the last thing on my mind. I know it's because things have been troubled between my fiance and me lately. Being in this lighthouse doesn't help. That's the real reason he keeps haunting me.

Except, it isn't really true. Because even when things were good, when I started thinking about what it'd be like to become Mrs. Reginald Drayton, Ryan still clung to the small, dark spots in my brain.

I sneak a glass of wine from one of the servers and take a seat near the back, hoping the alcohol will numb what's coming. With a drink in hand, I let myself wonder just where the hell Reg is, anyway.

Last night, before he slipped into bed and gave me the cool peck on the cheek that's replaced our old fiery kisses since the troubles began, he told me he was going into town.

Something about meeting with his financial advisor to manage new distributions from the trust left by his great uncle. He tells me there's probably going to be a big surplus this quarter, and maybe we can get away from it all for a couple weeks, go down to Chicago like we have twice before for a getaway dripping in luxuries.

I never did anything except nod my head, not wanting to risk another argument. I'll have to save it for our counselor, the fact that I'm so low on his priorities he's already forgotten I can't just leave the bakery for two weeks at a time.

I promised I wouldn't get into it before this party. Reg comes from a different world than I do, and he doesn't understand how life works. When you're born into a massive trust ready to spit cash every month like a magic ATM, it's easy to forget other money can only be earned by hard work and active management.

"I'm sorry, honey. He couldn't make it tonight, but he wants to have lunch tomorrow." My heartbeat spikes when I turn around, worried somebody means Reg.

No, it's just mom, her happy eyes shining down softly. She's talking about Matt, who's on his way home right now for several weeks of leave. He said he'd make my engagement party tonight if he got in early, but clearly that isn't happening.

I shrug. I'm not that disappointed – I've mended fences with my big brother since daddy's funeral.

Our relationship is cool and peaceful. I'm not about to rip into old wounds by laying into him over missing the most important moment of my post-Ryan life – especially when he's gone through his own personal hell since daddy died.

"What is it this time? An early night out with the guys?" I gently poke my mother, my gaze going down to the smiling little boy in her arms. "Not more crap with Maggie? She wouldn't normally let you have Holden on a week night."

Mom's expression deflates, and she passes my three year old nephew into my waiting arms. "I told her it was your engagement party. I didn't want Matthew to worry about picking her up when he lands on the red eye tonight, so it's perfect timing for everyone."

"Funny. Since when has the bitch started caring about what's going on in our lives?" I'm careful to keep my voice low, so none of high class Drayton associates chattering around us will need to clutch their pearls over hearing me swear. "Does she have another date or something? I know the latest didn't last long…what was he, number three after Matt?"

"Kara…" Mom looks down and stops just short of wagging a finger. "What she does with her life is none of my business, as long as she's playing by the rules. She's not part of this family anymore."

There's a sour taste in my mouth. It fades when I bounce little Holden on my lap, listening to him babble something that sounds like Auntie Kara a few times.

My brother's marriage to the unfortunate woman who's Holden's mom only lasted six months. He came home from a tour in Afghanistan and found her in bed with the neighbor. He's a hundred times more qualified to raise his son than the cheating slut, and so are we to help him, but the courts are never kind to military fathers looking for custody.

It's incredible how fast everything transforms. I hug my nephew closer, holding him as he yawns. I want someone to swoop down and tell me I'm not walking into the same terrible mistake my big brother made with his marriage.

Mom keeps me company. I pass Holden back to her and casually sip my wine, shifting my knees under the table while I wait for some word from Reg.

Patricia isn't kidding about the embarrassment if he comes in an hour late. Anger courses through my blood.

I don't know what's going on with him lately, and the uncertainty hurts.

Half an hour later, there must be dozens waiting. Every table is packed with men in suits and women who have never done a day's worth of thrift store shopping in their life. Their dresses are new, their purses are imports, and they're talking about trips to warm islands I've never heard of. Soft classical music pipes from the custom speakers installed just for us overhead, echoing through the lighthouse, but it's easily drowned out by the voices.

Patricia stands near the podium, giving me a nervous glance every few seconds. When she stares a little too long, I shake my head, telling her I haven't heard a damned thing from my other half. Reg's father, Harold, stands next to her. He reaches up and clears his throat, an anxious tic I've seen several times at their stuffy fundraisers and corporate parties. Can't blame him for being as worried as the rest of us about how this is going to go if Reg blows it.

This lighthouse used to be so beautiful. Why does it feel like a fucking prison now?

I'm practically kicking myself underneath the table for not speaking up when he pushed for our engagement party here.

This place is cursed, and I should've known it.

My mind wanders while the wine warms my veins, a pleasant distraction from the rising panic over Reg's mysterious absence. A few minutes later, Patricia pulls her keynote speaker into the corner. I don't need to read lips to know she's gone nuclear.

"Kara-bell. Sorry I'm late." Reg grabs my shoulder. By the time I look up, half the room around us is staring at us, cheering and applauding.

The Prince has returned. I try not to glare.

"Where the hell were you?" I whisper, remembering at the last second to smile and wave to the happy crowd.

God. I don't know how celebrities and politicians do this public persona crap.

Stuffing my real feelings down my throat, and keeping them there in front of hundreds of strangers, threatens to make me sick.

Is this how that California girl in the tabloids felt when she shacked up with Prince Silas overseas? I read about her fairy tale romance a few months ago, how she married him to save her father, and then fell in love for real. Some people get all the happy endings.

Reg doesn't say anything, just plops down into the seat next to me. He grabs my hand, pulls it into his firm grip, and lifts the back to his lips like we're prudish aristocrats who haven't ever locked lips.

Way to feed the ridiculous lie we're presenting here.

I go along with it, keeping my grin as wide as humanly possible. Several cameras flash, exploding around us, lighting up the fancy silver and gold balloons swaying against the walls. My fingers ache when they brush his lips because I want to slap him for leaving me hanging in front of everyone.

At least Patricia and Harold look relieved. His parents are walking smiles with the keynote now, Mr. Williams, who's about to step up to the podium and heap praise on the youngest, brightest, most upstanding young man he's ever had the pleasure of mentoring at Drayton Financial.

My predictions are dead on. Reg holds my hand through the entire flowery speech. His near constant smile turns a little more tense when he catches me scowling. His big grey eyes would outdo a whimpering puppy's.

"What's wrong?" he whispers, during a big round of applause near the end of the speech.

"You couldn't have even sent a text?" I'm pouting, and I don't care. "Seriously, Reg, how hard is it to tell the woman you're going to marry why you're late to our first big outing as a couple?"

"Correction, I wasn't late. I had two minutes to spare." His smile weakens. I wonder if he actually remembers how much I hate it when he says *correction*. "Kara, I'm sorry.

When my dad's guys heard about the engagement today, they all insisted on buying me a drink. We had a few rounds in the office, and I had to sober up before the drive. I let it get to me. Here I am, babe. You know I wouldn't miss this for the world."

He squeezes my hand. I stare into his eyes, wanting to believe him.

They're a pretty shade of grey, but they're also dense as the heavy storm clouds drifting over Superior. They're not blue, at least. After Ryan, I don't think I'll ever trust another man with his sky blue eyes again.

"Let's not ruin the night. Remember what Dr. Evans said last week? Forgiveness is divine."

My fingers tighten in his, and I let out a sigh. Thankfully, we're alone in the moment. Everybody around us is distracted, laughing at some charmingly subtle joke Williams just made.

Yeah, divine, like the counselor said. I'd love some divine intervention right now to put a stronger drink in my hand.

As much as I don't like to admit it, the jerk I'm going to marry might be right. The fact that he's thinking about our therapy at all tells me he's *trying*. I'm obligated to follow his lead.

"I'll hold my fire until we get home," I whisper.

Reg puts an arm around my shoulder, pulling me into him. "That's my girl. If you still want to fire away after tonight, I'll get down on my knees and let you put one right between my eyes."

He reaches up, taps himself on the forehead, and makes a jerking motion. He gets a point for making me want to laugh – for real – mostly because I remember the time we went to the gun range last year.

He dragged me with him as part of this country club get together with his firm's clients. I wound up being a natural the second I picked up my first gun and took aim at the targets.

Reg, on the other hand…my poor darling fell over when he felt the kick from the rifle. He never hit a single bullseye We've laughed about it ever since. It's funny because it reminds me how different he is from Ryan.

Unlike the ass who left me behind, Reg is honest. This imperfect, but sincere man who's about to step up and promise me his heart doesn't hide who he is. There are no grand secrets or masculine games with him. He doesn't need to get dirty in a garage, or waste a weekend cleaning his guns to go off hunting.

Sure, it's less exciting sometimes, but that awful night I lost my first love five years ago gave me a lifetime's worth of surprises. I'm done with all that.

I need stability.

I need devotion.

I need to be loved.

Reg offers everything, even when he screws up. My fingers lace tighter with his, and we share a look. It's happy, energetic, and just like old times.

A smile warms my lips, and then curls his, too. I see the spark we're going through therapy to reignite before we say our vows.

It's not so hard to recapture after all, is it? Maybe it never went actually went away, I don't know.

Every couple has disagreements, tensions. That's what we're working through, and we're going to beat it.

Williams is wrapping up, about to give up his speaking slot to Patricia, who's going to introduce us. I won't let Reg totally off the hook once we're done here tonight. But for the next few hours, I'm grateful everything is okay.

I'm going to get up on the stage for a little while soon and act like I'm happy he's about to put a ring worth more than most homes in our town on my finger. If we can just grab onto our old spark a little longer, breathe new life into it, then I won't even have to play pretend.

Our love will be good. It's going to be authentic. Everything I've always wanted, and more.

* * * *

"I met her at the coffee shop," Reg begins, speaking to the crowd when it's his turn at the mic. "You all know it – the only place in town where you can get that fancy feather drawn into your steaming cup of Joe. I told her the answer to the trivia question for the daily discount was all wrong. She told me I had all the answers. Lucky for her, I still do."

Reg smiles, throws an arm around me, and pulls me close. I'm smiling at the memory.

Just a year and a half ago, I hated him. I thought he was pompous, arrogant, too buttoned down whenever he came into my cafe, ordering boxes of coffee and pastries for his associates.

Some days, after I first opened, he was my only customer for hours.

"Look at her up here, playing coy." My fiance pauses while everybody laughs. "If you've had the honor of meeting the real Kara Lilydale like I have, you know spitfire doesn't begin to describe her. She's defiant, sassy, and special because she throws down the only criticism I'll ever listen to, smiling like a fool. Today, I'm honored to tell this town I'm going to make it permanent. I'm making her my wife. I'm ready, able, and waiting to hear her wit for the rest of our lives. It takes a sharp tongue to make a man better, and Kara –" He pauses, turns, and looks me dead in the eyes. "You'd better believe I'm going to be my very best for you, babe."

Reg shifts his eyes to me while waiting for the laughter to die down again. It's a perfect speech, the kind he's had a lot of practice with since college debate. His jokes are in just the right places, wedged in his measured delivery and oscillating tone.

Whatever's been going wrong with this boy lately, it's gestures like this that remind me we're right. My lover, joker, and adoring husband-to-be in one neat package.

I want to believe it's true. Still, there's a faint sour taste on my tongue when I lean in for a kiss.

He didn't appreciate my 'sharp tongue' so much last week, when I told him he'd better start taking our sessions with Dr. Evans seriously, or this wasn't going to work.

He stormed out. Didn't come home all night, and didn't offer much explanation. I didn't ask.

Even his kiss is cooler and softer than it should be when our lips touch.

I try to lose myself in the moment, focus on the happy throngs of people clapping around us. My face heats a little, but only because I know there's probably half a billion dollars staring at us right now. Everyone who's worth something in the whole U.P. is watching us.

To be fair, his kisses rarely curl my hair. Reg doesn't live life on gross, drunken passion. That's why he's stable and ridiculously successful, everything I need to live a happy life, to make up for the losses and failures darkening my earlier years.

I kiss him back, forcing myself into it, wondering if I can turn our little spark into a crackling flame. My face melds into his for one brief moment. When I push my tongue into his mouth, touching the tip to his, Reg pulls back with a startled look.

Predictable. He smiles, waves to the crowd, and soaks in his family's rich friends hooting and hollering like they've seen something truly wild.

Disappointing? Maybe, but I can't get mad at him for being who he is. He'll never make my panties puddle at my feet, and I'm okay with that. I love him because he's *good* for me, damn it. He's the complete opposite of –

No. Don't you dare think his name.

"Babe, would you like to say a few words?" Reg whispers, once the applause begins dying down. The firm hand on my back says the answer better be *yes*.

I give him a shallow nod, shuffling up to the microphone. I clear my throat once, and everybody quiets down.

"I just want to say thank you all for coming out here tonight. It means so much to Reg and me that so many of you fine folks are here to support our love." Turning, I look over my shoulder at his face, hoping it'll inspire the words I need to make an impression. "I'm not going to lie. When we met, I wasn't having an easy time. I'd just lost the man I loved most – my father – and I was trying to change direction after college. I was in a bad spot."

Several people pop big sympathetic smiles. They don't know I flunked out, and probably think I'm talking about starting a new million dollar charity, or something.

"Reg helped pull me out. He taught me to love again, proved I can have a future better than anything I ever imagined. He taught me to appreciate a good man – even when he's being the world's biggest know-it-all."

I pause, looking back at my fiance. It doesn't take much to make this crowd rumble with laughter. Reg smiles softly, knowingly, approval glowing on his face.

Time to bring it home. "Tonight, I'm touched. Honored. Really, I am. I worried this town would never make us feel welcome again after the tragedy that unfolded with Nelson at my father's auto shop several years ago. I'm thrilled to say I was wrong. This town's better than its past, and I'm smiling when I dream about our future. If our wedding is even half as lovely as this engagement party tonight, I know we'll be happy together until the end of time."

People clap unevenly. When I turn, Reg is staring at his feet. He doesn't look up, just grabs me by the wrist, leading me away from the podium.

"Isn't she incredible?" Patricia screams into the microphone behind me, the instant I'm gone. "Another round of applause for happy couple!"

"Okay, stop!" I dig my feet into the floor when we're halfway out the back door, tearing my hand from his grip. "Mind telling me what I did *this time* to piss you off?"

"This was supposed to be our night, Kara," Reg growls, his eyebrows furrowed. "Did you really need to go and remind everybody Uncle Nelson died at your family's stupid fucking chop shop?"

"I wasn't planning on it. Guess it just came out." I'm angry, but I'm honest. "Sorry my speeches aren't as polished as yours, Reg. I didn't have the luxury of a private debate tutor when I was too busy working at that 'chop shop' you're happy to take potshots at."

His lips curl in a fresh smile, a nasty one. "Oh, so it's okay to bitch about jabs at family, and then you take one at mine? Don't be a hypocrite, Kara-bell."

Better a hypocrite than an asshole. He starts walking ahead, down by the trees near the parking lot, reaching into his pocket.

I won't follow him yet. I know by the time I get down there, I'm going to see Mr. Perfect with a slim cigar stuffed between his vicious lips. It's his lone vice, one he's told me a million times he wants to quit.

The wind chooses to pick up just then, billowing in from Superior, sending foamy waves hard against the rocks. Awesome.

I stare out into the night, watching the flickering

shadows through the lighthouse's windows. Up near the beacon, it's pitch dark. Reg couldn't convince the historical society who manages the place to light it up for us tonight.

I don't know why it makes me think about Ryan. For all his faults, he never would've left me standing here after our engagement, wondering more than ever if I'm about to make a gargantuan mistake.

I'm trying to warm myself in the cool night when I smell the asshole's smoke. "Let's go home," he says.

"Already? We're not staying for dinner after the speeches are done?" I jerk away from his hands again. I've lost count how many times that's happened tonight.

"We've made our appearance, Kara. That's all we're expected to do. The rest of the evening belongs to the guests."

"It's supposed to be *our* night," I say, repeating his words from earlier. "Did you really mean that, or were you just hoping I'd play along?"

He snorts. "It's really for the guests, babe, and I think you know that. We'll have our fun at the wedding in a few months. Don't worry."

He starts heading for his big black Escalade. We're leaving in separate cars. I'm sure we'll spend the entire night sleeping as far away from each other as we can get, too.

I don't start crying until I'm pulling away from the lighthouse, watching it fade in the rear view mirror. Part of me wants to take the ramp to the highway and forget about pulling into the heated parking lot of our million dollar condo.

All the material comfort he's given me can't take away the doubts bleeding into every corner of my brain. They're making me dizzy, and the old fear that I'm about to fuck up my life yet again comes swooping in behind them.

There aren't many lights in this town on a sleepy autumn night. The big new construction off Angus street, just before you hit the residential areas, is the only exception.

It's some kind of new office, or a factory. Maybe both. It's glassy, glamorous, so huge in its splendor it's like a miniature skyscraper. Totally out of place in Split Harbor – especially with those lights.

God, those hot white lights. I have to shield my teary eyes when I go past to stay on the road. The thing looks like it's prepped for its grand opening, an event I'm sure Reg and every other rich asshole with a political background will be there to attend.

Nobody heard of Punch Corp until they were building on our doorstep. Now, it seems like the chatter never ends. There's a million stories about how it's going to bring so many jobs, higher revenues, plus a lot of long lost prestige. No thanks to the whiz who manages it, Tanner Brooks, some kind of twenty-something start up freak from the West Coast with a genius IQ.

He's a billionaire already, they say. I hear the girls around my own age chattering away at Grounded, spilling their anxious dreams in the open. Ones where they bump into Tanner, and he becomes their Prince Charming, whenever he decides to grace our little town with his otherworldly celebrity.

It's good people can be still get excited over more than failing relationships.

Me, I'm too busy wondering if this marriage is done before it's started. I don't care about Tanner fantasies, or Punch Corp, or any of that.

My foot taps the accelerator hard, and my car roars on into the night. I'm desperate to get home so I can have a hot bath and close out this miserable day. Maybe I can get the usual fight with Reg over with early. It'll exhaust all my energy so I won't sit up by the fireplace, staring across town out our big bay window.

Then I won't have to think about the last time a man ripped my heart out. I won't have to think about the high turnover with the high school kids at Grounded, or the brake job my car needs that I refuse to let him pay for, or even the last thing daddy said to me before he slipped away into his medicated coma and never woke up.

You're a beautiful, intelligent woman, peanut. You've got your whole life ahead.

I hate the way that memory, the last one I have, seems to dominate all the others. Remembering his words makes the tears come hotter, more frequent, scalding rivulets running down my cheeks.

I love you, daddy. I gripped his hand so fucking hard that night. It was just him and I. I'm glad he was pumped up on constant painkillers, or my death grip probably would've hurt. He'd gotten so much smaller, so frail, just a shell of the brawny soldier and mechanic he used to be.

Kara. He strained to say my name, opening his eyes one

last time. *Come closer. There's something I need to tell you…something about that night…something with him…*

My heart swung down like a pendulum, and I was almost afraid to ask. But I had to.

Daddy, who?

His jaw clenched one more time, as if it took all his energy just to open his lips. *Ryan…*

Ryan was the last word he ever said. He closed his eyes, his body releasing, and died several hours later.

I still wonder if I heard him right, even though my ears imprinted that word into my head like a permanent echo.

I hear it to this day, a curse from another time, haunting and mysterious. I ponder, obsess over it, especially when life decides to twist my nipples in a vise.

Why in God's name was Ryan the last thing on his mind? Was it the drugs, the trauma, or something more?

And why did I have to hear it so clearly, leaving no doubt? Every possibility feeds a thousand more, each one pounding in my head so viciously it makes me sick.

The rest of the short ride home is a long, painful blur.

When I step inside, there's a flickering glow in the living room. Reg beat me there. He has a fire going under the mantle, a glass of red wine in one hand.

"There's another glass for you on the counter," he says, giving me a slow look. "Sit down, babe. I want to talk. I'm sorry for what happened earlier."

Sorry. There's a lot of words I despise these days, but it's near the top of the list.

I have no choice but to humor him. I put away my coat,

pad over to the counter, and grab my glass. If I drink it down fast enough, maybe it'll take the edge off. Luckily, if it doesn't, there's plenty more in the bottle.

It takes me several seconds to bite my tongue hard enough to walk across the room, and sit down on the leather chair across from him. He tries to smile at me again, but I don't return it. I'm not in a giving mood. Not after what he did earlier tonight.

"I don't want it to be this way," he says. Could that be more obvious? "Listen, if there's anything I can do to make this right, just let me –"

"Start by telling me why you got there so late." Pinching the stem of my wine glass harder, I glare at him, conjuring my inner bitch.

She won't be easy to satisfy tonight. I don't care how many times Dr. Evans extols forgiveness. It feels like a burden more than something divine. I'm not interested in flowery mumbo-jumbo tonight, unless he's willing to come clean about everything, and apologize.

"I told you already. Too much drinking with dad's associates." He sighs, briefly closing his eyes, trying to be patient. "I let it get away from me. I messed up. I told you, I'm sorry. I've apologized before, but I'll do it again, because I mean it, Kara-bell. I should have called."

"Yeah, *should*. Just like you're about to tell me you should have kept your cool, instead of dragging me out of our own engagement party like a spoiled brat, right?"

"Kara…" He pauses, takes a big pull from his wine, and I inwardly smile, knowing that's exactly what he was about to say.

His glass goes down, clinking on the little table between us. He folds his fingers, staring into me with his cool grey eyes, until I look back.

"I'm not going to apologize for that. I know you're tired, sick of the excuses. Let me give you the truth instead. Truth is, I'm stressed out. I'm human. I'm having a hard time getting things back on track, managing my role in the family business, trying to deflect mom when she calls up every day with another hundred things to do before the wedding happens."

Oh, okay. You're stressed? My first reaction I hold in, because the second is amazement that Mr. Perfect just fessed up to being fallible.

"Go on," I say, slowly draining what's left in my glass.

"You deserve better than this, babe. You need me to do better, and I will. I'm going to make mistakes along the way, I'm going to piss you off, but for fuck's sake, I'm trying. I'm going to call Dr. Evans in the morning, and ask him for advice about how to handle this, because I don't know how I should. If you want to put it on hold until then, go straight to bed, I won't blame you. I'll sleep in the guest room tonight, if you need some space."

His eyes are huge, almost watery. I've never seen tears clouding his eyes. Honestly, it scares me.

He lets out a long sigh. I can see he's about to walk away, if I don't first. "Wait. Don't sleep in the guest room, Reg."

I reach for his hand, give it a squeeze, and manage a ghostly smile. "I appreciate you for trying. I'll agree this hasn't been easy on either of us. That has to change."

"It will. I can't give up, Kara. I'm serious, more than I've ever been about anything in my entire life."

The anger I had before melts into sad resignation.

I can't stop staring into his eyes, wondering why it's so hard to love, and *just be*. He stands up, moves around the table to me, and crouches on his knees. He throws an arm around me, runs his smooth hand across my face, slowing when he senses the fire in my cheek.

"Jesus. You were crying on the way home, weren't you?"

"Not just about tonight," I say. There's no point denying it. "It isn't all you, or this wedding. You're stressed out, and so am I. There's a lot to get done. I'm overwhelmed. I'll need to see my accountant next week about the quarterly taxes again."

"Kara-bell, use my guy. For the hundredth time, he'll do it right, do it fast, and save you a ton of money."

I open my eyes. Reg stops there, and gives me a sheepish smile. At least he realizes the last thing we need tonight is another fight over why I'm adamant on doing things my way, instead of taking the easy route with his family's resources.

"Do you want me to run you a bath?" he asks, something he hasn't done in months.

Nodding, I lay my fingers on his neck, just enough to feel his pulse. "That sounds really nice. I'll be in bed shortly. I just need a little time to myself to digest all this."

"I love you, babe. Don't ever doubt it."

Before he slips away, I dig my nails into his neck, and bring my lips to his. We kiss, soft and sweet, for just one second.

It isn't much, true. But after everything that's happened, it's enough to stave off disaster.

Later, after I've had a couple more glasses of wine and soaked my skin to pruning, I slip into our silky sheets. He's fast asleep, snoring gently on the far side of the bed.

Baby steps. There's no need to hold him tonight, much as part of me might want to, much less do anything that doesn't involve our clothes.

It's been months since we had sex. Probably twice as many since it was normal. That part of our relationship has never been perfect, but there was always enough good outside to make up for it.

Reg has...unusual tastes. When times were better, I did everything I could to indulge him, even though it didn't do much for me.

No, it wasn't a total waste.

I let him spend big on his habit. I still have weeks worth of pedicures to cash in, and rows of heels to show for it. They're useful outside the bedroom, at least.

Just worthless for making me wet. It's the same when he asks me to let him rub my feet, or run his tongue across my shiny new Louboutins.

If you can't imagine getting sick of foot rubs, try being with a fetishist. I wish I could trade them away most nights.

I need to be fucked in our bed, and hard.

Our sex life has barely come up in therapy, and I cringe when I think about it. Tonight, I'm too exhausted to dwell on it. We need to fix the emotional gap between us before we can talk about the physical one.

I'm content that our drag out fight has been diffused. Thankful for small victories, I drift off staring at my fiance's face. It reminds me that I really do love him, and we're going to get through this.

I'd rather work through these issues now than revisit them when we're forty with three kids. As long as we're upfront, motivated, and honest with each other, we'll survive.

Jesus, we have to.

Losing another engagement when I'm leaving my early twenties isn't an option. I can't stand another heartbreak.

It's get through this, marry Reg, imperfections and all…or else I'll wind up asking myself why I'm doing this. Why I need him, or any man, to fill the craters blown open in my life.

There's no way I'm going into that dark place. It's taken five years, but I've learned my lesson, over and over and over again.

Cope. Never look back. Don't ask too many questions with painful answers.

There's nothing more dangerous than *why*.

VI: Peephole (Ryan)

I'm at my new desk, so shiny it's almost blinding, staring at my laptop. It's all there, the video I shot with my military grade spy cam around seven o'clock last night. I'm watching the footage, fighting the urge not to put my fist through my nice new screen.

He comes out of the hotel with a woman hanging on his arm. She's decked out in a silky purple dress. He kisses her one more time before he climbs into his car, making damned sure to let his hand swoop down her low back, grazing the top of her ass. Both their smiles say they've just finished fucking like it's Valentine's Day.

I want to kill the cheating bastard.

I want to wrap my hands around his throat and squeeze until his eyes pop like marbles. I want him to die slowly, painfully, and without mercy because he's fucking her over – literally and figuratively.

He fucks her once with his dirty little secret, the secret life she knows nothing about, and again when he comes home and climbs into her bed.

Meanwhile, I'm being fucked by my own jealousy. It

wraps around me like a snake, glues my eyes to the screen, and makes me look at the man I despise for one simple reason.

The lying, mild mannered little prick is having her, and I'm not.

My fist comes down hard. It echoes in the office like a gunshot, and there's someone at the door a second later.

I can't help it. I haven't been this upset, this pissed off, since I saw it go down with my camera last night, hunkered down in my Tesla with my coat pulled up over my mouth. And before last night, I haven't been that pissed since the night I lost her, sent her like a lamb into the arms of this skirt chasing wolf.

"Mr. Brooks? Is everything all right?" Becky jiggles the doorknob when I don't answer quickly enough.

"Yeah!" It takes me several seconds to have a long swig of coffee, and then compose myself. "Come in."

She enters, all smiles. I ought to be grinning too, considering the way everyone's bonuses around here have bloated five times bigger this quarter. It takes every muscle in my face not to scowl.

"Are you okay?" she asks me again.

"Not exactly, Becky," I say, standing up and straightening my tie. "We're better than okay. It's going to be an incredible day. Are they ready for us?"

The uncertainty on her face melts in another sun beam smile. "That's why I came up to get you."

We make small talk on the way out. Leonard is already waiting in the limo, looking more sleepless than usual. His newborn is forcing him and his wife to burn extra hours on no sleep. He'll get a break soon enough, but it's been rough with the duty I've had him pulling, making certain our grand opening in my old hometown goes off without a hitch.

"Can you believe it, boss?" he asks, just when the big crowd in front of the factory comes into view.

"I can. We worked our asses off to get here, and we're not leaving until everybody's a whole lot richer. That means us, plus the good people of Split Harbor. You're not allowed to quit when your company crosses the billion mark."

He smiles. "Only a year ago. Jesus. Some days, it gets to me, trying to believe this." He spreads his hand across his chest, an exaggerated display that makes Becky laugh.

"Yeah, it better. Appreciate it. We're big enough for other companies to start poaching talent. If I don't keep it rolling in, there's no way either of you are going to stay with me in this little town."

"It's really very quaint," Becky says, staring into her phone as she applies more lipstick. "Quieter, I mean. More peaceful than the little towns down the coast from Seattle."

"Almost too quiet." Leonard wrinkles his nose. "Can't stand the energy here in all honesty. Without the private jet home, we'd be screwed."

"Tell me that again when you see how many good, hardworking people we snatch up in this town. The whole U.P. is teeming with people who just need a break. Besides, we don't need geniuses with PhDs and ten years experience to operate our machines. That's why we're a perfect fit."

"Yeah, but why here, boss? I'll never understand how you found this place. Marquette is small enough. This place, down the highway…it's like we're in Timbuktu. There's only two shops serving coffee in the morning in town, for Christ's sake!"

Becky and I laugh. I'd better keep smiling, or else I risk revealing history no one needs to know about.

"Used to spend my summers in Michigan," I lie. "It doesn't take too many drives up and down this shore to fall in love with the scenery, plus the little towns. You should try it sometime, Leonard. Better way to pep yourself up than tossing down three espressos a day."

"Shit, only three? That was before the kid. Boss, I'm up to *five* with Billy keeping me up!"

I smile, laying a brotherly hand on his shoulder. "It's going to get easier. Trust me."

I'm pretending I know, but I don't have a clue. Ignorance stings.

Yes, I'm happy for him. Doesn't mean it isn't a wicked irony.

I'm sure my advice sounds just as ridiculous to him. As far as anybody with an exec title knows, I'm still playing the field, plodding my way through the finest clubs in Seattle, leaving heartbreaks and hangovers in my wake.

I haven't fucked in almost a year. Not since our company got its biggest contract, and I saw the blueprints for this place with my own eyes.

Several valets rush up from the spot where the mayor is waiting, opening our doors. I step out with the firm smile

I've cultivated over the last five years and wave to the people like I own the world. Today, in this town, I do.

I'm careful to check my cuffs one more time, just to make sure they're covering the ink expanding on my skin.

Deep down, I'm nervous.

It's got nothing to do with the first day jitters where hiccups in component production are bound to happen, or the fact that I'm about to address people who knew me under my old name.

I'm not worried about being recognized. I've spent enough time in town to know nobody places this face to the kid who disappeared. Even stopped wearing the contacts to change my eye color when I realized how dead and forgotten Ryan really is to this town.

It's like he never existed. Maybe they never wanted him to, after they think they found out who he really was.

My speech is brief. I'm here to pump them up, not give them a lecture. I give them the usual spiel about prosperity, jobs, creative energy, and a Seattle sized drive to kick ass in the Midwest.

By the end of it, the mayor wraps her arms around me. We both share the oversized gold scissors, more like garden shears, and cut the red ribbon near the doors.

Everybody cheers. Leonard, Becky, and so many more I've worked with for years lose their shit, lost in the moment, drunk on our triumph and dreaming about tomorrow.

For Punch Corp, it's a victory. Growing up here, this was the moment I fantasized about, the day I'd know beyond any doubt I'd made it.

Too bad it isn't her.

No factory can compare to Kara. Neither can the dozens of lucrative contracts, or the millions in personal investments I'm accumulating every week.

Richer on paper. Poorer in heart.

Once upon a time, I thought that 'money can't buy happiness' schtick was the biggest BS I'd ever heard. Now, I'm afraid it might be true.

The rest of the ceremony drags. I keep the same beaming grin plastered to my face, hobnobbing with my associates and a hundred people whose names I won't remember tomorrow.

The instant we're done, I'm back in the limo with Leonard and Becky, listening to them chatter about priorities impatiently when I just want to get back to the office.

"Len, I want you to sort out the kinks," I tell him, drawing a surprised look from Becky. She can't believe I'm trampling on my inner perfectionist. "You two are smart, you're capable, and you've been with me the longest. It's time for me to stop micro-managing and focus on the big picture. I'm leaving early today. There's something I have to do, but I'll be in tomorrow for the full rundown on what's going right and wrong. Do your best."

They don't say anything except "yes, sir." I'm out of the limo before I can get any more weird looks, heading for my car.

It's a tense ride to the place where she lives with the cheating asshole. I refuse to call it her home when he's got her trapped in a lie.

The last time I gripped a steering wheel this tight, I was leaving town in a stolen yacht. It's strange to drive through it, taking the twists and turns through the forested boulevard on the edge of town, then down to the wealthy lodges and condos along the waterfront.

I'm bigger, richer, and more successful than anybody here. Doesn't seem to matter. Part of me still feels like that kid, helpless to forces bigger than I can understand.

When I pull up to the curb outside her condo, I don't get out right away. My eyes scan the walkway near the heated garage. The small slanted windows there are just big enough to let me peer inside.

I see her car. She's home.

It's been months since I seriously worried about being recognized here. When I walk into the entryway and look for the attendant to ring her, there's a cold sweat prickling my brow.

Will she recognize my voice?

Will she remember my face?

Will she turn me into the police, or maybe kill me herself, the second she figures out who I am?

* * * *

"Ms. Lilydale, there's a man here to see you," the desk clerk says, holding down the button to radio her condo. "He says he has business concerning your cafe."

"Business with Grounded? Really?" Her voice crackles through, soft and surprised. She hesitates for several seconds. "Okay, whatever. Send him up."

The man stands up, walks over, and slides his card through the elevator. We exchange friendly glances as he holds it open for me. Soon, I'm heading up to the third floor, second guessing myself more in those agonizing seconds than any other time in the last five years.

There aren't many units to walk past. It's a lot like my place in Seattle, private and exclusive, except here there's fewer luxuries and a more old world charm.

My fist is clenched while I head down the hall, ready to knock with just the right pressure.

Except I don't have to. She's hanging out the door. Blond, green eyed, and beautiful as the day she said yes to me. Prettier than the day I kissed her for the last time and said goodbye.

She looks at me and smiles. I'm still about eight feet away. If she knows who I am, there's no recognition.

The biggest surprise of all is the kid. He's hanging off her leg like a little monkey, a toddler just learning to walk, bashfully pulling behind her when he sees me coming. Maybe he can sense the atmosphere coming undone all around me as I'm heading for judgment.

"I have to say, this is a surprise. I didn't think I'd made any real inroads at that roasters convention last month. Who do I have the pleasure of meeting, Mr. –"

Her tongue turns to stone. I'm standing right in front of her, and I watch her eyes go huge in slow motion, filling up like she's sucked in a storm, desperate to hold it. The kid at her feet smiles, and giggles.

"Oh my God. Come on, Holden, we're way overdue for

your nap." She reaches down, starts scooping him up, ready to retreat back inside and slam the door in my face.

My hand shoots straight past her, knocking it into the wall. "Wait."

"Leave!" she hisses, one word like an arrow through the ribs. "Leave now, Ryan, or I'm calling the cops."

"Just like that? The old Kara would at least ask why I'm here." I smile, gazing deep into her eyes for the first time in years.

They're beautiful. Electric. And so damn alive, even when she's afraid.

I'm placing bets doing this, but I'm also drawing lines. The kid throws a wrench in everything. He's the reason she's being so careful, but I'm not going to take advantage of it. I won't do anything that scares him.

In all my planning, all the times I imagined this fragile moment, I didn't account for any visitors. *Fuck.*

"I'm a married woman now," she says quickly, her eyes darting around. "Married, with a family. There's nothing to talk about. You have no right to barge in like this."

I hold in a nauseating laugh. She's a horrific actor.

What the hell happened to the woman I loved? She never would have lied like this in the past. She's either petrified, or she's changed so much I barely know who I'm seeing beyond the surface.

"We can stop pretending. I know he's Matt's son, Kara. If you want to talk, lying to my face isn't a good way to start."

"I *don't* want to talk to you, unless you're going to admit to being a stalker freak. Christ, it's hard to even look at you." She turns her face so hard a brilliant golden lock of her hair whips across her shoulder. "Nothing you can say will *ever* change my opinion. You think you're so smart, don't you?"

Yeah, launching a billion dollar company will do that. I hold my tongue, keeping my ego in check, because the last thing I want to do is piss her off more.

"I don't give much thought to my intelligence. I think you're still beautiful." My hand uncurls and reaches for her face, cupping her cheek. It's like lightning, my skin on hers, a jolt filled with memories, passions, and dreams unfulfilled. "I'm not here to scare you, Kara. I came home to make things right, including with you. Give me a little of your time. That's all I'm asking. We'll meet somewhere after your nephew's home. I'll explain everything, I promise."

"Time?" It comes out like a curse.

She shakes her head, turns around, and starts walking. Too bad she's got the kid, or I'd be going after her. No, I don't care about tromping on the cheating asshole's Turkish rug. I've got five of them worth thousands more in my own place. I'd roll her fiance up in it and drop him off the nearest bridge if it brought her back to me.

Why won't she look at me?

I'm pissed. Volcanic blood surges through my veins, electrifying my temples. I try to look cool, holding myself up in her doorway, waiting until I hear her footsteps coming toward me again. I'm surprised she doesn't have her phone out, ready to make good on the threat to dial the cops.

She's empty handed. Her arms are folded. She's glaring,

and I've never seen those eyes I fell in love with burn with such hatred.

"You want time, Ryan? That's what you came to ask me for?" I open my mouth to answer, but she never gives me the chance. Her little hands fly out. They're slapping my shoulders. I'm so taken aback I stumble into the hall, and she follows, still hitting me, this time in the face.

"The nerve...you're a sadistic, creepy, backstabbing asshole! I can't believe you have the fucking *nerve* to ask for time after everything you stole from me. You robbed away *years* from my life."

"Kara-bou – stop!" Catching her wrists, I squeeze them hard, and push her against the wall. "It isn't like that."

It's not my hands that overpower her. She locks up when she hears the old pet name, the one that's as alien to her as Ryan is to me.

"Let go. And don't you ever call me that again." Her eyes are daggers, eager to cut me to pieces.

Growling, I slowly release her, lowering my arms. My hands go out. Pleading, imploring, desperate to make her listen for one golden minute.

"I didn't come back to turn your life upside down again," I tell her. "Your fiance, Reg, he's not who you think he is. There's something you need to know, Kara."

"No." Her eyes narrow, sharpen, and cut me like green knives. "You fed me the biggest lie of my life, Ryan. If you think I'm going to stand here and listen while you try to ruin my marriage, you don't know me. Hell, you don't have a clue anymore."

I stare her down, trying to find the right combination of words. "Give me one chance. Five minutes of your time. *Please.*"

"Get out! Leave, leave, and never come back." She closes her eyes, forcing a hot tear down her red cheek. "I'm not going to say it again, you fucking murderer."

Ouch. Hell is hearing her say what she thinks I've become.

I blink, too pissed at how badly this is going to do anything else.

Murderer. It's the dreaded word, one that's kept me up at night for five years, imagining its weight on her lips.

I told myself I was ready to deal with it. I must've been insane to believe it.

"Kara –"

"Fuck off!" She swats my hand away when I reach for her, backing into the wall on the opposite side of the hallway. "How many times do I have to ask you to leave? Turn around and go. *Now.* I'm not interested in excuses, catching up, or whatever big secrets you think you're entitled to drop in my lap. You abandoned me, Ryan. You missed *everything*. My suffering, Matt's purple heart, the night daddy got diagnosed with cancer, the night he fucking died!" Sighing, she closes her eyes for a second, shaking her head.

It's hard not to wince. She doesn't know how torn up reading her old man's obituary made me not so long ago. If it weren't for Bart, I wouldn't be standing here, taking this abuse, absorbing it patiently because I deserve every last word.

I left her. If I'd had another choice, it's the last thing in the world I ever would've done.

"Kara..." I try to reach out to her, but she gives me a look like she's going to bite me if I touch her again.

"No. We're way past over. You took weeks, months, years off my life," she says. "Let that sink in for a second, jackass – *years*. I'm going to count to five. If you aren't on your way to the elevator by the time I'm through, you'll be in prison."

I study her eyes. It isn't just fear clouding them.

It's real hate. Loathing. Years of pain fermented into poison, inflicted by me, unearthed when she least wanted it.

I can't give up on this. I need to convince her, but her face is telling me the obvious – today isn't the day to do it.

Fury churns in my guts while I turn away, put one foot in front of the other, and force myself to leave her a second time.

Before I'm to the elevator, I hear her door slam shut. The metal doors close, locking me in. There's a few brief, hot seconds where my fists are flying and I'm screaming, before I hit the button. I'm so sick and disappointed in myself I can't even remember to check whether or not the elevator has a camera.

Thankfully, this town is so small, even the million dollar condos don't need to be crawling with surveillance. The attendant looks at me when I stop next to his desk, fish out several hundreds from my wallet, and throw them on his desk.

"Sir?"

"That's for the damage in the elevator, plus extra for your trouble." I also leave Becky's card, knowing he can reach her if he needs more. "I'm sorry."

I'm clenching my hand, trying to stop the bleeding. I only glance back once, over my shoulder, before I'm heading through the big glass doors to my car. The entire floor inside the elevator is covered in sharp fragments from the mirrors that used to line its walls. I shattered every single one of them with my bare fists.

* * * *

Later, when I'm at the hotel where I'm staying with a drink in my hand, I realize my mistake. I'm staring across town at her condo. It's the only building taller than this one, before my new factory was finished. Now, it dominates Split Harbor's vacant skyline.

I never should've confronted her at home. There were too many unknowns, like the kid she had to put down for a nap before she could even talk to me. Plus it meant invading her personal space – something she'd never welcome since she's chosen to believe the worst about who I am, what I did, and why.

For a second, that night flashes through my head again, and I swallow the rest of my drink. I can only remember the blood, the panic, the gut-wrenching pile of evil shit I found in that old man's car, and then sailing for my life across Superior's inky unsettled black waves. Each one crashing down over the hull, threatening to snuff me out like a mountain falling on a mouse.

I'm staring at my phone, watching the line on the map. The GPS tracker I put on Reg's car rolls into Marquette. He's so predictable it hurts.

Asshole goes straight to their usual place, the big hotel by the lake, where he lies to her again every time he buries his dick in his dirty little secret.

Maybe she can't forgive or forget what I did. If she hears me out, and still decides we're not meant to be, then I'm ready to walk away. Move on. Know that I did everything I could to win her back.

But I can't give up without opening her eyes. She can't marry this sonofabitch.

Whatever mistakes I've made, however I've stumbled back into her life this afternoon, I won't screw this part up.

Next time we meet, it's going to be on my terms. I'm giving her the truth about dear old Reg. Then I'm going to open my arms, pull her in, and put my mouth on hers until neither of us can breathe.

Yes, I'm officially a stalker, peeking into their lives, hellbent on chasing a second chance I don't know if I deserve.

I'm obsessed, guilty, and proud of it. I can't live the rest of my life saying what if.

We're meant to be. I'll live, breathe, and worship this last chance to have her back until it's crushed out of me.

Until it's gone, the last hanging shred of my old life, forcing me to bury what's left of Ryan for good.

Maybe I'm a fool, I can't save us, and I'm going to have to suffer to realize you can't bring back what's long dead. Doesn't matter.

I'm done looking through this peephole, staring into a life I'm never supposed to have.

I won't let go before I've exhausted every option, every chance, every ounce of wishful thinking.

I'm taking her back. I'll have her under me again, moaning my name, or else I'll feel every last drop of blood squeezed from my heart when she pushes me away forever.

VII: Shaken (Kara)

I'm too shaken the rest of the evening to do anything.

There's a fugue hanging over my head when I wake up Holden, kiss him goodbye, and hand him off to my brother, who's comes by to collect his little boy sometime around ten.

I don't know where Reg is. Again.

Working late again. Ask me about the chat with Dr. Evans later.

That's what his text reads, anyway. I shrug, instead of getting angry. There isn't any point. I don't think it's possible to know rage after seeing Ryan. There's too much confusion numbing my nerves. The cloudy, maddening blur sends me back through time and space, making me think about the bastard all over again.

He's just as mysterious as the day he disappeared. Getting him to leave was my only concern when we were standing face-to-face. Now that he's gone, I'm able to sit and wonder about the fancy suit clinging to every inch of him, plus the high end black car I watched him climb into through the window.

Did he come here dressed to impress me? Or is it just one more part of who he is – someone who's a total stranger?

Of course, he was gorgeous. More handsome than any heartbreaker with blood on his hands has any business being.

The years have been good to him. The muscular, sexy boy became a man. Full bodied, broad shouldered, his trousers tucked around hips that look like they could slam a woman into the next century.

It's hard to remember he's probably a killer. *Probably.*

I'm not going to get my hopes up about anything daddy whispered an hour before he left this world for good. Secrets almost killed me once. They'll do it again if I give them a chance.

I hate this. But damn, it's hard not to get wet when I picture what that body looks like underneath the suit, or whenever I remember how his hands didn't hesitate when he backed me against the wall.

His touch stopped me in my tracks. Owned me the way he used to during our brief, beautiful nights together. Reg never touches my face. I'd forgotten how good it is to have a man's hand there. Raw, masculine strength that can be as rough or as gentle as I want it to be.

God. Did I mention I'm *shaken?*

Nothing will take the edge off. I'm going to get sick if I resort to wine.

I settle in on the balcony, wrapped in my robe, a steaming cup of black tea in my hands. It's my fault I wouldn't let him speak, but I couldn't let him give me a mental breakdown.

I don't know what kind of game he's playing. If he really killed Nelson that night five years ago, then there's a good chance I'm dealing with a genuine psychopath.

There should be no sympathy. It shouldn't hurt to touch my phone every time I think about reporting him. One quick call to the sheriff's office, letting them know Split Harbor's most notorious fugitive is back, and I won't have to worry anymore.

He's not who you think he is. Ryan's words stick. They're death threats if they're right. Every one of them promises to detonate everything I think I know.

I couldn't survive it from any man, but hearing it from him? From the strange, heartless bastard who lost his mind, killed a man, and threw my heart in the trash half a decade ago?

No, I can't. I won't listen.

I can't, I can't, I can't, I can't.

I'm about to throw my mug three floors down to the parking lot when I hear someone behind me. Whipping around, pulling my robe tight, there's Reg standing at the door with a glass of wine, a worried look on his face.

"You're out here awfully late, Kara-bell. Come in and warm up. I just turned on the fireplace."

"It's almost eleven. You didn't call." Yes, he's taking the brunt of everything Ryan stirred up earlier, but I don't care. I really need to know where he was, especially after hearing *he's not who you think he is.*

"Babe, what's wrong? I sent you a text. Had a pleasant conversation with our doctor this morning. I told him about last night, with the party. You know what he said?"

"I don't care. You're deflecting my question," I step inside, resisting the urge to throw my mug again, this time at his face.

"He said we did good, Kara." Reg stops, sips his wine, and waits until I look at him before he goes on. "We're making real progress. Sure, there's a long way to go, and we're going to keep stepping on each other by accident once in awhile. Every couple does it. He said so himself."

His wine glass goes down. Hits the counter with a resounding clink, and then he's coming toward me, holding out his arms. His embrace is just about the last place in the world I want to be today.

But as soon as his lean, firm arms are around me, I fold. I'm only human. There's no resisting comfort right now. I think I'd accept it if a grizzly bear walked into the room offering a hug.

Desperation sucks.

"I have to ask you something," I whisper, wrapping my arms around him weakly. "You can't get mad. Just be honest."

"Anything, babe." He pushes his fingers through my hair, wearing a smile as soft as the sun.

I don't remember the last time I felt this much at peace with him. Shame it's going to go up in smoke as soon as I drop my question.

"Are you having an affair?"

His fingers slip through my hair a little more quickly,

tangling the ends of my locks. He's extra fluid when his eyes find mine, every part of him animated at once. Just like the way he used to get when we'd stay up half the night, talking about the places we're going to see after we're married, trekking the globe together as husband and wife.

"No. That's crazy, babe, and not something you'll ever need to worry about." He leans down, his voice strangely soft. His warm lips touch my forehead. "I'm not mad, but I'm going to ask you where the hell you got the idea?"

"You're late all the time, and you won't say why. Is it really all work, or is there something else going on?" My eyes scan his, searching for dishonesty, however faint. I can't tell. "If it's not another woman…then what? Are you drinking too much? Wrapped up in something illegal?"

For a second, he hesitates. But his eyes aren't lying. He smiles, letting out a lengthy sigh.

"I wanted it to be a big surprise. I've been spending a lot of time down in Drayton Financial's marketing firm, Karabell. You won't accept any help from me with your business, I know. I get it. Hell, I respect it." His fingers move through my hair again, softer than before.

"Marketing? What are you talking –"

"Since you won't let me give you the money you need to run proper ads for tourists, I was going to do it myself." He holds a finger up with his free hand, and pushes it gently against my lips as soon as they open. "Don't say anything yet. I'm *not* building your business for you. I'm simply promoting my favorite coffeehouse. And since my family runs so much of the tourism here, it only makes sense the good people from out-of-town ought to have the best recommendation for their morning cup."

I'm melting. There's nothing in his voice that says he's full of it, even though a voice deep down inside is telling me it's too good to be true.

Too convenient, perhaps. But the alternative to continuing to dig into him, insinuating he's full of it, is recognizing my own creeping cynicism. That's the last place I want to go.

So, I don't say anything. I'm satisfied for now.

He holds me gently, swaying in the middle of the kitchen, rocking me. I let him because I'd better get used to feeling the earth moving beneath my feet.

Ryan's reappearance is proof the earthquakes aren't going to stop anytime soon. They're going to get worse, and someone is bound to collapse before it's over.

* * * *

It's an uneventful week. We go our separate ways, have our weekly session with Dr. Evans, and talk to his parents a few more times about food options for the wedding. I try my damnedest to get back to my normal life and forget I ever saw a ghost from my past.

One morning, I'm at Grounded like usual. Working my tail off to make sure there's enough beans roasted for a media drop-in scheduled this afternoon. It's something to do with breakfast and coffee recommendations for the new Punch employees on the edge of town, and I'm eager to make a lovely first impression.

I'm still in the back, barking orders to the half dozen kids I manage, plus one single mom picking up part-time hours. The second I hear the chime for the front door ring, I'm flying out to the register, a huge smile on my face, carrying two steaming sampler mugs of our best coffee to the man waiting there to greet me.

"It's a pleasure, Ms. Lilydale." His voice stops me dead in my tracks before I even see his face.

It's Ryan. Standing there with the world's smuggest smile, extending a hand, surrounded by at least three men from the Harbor Gazette priming their cameras.

"Welcome to Grounded." My voice threatens to crack, but I won't let it. If he's here as some kind of sick joke to throw me off on a big day for my cafe, he's wrong. I'm not giving him the satisfaction.

"Have to say, I think I'm already in love with this little place." Of course, the bastard beams his ocean blue eyes into mine when he says the dreadful L-word. "Give me your best. Black, please. Before I leave, I'd like you to know I've dropped a check in your donation box for the cancer foundation you're advertising. It's wonderful to see business being charitable."

He motions to the big pink banner hanging up above our charity billboard.

Charitable? Really? Is that what you call it when you left me behind to watch him suffer? When you weren't around for daddy's funeral, the whole fucking reason I'm hawking cancer research here in the first place?

I'm so caught up on wondering how I can punch him in

the face and get away with it, that I barely stop to wonder why he's here with all these cameras. He can't be Punch Corp's marketing rep…can he?

No, I never saw Ryan working a corporate job. But we've lost a lot of years, become different people, and I can't rule out anything.

There's nothing I know about the pompous ass in front of me except that I hate him. He looks at me while I order up his drink – a premium cup of steaming *get-the-hell-out*.

"Can I have a look around?" I nod quickly, once, and he smiles. "Good. I think the press with me here today have a few questions of their own. This is your spotlight, Ms. Lilydale. The last thing I want to do is get in the way."

"It's Mrs. Drayton soon," I snap, a sinister satisfaction lighting up my blood when I see jealous storms rolling through his eyes. "Just a friendly correction."

He turns, a fake diplomatic smile on his face, and starts strolling around my cafe like he's fascinated with everything I've built. I order coffees and donuts for the media people, letting them know I'm happy to sit down anytime for an interview.

A tall journalist named Tom guides me over to the nearest table. He's shaking his head by the time we sit down with our coffee.

"Before our interview, I just want to say, you're doing a *hell* of a job handling yourself in front of a celebrity, Ms. Lilydale." I don't bother to correct him on the name because it won't get under his skin, like it will Ryan's. "Did you ever dream you'd have this little place getting so much attention?"

It's my turn to shake my head. I'm not understanding.

Celebrity? What the hell is he talking about?

I look up, my eyes shifting over to Ryan, who's standing in the corner, staring up at the huge oil panting of old ships coming into Split Harbor, hauling ore and grain across the Great Lakes.

"Who, him?" I nod toward the asshole in the suit who's come back to ruin my life after I worked so hard to undo his damage.

Tom's cracks a grin. "Excuse me? Are you saying you've never heard of Tanner Brooks?"

"Wait...you're telling me that's him? *The* Mr. Brooks?" My mouth hangs open a little.

The reporter just laughs. "I'm blown away. You really didn't know? I may be a small town journalist, Ms. Lilydale, but I know bait. Nobody can be that ignorant. Listen, I'm not going to walk into whatever PR surprise trap you've set with him."

Holy shit.

It finally makes sense. The reason a corporate Goliath magically decided to set up shop in our little town...it's to bring him home, closer to me.

"There's no trap, Tom, let me assure you." Ryan – or Tanner's – hand hits my shoulder and gives it a reassuring squeeze. "We've never met before this morning. All the contacts to set this up were through my chief of executive support, Becky Grahmer."

I look between the two of them. The old, balding reporter pushes up his glasses, his eyes suspicious.

"Why don't we get on with talking about coffee, rather than badgering the poor woman over putting names to faces?" Ryan smiles, pausing for another long sip of rich black brew. "To get things rolling, I think this coffee is goddamned incredible – and you can quote me on that."

I stare up at him, my blood running hot. Every instinct I have wants me to shove his hand away, but I can't when I'm sitting in front of this reporter.

He's actually trying to help me. Somehow, that makes him a bigger bastard than before.

I can't let him know it. Better to keep my hostility in check, rather than give the local gossip mill something to really talk about.

The tone shifts after that. Tom seems content to ask me about the boring stuff. Everything about the cafe's hours, it's goods, it's ability to serve the new arrivals quality coffee, which of course they're expecting since many of the managers are from the West Coast.

Tanner the fake does more talking than I do. It unnerves me how easily he's got the reporter wrapped around his finger by the end.

"So, Mr. Brooks, what can we expect next from you? Not the company, but the man who's in its beating heart."

He pauses a moment. Pulling out the chair next to me, he sits down, and gives me a hard look before he answers. "I'm going to keep building the greatest automotive tech company this country's ever seen, no doubt about it. Then I'm asking for more."

"More?" I say it before reporter Tom, turning up my nose.

"I've never been satisfied with half-assing anything, Ms. Lilydale." He stresses my soon-to-be maiden name, ignoring my earlier request, which only sharpens the needles in my blood. "I know what the tabloids and the blogs say when they name drop me. They're always calling the latest girl I've brought to my big events *the one*. They're always wrong, but one day, that's going to change. I'm getting to the point where I want to settle down, have a family, and do what people are meant to, regardless of billion dollar empires to run."

"Very touching, sir." Tom scribbles a few more notes, nodding along.

I'm ready to get up, walk out back, and hope the cool air will put out the fires roiling my center. He isn't helping himself, talking about other women, or the grand old future he's planning for his arrogant self.

Christ, why am I jealous? I don't give a damn what Fake Tanner does with his time, or who he's with, as long as he stays the hell away from me.

That's what I try to tell myself. Never mind that it's an obvious lie.

"Thank you both very kindly for your time," the reporter says, standing and grabbing his coffee. "I'll be sure this gets printed in our next issue. This place should be a lot more crowded soon, Ms. Lilydale. I'd better swing by a little early for my morning cup."

"We'll be ready," I tell him, ignoring the way the bastard at my side decides to shift his knee into mine just then. "Thank you for the thorough interview today, Tom."

He's gone. The second I see the journalist open the door and step outside, Ryan's hand moves against my wrist. It's a gentle stroke, but it's also a movement that tells me he can grab me anytime if he chooses.

If he does, I'm going to scream. I don't care how many people hear me. I'll tell them everything.

"No thanks for me?" he asks, the same annoying smoothness in his voice as the kind that disarmed the reporter. Well, it won't work on me.

"If you're smart, you'll pick yourself up and walk away now." I snatch my hand away, glaring. He's bigger, stronger, older, and clearly a lot richer.

One thing hasn't changed: his eyes are so familiar it hurts. They confuse me, and that's very, very dangerous.

"Not like this. We can't say our goodbyes just yet, Karabou. I want to talk. Come out tonight, around nine, and meet me at the lighthouse. We'll go up it like old times, and catch up properly."

"I can get that out of your way if you're finished, Mr. Brooks?" Karen has the worst timing in the world.

The seventeen year old kid chooses the very second I'm about to tell him to fuck off forever to stop by our table, collect our cups, and flashes her awkward smile.

"Go right ahead," Ryan says, leaning back in his chair so she can take his mug.

I'm about to explode. The bastard probably wants me to spill blood all over my business. Some kind of sick satisfaction because he obviously has the control to create something a thousand times bigger than my little shop will ever be.

When she's gone, I turn to him, keeping my composure. "You're insane if you think we have anything left to talk about."

"Better to be insane than delusional. I'm afraid the second one's what you're flirting with if you keep ignoring me, Kara. You're going to make a terrible mistake with him. I want to stop it."

"*You* don't have to stop anything!" I catch my voice rising above a harsh whisper, and close my eyes, remembering to breathe. "You're not part of my life anymore, Ryan. I told you to butt the hell out."

"Kara, it's Tanner. Whenever we're in public like this –"

"Oh, you're nervous, Mr. Caspian?" I lean toward him, using his real last name, until our faces are only inches apart. "Good. Now you know how you've made me feel since the second you showed up at my door yesterday."

"Wait," he growls, going for my wrist.

His fingers catch me, tug me backward. His touch keeps me sitting, even though I've pushed my chair out, screeching across the wooden floor. I hate having his skin on mine. There's too many memories every time we touch. Far too many I fought to kill, bury, and forget.

But I'll never forget the first time we spent a night together. Naked, young, blissfully ignorant. He held my hand half the night, even when he was inside me. He pinned me down and didn't let go, nestling my fingers between his, feeling them twitch every time he caused me to come all over his cock.

I've never had sex that good since. Reg's fetish has

something to do with that, but it's also the spark that's missing.

We had chemistry, and it makes me sick that it's lost forever. It's gone, *G-O-N-E,* because I'm not going to let this asshole seduce me a second time with those cold, beautiful blue eyes.

I don't know what to do. Then the sick realization hits me that there's only one way to make him leave.

"If I come out there tonight, my friends will know." Telling him that I'm considering it makes me want to bite my tongue, but I need to get away from him. *Now.* "They're going to know exactly where I am, and who I'm with. I don't care what name I use. They're going to know it's you, and you're not getting away a second time if I don't check in when I should."

He smiles, softening his grip. "I'm not a murderer, Kara. I would never, ever hurt you. That's everything I'm trying to prevent."

"I don't know that. I don't know you anymore. I'm not interested in whatever it is you want, Tanner." Ugh, that name sounds so strange on my lips. "I'm agreeing to meet with you tonight because I want you to go away. Ten minutes. That's all I'm giving you, and then we're done meeting forever. If there's anything else you want with Grounded and Punch Corp, you can send one of your thousand employees to do your bidding."

"There's only three hundred between here and Seattle. I run a lean machine, babe, and I'm proud of it."

No more. The chair screeches again as I stand up,

whipping my head around to see if anyone is paying attention to us. Thankfully, my employees are too busy, ringing up a few new drive through orders, and cleaning up the tables in the back for the lunch hour rush.

I look at him one more time, making my voice like ice. "Stop calling me babe. No darling, no baby, no boo, no Kara-bou."

Slowly, he gets up after me, picking up his coffee cup. He takes a long pull, giving me more than enough time to drink in the huge, powerful, infuriatingly handsome edges he's hiding underneath his five thousand dollar suit. "I'll see you tonight."

I'm not impressed by his wealth. I have that with Reg, and I'm not doing too badly on my own with the earnings from this place. His body, on the other hand...

The jackass never responds to my only condition, not to call me those names. I should run after him, snatch the cup from his hand, and throw it in his face. Then I should tell him there won't be any meeting tonight, and I'm going to file a restraining order if he gets in my face again.

No, I don't care if he pulls his business from mine – I don't fucking need it to make this place a success.

I don't do any of those things. I stand there, staring out the window at the ghost who's decided to haunt me after a five year absence.

Why can't I just let go? Why can't I give him the same respect he gave me – none?

My stomach sinks, watching him through the window. I know what's going to happen tonight. He'll try to ruin another engagement after he demolished my first chance at happiness because he took himself out of the equation.

I'm a fool for letting him back in. But I'll be a bigger fool if I ignore his claims about Reg.

My heart can't take another betrayal. If he's going to give me the truth, with proof to back it up, I have to listen.

I'll deal with the devil himself if it saves me from another heartbreak. And as far as I'm concerned, Ryan is close enough to Lucifer thanks to the strange, intoxicating power he has over me after all these years.

* * * *

Later, I'm sitting with Reg and Amy, our wedding planner. We've been going over our floral arrangements again. Now, it's time to talk about chefs and caterers.

He wants fine wines, champagne, pate and oysters, plus a list of fancy duck entrees I need to draw on my rusty French to pronounce. It doesn't help much, considering the fact that I've barely sampled any of these things.

Fancy cuisine doesn't appeal to me anyway. I want barbecue, something that will go over well with my guests. I'm telling him Eddie's will bring us the best from several towns over, and there'll be more than enough to go around so no one will go home hungry, picking at their million dollar bird food.

"Kara, I'm not dismissing your suggestion, but it's very unusual. The food you're suggesting would be out of step with the overall atmosphere we're working to create." Amy flashes her huge grin. She's roughly my age, and still in braces.

I despise meeting with her. Her family's close to Reg's, part of the same class, and almost as stuck up. She always shoots down more than half of what I want, siding with him.

"It's my wedding," I remind them both.

"Ours," he corrects, stabbing his pointer finger down on the list of recommended caterers in front of him. "Look, Kara, we can do barbecue for practically anything else. The people we're trying to impress, they're not going to be satisfied with ribs and baked beans. They want something on par with the best in Minneapolis, Detroit, or Chicago."

"Of course. It's only impressing your relatives and jackass business associates that matters. I should've known."

Amy holds her hands up defensively. Her and Reg share a look, and I'm left feeling like the odd bitch out for the millionth time. I want to stand up, sweep the papers off the table, and tell them the whole fucking thing is on hold until we fix our relationship.

But his parents are paying for the entire thing, and they want answers. We already have a date, and unfortunately, it's coming fast.

I can't buckle, or give up, or let several hundred people down. Biting my tongue is what I do best in this relationship. Too bad there's more incentive to do it because he's actually trying to fix us. I have to honor that.

"Kara, babe, why don't you pick out the drinks?" he asks, softening his gaze. "I don't want to fight about this. If you're wanting to put whiskey or cocktails on the menu along with the wine and champagne I know everybody will be after, go right ahead. I won't get in the way."

It's a small consolation. Just enough to prevent me from chewing his head off in front of the uptight bitch grinning across the table.

"I love that idea. Here, I was just about to go over this list of vineyards we're able to work with, if you'd like to do something domestic. We'll have the usual European selections, of course." Amy slides yet another piece of paper over to me.

One thing jumps out right away. "Nothing local?"

She looks at me, baffled, just like I'm asking about a ten foot rabbit standing over her shoulder. "Well, I *could* check with several places in Door County if you really want a cherry wine from Wisconsin, but I'm afraid Michigan isn't really known for its –"

"Forget the local crap," Reg cuts in, eyeballing me with even more contempt than our planner. "Jesus, babe. When I told you I was fine with whatever, I didn't mean go crazy. We're trying to plan a wedding here – not a circus. If you want something to make your brother and his buddies happy with the local stuff, why don't we look at beer? I'm sure we can manage a few cases of craft brewed swill to keep our guests with simpler tastes satisfied."

Amy clears her throat. I'm about two seconds from getting up and walking out the door. The meeting with Ryan tonight, just a few hours away, is the only thing that makes me hesitate. I don't want to drag myself out of here on bad terms with my fiance.

Reg deserves a fair trial, and an objective eye on whatever

the bastard is going to drop on my head. If I walk out of here pissed off, hating him, knowing this entire thing is wrong, then there's a scary chance I'll lap up anything Ryan gives me without scrutinizing it like I should.

The asshole across the table is the one I'm supposed to marry, after all. Not the ass who left me.

I have to repeat my mantra.

Keep it together.

Keep believing. Because thinking about the alternative – another heartrending loss – turns my stomach a hundred degrees.

"Fine. We'll do the beer," I say, leaning over to whisper the rest in his ear. "But don't you ever imply Matt's just a stupid peasant drinking cheap beer. He's taken more risks than you ever will, honey."

When I pull away, he's glaring. I couldn't help it.

Amy clears her throat yet again, shuffling through several more papers. She looks up with a smile after the clip holding all her stuff together snaps in place.

"I think we can leave off here for today. We're making progress!" She gets up without either of us saying anything.

Her tall, black heels sound like horse hoofs on the ceramic floor. When I look at Reg again, his eyes are fixed on her feet, giving me one more sickening thought I don't need.

I need to get out of here. "I'm catching up with Courtney tonight, so don't wait up for me. She's only staying in Marquette tonight, and it's been awhile since we've seen each other."

He nods, something like relief flowing into his expression. "Okay, good. I was just going to tell you, I'll be out for a few hours myself. I'm glad there's a few things we're still on the same page about."

Nodding, I ignore his last jab. We get up and walk to our cars together. It's silent, awkward, filled with tension rippling beneath the surface.

"You're going to be here Friday, right? We're supposed to see Dr. Evans again. I'm sure he'll want to go over everything you've talked about by yourself in person. I'm looking forward to his take on the past week."

For a micro-second, his face twists. I wonder if I've caught him in a lie, maybe several. Has he been talking to our counselor on the side at all? Or am I letting the paranoia injected into me by Ryan take over?

"I'll certainly be there," he says, forcing a smile as he splits off and heads for his car. "Did everything go well today with the Gazette's interview?"

Now, I'm the one twisting my face, keeping my back turned to him until I'm ready to climb into the driver's seat. We sat together for almost twenty minutes before Amy came to meet us. He could've asked me about my day any time.

He didn't. He doesn't really care, except as an afterthought. No different than the rest of our relationship, including the wedding planning.

"It was fine," I tell him.

Yes, just dandy, considering I'm about to meet the man I used to be engaged to at the place where he first proposed.

All to bad mouth the man I just finished talking marriage with.

Reg waves half-heartedly when he pulls out of the lot. I slide into my car and watch his tail lights disappear. The steering wheel feels so cold I reach into my glove compartment and grab my gloves for this first time this fall.

Who am I? My faint reflection in the mirror doesn't hold any answers. *What am I doing here?*

Deep down, I think I know.

I'm scorned. Frightened. Sick of being yesterday's news.

But like I told myself earlier, I'm nobody's fool. The Kara Lilydale who lost years off her life going to pieces for a man is dead. She died the second she moved in with Reg. I tell myself again I'm not going to let myself be used by either of these men, especially the one who almost seems easier to deal with, after the hideous session that just went down with my fiance.

That doesn't mean I'm lowering my guard. With Ryan – new, gorgeous billionaire Ryan – I know that's a fatal mistake.

I also know, after all these years, I'm not over him. And that tears me up more than anything tonight, warming my face a hundred degrees, makes it so hot I don't even need to turn on the car's heater.

* * * *

There's at least a little truth to talking to Courtney tonight. I've had a long lasting bond with my old roommate from the first and only semester I spent at Ann Arbor. She gladly accepts my texts about the strange meeting I'm about to have, promising she'll contact the police if I haven't checked in by ten.

It's the last thing I do before I get out of my car, eyeing Ryan's empty vehicle, and head into the lighthouse. He's upstairs. Something so predictable and ironic it makes me want to either laugh or vomit.

When I walk to the upper floor, beneath the historic glass, he's dressed casually. He has his back turned to me, wearing a tight navy blue shirt and grey jeans hugging his hips. Like I need more temptation.

"Five years since we had happier times here," he says, without turning around to face me. "Where does the time go?"

"Goes by pretty fast when you're left without any answers." I walk up next to him, sighing because I want to get this over with. "I'm not here to rehash you and me. That's over with. Done. If you've got something to tell me about Reg, then do it."

His body pivots to face me. I'm trapped in his eyes again. They're deep and furious as oceans tonight. I should know ordering this man to cut straight to the point is hopeless.

"We'll get to that," he says, looking me up and down. "I know you think you're going to be a married woman. After tonight, I hope that won't be the case. Before I say anything else, I need you to tell me one thing – does he tell you you're beautiful, Kara? Because you look fucking stunning. If we hadn't lost five years, I'd have you bent over right now, begging for every inch of me."

Begging?

I'm lava. I look down awkwardly, trying to put more space between us, the heat on my cheeks betraying me.

No. I can't let chemistry take over.

One rough compliment from Mr. Disappearing Act doesn't erase the anguish he caused. I need to remember why I'm here. I have to keep him on my leash, and do the same with myself.

"Reg." His name comes out of my mouth so loud, it echoes. "Why don't you want me to marry him? What has he done?"

Ryan reaches into his pocket. He pulls out a tiny black thumb drive, and holds it out to me. "He's cheating on you. I don't know how long it's been happening, or who the other woman is, but it's all there. Data from the GPS tracker I put on his car, photos of the two of them together, even hotel receipts. Trust me, those were an utter bitch to get, but I did it. I'd chase my tail across Superior if it kept you from tying the knot with the wrong jackass."

It's worse than I thought.

My stomach sinks into the pit opening up inside it. "Don't bother. You already did that once."

He clenches his jaw. My hurt spreads to his face, and soon he's coming toward me, offering those arms I've dreamed about. Always a joy in my mind, before they turn to ash and disappear, making my dreams into nightmares.

"Take the drive, Kara. Sit down with it when you get a chance, whenever you're good and ready. I know this is hard." He pauses, lifts me into his embrace, and pushes his fingers through my hair. When my cheek hits his rock hard chest, it becomes very real. This is no dream, however surreal it feels, and he isn't going to disappear. "Your fiancé's a demon. I know a lot, but I don't have every detail. I think he's marrying you for a PR stunt. He wants a good wife who will take his name, smile, put up, and shut up. He doesn't love you. Hell, he's barely one step below his pig of a great uncle."

Enough. My hand flies up as I'm squirming away from him and hits his cheek. The resounding slap resonates around us.

Neither of us know what to do. The sting on my palm matches the red mark blossoming on his face.

Tears are coming now, hot and sudden. I don't want to look at him. I'm struggling to hold onto the small black coffin he's pushed into my hand, the data inside it as grim as a corpse.

It's the final splash of kerosene that's going to burn my world alive, more than even his words damning my marriage.

I already know they're true, unless he's truly insane. But this can't be madness.

He couldn't look at me the way he does, speak with this much conviction, if they were lies.

"Why did you come back, Ryan? *Why?*" My voice cracks on the last word. "I never thought I'd say this...but all I want is to be left alone."

He starts coming toward me again, but I hold out both hands. I'm ready to fight him if he tries to tangle me up in those arms again, an embrace I don't know I'll ever be ready for, however much part of me wants it.

"I'm back because I love you, Kara-bou. I'm going to make things right."

Love? He can't be serious.

I've lost years of my life just waiting for those words from him.

Waiting, wanting, and fearing them.

"Who do you think you are?" I ask, watching his handsome features blur as more tears cloud my eyes. "It's been too fucking long! You can't come back and say things like that. You can't just barge into my life, pretend nothing happened, and tell me I'm getting screwed over by the man I love."

For the first time tonight, Ryan's face darkens. He stops, several feet away, and tilts his head. "You love him?"

I don't say anything. It's like I'm in front of a firing squad, too stunned for last words. Every sane part of me says I should say *yes,* should spit it in his face, and then walk the hell away.

"I don't know anymore." Honesty hurts. Each uncertain word claws its way out of me, scratching my throat.

I roll my shoulders, stretching out the aches and pains invading my bones. This doubt and confusion is making me physically ill.

Turning away from him, I walk to the nearby banister, and lean against it, starring out across the cool dark sea.

"You're not happy, Kara," he tells me, laying a gentle hand on my shoulder. "Look at me."

The second I comply, my eyes burn hot again. Reaching up to wipe the tears, he stops me, grabs my wrist and pulls it down. His arms are around me, and his strong hand grazes my face, brushing away the agony streaming down my cheeks.

"You really want to know why I came back? I'm here to prevent this. No man should make you cry."

"Well, you're doing a shitty job." Pain twists my tongue. I can't believe he doesn't know he's the only reason I'm standing here in the cold, dark night, mourning another marriage going to ruin. "I didn't ask for you to play truth teller, Ryan. I would've found out myself, if what you're telling me is accurate."

"Yeah, you would have. You were always the smarter one. Unfortunately, there was a risk he'd pull one over long enough to do more damage."

"More?" I repeat numbly. How could Reg possibly do more than shredding what's left of my fragile heart?

"It's easier to break it off now, when you're sharing a home. It's a hell of a lot harder with a few kids, after being in the town's eye forever. Trust me, I know something about celebrity. The camera eye changes you the longer it's on. Makes it harder to escape."

"Like I care about any of that. If he's done wrong, I'll leave. Whether that's tomorrow, or ten years from now, I won't waste time with the wrong person. Nothing's going to keep me with a man who's screwing around behind my back."

He smiles, slowly running his hand up and down my back. I'm burning up despite the chill in the air. Ready to overload on hot, conflicted emotion, churning in my blood like magma.

"You deserve better, babe. You'd have it, too, if I hadn't left like I did."

"Better?" I turn my head to face him, my lips twisted sourly. "I'm guessing you mean I should be with you?"

He shakes his head. "I'm here to set you free, Kara. Nothing in this universe would make me happier than having a second chance, shoving your lips on mine, sharing my bed. I'm a realist, though. I can't imagine the kind of hell you've been through the last five years."

"No, you can't."

"If I can't save you from five more fucked up years, that's reward enough. I'm not here to twist your arm into loving me again if your heart says something different. All I want is to see you happy, and that's not possible with the bastard who's got a gold stick so far up his ass he thinks he's entitled to thieving more years off your life. I won't let you marry a liar."

It's not really up to you, I want to say. But the way he growls the last part – *I won't let you* – makes me feel strangely secure.

That's one thing Reg never did. He never laid claim to me like Ryan does every time he looks at me, his blue eyes blazing, ready to sink into me. Every part of him, too.

His words, his hands, his tongue, the bulge between his legs I feel every time I twist against him the wrong way.

I'm wet, and I shouldn't be. Sex should be the last thing on my mind when I'm caught between two men I hate, the only two responsible for casting me down to hell, several times over.

But the body does strange things when it hasn't been fucked good and proper for a long time.

No, I won't jump into bed with him tonight. It's a one-way ticket to more insanity.

I haven't even seen the evidence condemning my fiance, though I know it's true.

Walk away. That's all I want to do, and never look back. But I can't deny the attraction I've tried to snuff out and forget for five years is still lightning hot.

It burns, taunts, and draws me into him like a magnet.

So, I'll let myself wrap my hands around his neck, remember how good his skin feels against mine, and push my face into the protective nook of his shoulder, where his masculine scent says *everything will be all right, damn it.*

"Why did you leave?" I ask. He's in a giving mood, isn't he? I wonder if he'll tell me the truth about the night that ripped us apart. "Did you really kill Nelson Drayton?"

He pulls away, staring into my eyes. "I can't talk about that, Kara. Not yet. You need to deal with Reg without more distractions."

The Superior chill sweeping up my back has nothing on the one he's just sent through me. I untangle myself from his arms, wondering if I should trust anything he says.

It's so quiet, I jump when my phone pings. It's Courtney, checking in on me. I'd lost track of the time.

I quickly pull it out and fire off a message, shielding my phone when he walks up behind me. I tell my friend everything is fine. Technically a lie, but she can't exactly call the police over my heart being pulled in two directions at a hundred miles an hour.

Ryan's firm hand goes around my waist before I can protest.

"I don't want to lie to you, Kara-bou. That night, it's a fucked up story. We need to sit down and talk about it. This isn't the place or town."

"Tell me what is," I say. My hand goes to his face.

I cup his cheek, running my fingers across his dark stubble. His coarseness excites me because it's a reminder who he is.

This man can save me, or destroy me. It's like he thrives on secrets, and I want to know them all. Just so I can finally figure out which side of his sword I'm on.

"I need the truth tonight, Ryan. I told Reg I'd be home late tonight."

He ponders it for a second, then gives me the sly smile that makes my knees tremble. "I read the draft of the interview this evening. Grounded's supposed to have the best cherry pie in the whole U.P., isn't it?"

"Mom's old recipe," I whisper. "Same one you always loved at Thanksgiving. I can't do her pumpkin any justice, so I'm all in on what I do best."

"Let's go." He pulls me along, offering me his hand to help lead us down the steep, winding staircase. "How is she, anyway?"

"Struggling to make ends meet on what dad left her after the cancer treatment." He doesn't look back when I drop the bad news, but I'm not holding anything back, assuming he really wants to know. "Otherwise, she loves being grandma. She gets Holden a lot on his days with us. The bitch allows it when Matt's on tour, but rarely when he comes home."

"You're talking about his ex?"

I nod, following as we head for the parking lot. My hand blazes in his, warmer and happier than it's been in eons. I pull my fingers away before we get to our cars.

I'm playing with fire. This is happening too fast. I haven't found out what's going on, much less forgiven him, and everything about the way this insane attraction is reigniting screams *wrong*.

"I'm sorry it didn't work out for him," Ryan says, stopping next to my car. "Shit, I regret everything that's gone sour for your folks since I left. You guys were like family. Could've been my own flesh and blood when I was that miserable orphan kid, trying to find my place. They'll always be my parents, and my brother. Kin by choice. Everyone except you."

His hands goes to my face. I'm already blushing because I know he's always seen me as something more than a little sister.

I was the love of his life. His expression tells me I still am.

"I'll meet you at the store. Give me a minute's head start. Should have the doors unlocked and the lights on by the time you pull up." I turn away, opening my door, but I stop to reach out, pulling on his shoulder. "No more games, Ryan. If you're going to be honest with me, I need the truth tonight. I have to know I'm not dealing with a killer."

Please, I think. *Please tell me I'm not making another mistake, destroying my pending marriage because I have a lingering crush on a disappearing murderer.*

He doesn't say anything, just smiles and heads for his sleek black Tesla. I drive on through the night, making the ten minute trip to my cafe in silence, hoping the chasm in my stomach that keeps growing tonight doesn't swallow me up.

The truth that's on the thumb drive he gave me should cause more dread than whatever secrets are rattling around in his head. But he never denies it when I ask about Nelson's murder.

Something awful and completely out of place happened that night. Too bad I've been let down too many times, by too many people, to assume the best anymore.

I'm going to pry it out of him. I have to know what happened that fateful night was a mistake, he was framed, or the blood on his hands is only there for a damned good reason.

* * * *

He's at the counter with his hands folded, a steaming cup of coffee at his side. I carve out two big pieces of my best cherry pie with the crumble crust for us.

He digs his fork in and takes a big bite as soon as I slide it across, topped with a scoop of vanilla ice cream. Ryan closes his eyes, savoring the taste, not caring about the tiny crumbs rolling down his expensive suit.

"Christ, that's delicious. They can't get the tartness right out west. I've missed a lot in this town, and Lilydale cooking is definitely near the top of the list," he says, reaching for his coffee.

I sit next to him, toying with mine less enthusiastically. It's hard to eat with the elephant standing over us, the one who's threatening to bitch slap this happy moment away if I find out the truth about Nelson.

"I'm glad you're enjoying it, but now I need something from you."

He gives me a knowing expression, the satisfaction on his face melting as he chews another bite, and slowly swallows. "It's too soon for that, Kara-bou. I'm not throwing you down in the sheets before your engagement's off."

"Ass!" I punch him in the arm, catching myself laughing.

He is, too. For a second, it's like we're both in our teens again, and the last five hellish years are nothing worse than a long nightmare.

He turns on his stool, quickly finishing up his pie. I give him a few more minutes, hoping he'll be ready once he's had his fill. I tell him about the situation with Matt and his ex, Maggie, who twisted the knife deep when he found out she was cheating.

"Does he ever think about leaving the Marines?" Ryan asks, reaching for my hand.

I let him hold on without fighting to pull away since the first time he's come home. I shake my head, sipping hot cider. "We both wish he would, mom and I. Don't think he wants to give up the pay, and there's nothing here in the U.P. for him. He talked about trying to rebuild daddy's old auto shop last time he came home for Christmas, but it isn't going to happen anytime soon. We don't have the money for that. Especially if Reg is out of the picture."

Yes, my fiance made noise about supporting my brother's effort. That was back when things were good, before he started screwing around, assuming he hasn't been playing me all along.

Ryan looks at me. The next time I blink, he's pulling out his checkbook, pushing a silver pen to paper.

"What are you doing?" My fork clatters on the small plate holding the remains of my pie, and I wipe my mouth, eager to make him put that thing away if he's doing what I think.

He doesn't say anything until he's finished. The check comes out, and he slides it over. My eyes pop when I see the amount he's written.

"No way. I can't accept this."

"It's not for you," Ryan says, gripping my hand. "Give that to Matt. Tell him it's from an old friend who wants to make things right."

I chew my lip, nervous when I imagine how it would go down. "He doesn't like you anymore. He believes the worst – the same thing most people in town think about what went down with you and Nelson."

My foot taps the floor. I'm annoyed we're debating charity for my brother, when the big secret is the only reason we're here, sitting together like he never abandoned me.

"Keep your money, Ryan. Seriously. We'll figure things out." I lean in, staring into his gorgeous face, refusing to let his blue eyes swallow me this time. "I can feel Matt out the next time we're hanging out, if it makes you feel better. Of course, it would *really* help if there's anything you want to say to clear the air about what happened."

"Okay, yeah. Guess it's finally time," he says, pausing to smooth one hand across his face. He stretches his skin, as if he needs to smooth out the tension caused by holding in his secrets. "Before I say anything, you need to know it went down this way because I made a promise. I –"

He stops talking the second I hear the door chime. We turn around, and I'm halfway off my stool, ready to tell the intruder we're closed for the evening. It's my fault for forgetting to lock up.

Except it's not just a random interloper, looking for a midnight snack. Matt stands there like a deer in headlights, his big arms bowing out, fists on his hips.

"Kara? Ma sent me out to grab some muffins for breakfast tomorrow. Gave me the spare key, and said you wouldn't mind. What're you doing here so damned late?"

He hasn't recognized Ryan yet. Thank God.

I want to lean down, tell him to walk in the back for the pastries, and keep on going.

But it only takes a second for my brother to notice Ryan's fingers still wrapped around mine. This causes him to study the stranger next to me in greater detail.

I see it the instant recognition hits.

Then all hell breaks lose. My Marine brother sends all

two hundred and twenty pounds of muscles flying across the room, straight into my old flame's chest. Ryan's a big man too, and it takes a lot to knock him down.

It's like two bears slamming into each other, rolling and swearing when they hit the floor.

"What's he doing here, sis? What the fuck's this piece of shit doing with his hands on yours?!" He's still yelling to me as he tries to punch Ryan in the face.

He's quicker than my brother. Ryan catches his wrist, holds it, and strains to prevent the blow from landing on his face.

"Matt, stop! It's okay! Calm your ass down."

"Bullshit!" My brother's voice echoes like a cannon shot. I'm digging my nails into his shoulders, trying to pry him off, but he bucks once and throws me down, knocking me on my knees. His attention turns to Ryan. "You never should've come back here, you goddamned idiot! I'm turning you in."

"No, you can't!" Oh, he can, and that's why I'm crying.

It's a small mercy because my anguish seems to break up the fight. Ryan takes the break in my brother's drive to knock his teeth out to throw him against the counter. He hits the floor next to me, sweeps me up in his arms, and buries my face in his chest.

It's a smart move. Matt won't do anything while I'm there except bark. I would've put myself between them anyway if I'd had a few seconds notice, before the last shred of sanity holding this night together snapped.

"Kara...I can't believe this," Matt growls. "How long

have you been seeing him? Do you know what people are gonna say if they see you with this asshole, right underneath Reg's nose? Let alone if they realize who he is…Christ!"

"That's my problem. Not yours." Ryan stands, cradling me against his chest. I'm clinging to him, ready to fight if he tries to push me away, because I'm the only thing that's stopping Matt from ruining my cafe and tearing into him again. "Let's talk about this like men."

"Fuck you, Caspian. There's nothing manly about what you did to that rich old fart, or how you ran away from town leaving blood all over dad's auto shop. He never should've hired your lying orphan ass." He bares his teeth, shaking his head. "Shit. If only we'd seen right through you since the beginning…"

"Nice to see you too," Ryan says, reaching to the counter. "Honestly, I'm glad you're here tonight. We were just talking about you before you came storming in. I've got something with your name on it."

He holds the check out for what seems like forever before my brother walks up, and snatches it from his hand. I keep holding in my breath.

"What the fuck is this? A bribe? You're an even bigger asshole than I think you are if you're telling me I should take your money and walk away," Matt snarls. It takes a few seconds for him to speak after he sees the amount on the check.

Then he holds it up to his face and takes the corners with both hands. I know what's coming next.

"Wait!" Ryan jerks in my arms, holding out one hand.

"Before you tear that thing up, I want you knowing it's not a bribe, Matt. We used to be like brothers, before everything went to shit. Give me a chance to explain all this. That's all I was trying to do here tonight with your sis. If you'll hear me out, you'll see I want you to have that money, and I've got more with your name on it for the vets' charity I know you're trying to set up."

"You've been watching me? And her?" Disbelief sizzles in his tone. "Fuck you, creepy ass stalker. You've got no clue how much you blew our lives to hell after you left, especially Kara's. We don't want a damned thing from you. Sis, just say the word, and I *will* call the sheriff. I don't care who this fucknut thinks he is with his suit and his money. He belongs behind bars."

"Matthew, I swear to God," I say, closing my eyes. "Let him go. This isn't what you think."

At least, I hope it isn't. Thanks to my brother's crap, I still haven't found out the big secret. Now I'm afraid I won't get the chance tonight.

"Just go home. The family doesn't need this, and neither do you. Go grab your muffins in the back. Take whatever you want home to mom and Holden."

We stare across at each other for several fiery seconds. Then rage snorts out his nostrils. His fingers finish ripping the check into a dozen little pieces and they fall on the floor like snow.

"Sorry about the mess. I'm not taking this fucking backstabber's money. As for anything else…we'll see. I'll think about what I'm gonna do on the way home."

He marches past us. I hear him slamming drawers in the kitchen, looking for the day's leftover baked goods, which would've gone to the local shelter in the morning. His fist bangs the back door on the way out, and it swings shut, closing with a *thud*.

Ryan gives me one more squeeze before he walks over and bends down, picking up the remnants of his shredded check.

"Jesus, Ryan, I'm sorry. Didn't have a clue he'd be coming by tonight. We should've went for a greasy burger instead."

"Don't apologize," he says, more adamant than ever. "Kara, this wouldn't be going down if I weren't here. I've got a lot to fix, as soon as I give you the explanation I promised."

I wrap my arms around him when he comes back to me. I'm shaking my head, hating myself for the next words out of my mouth. I want to know what the hell happened, but not if it means putting him at risk.

"We don't have time to rehash the past tonight. You need to go home and rest. So do I. There's no telling what Matt's going to do after seeing you like this."

"Fuck. You're right." He leans down, touching his forehead against mine.

We stay like that for a little while, just savoring our old, familiar warmth. Hating the confusion, the uncertainty, but loving this closeness. These are possibilities, poised between new disasters and miracles.

I'm not going to find out the ending to this story

tonight. "Go," I tell him again. "I'll be in touch. I need a chance to get home and look at what you've given me, too."

Reluctantly, he nods, and walks me to my car. I give him my number, hoping I'm not making another mistake.

Whatever's coming next won't be easy. Looking into his eyes, I see horrors up ahead. It's going to get worse before it gets better.

Even if he's squeaky clean – and I seriously doubt that's the case – I'm facing a hurricane when Matt spills the news about Ryan's reappearance to mom, and that's separate from the hell coming whenever I walk out on Reg.

If I walk out on him. Ugh. It's hard not to get ahead of myself after being plunged into darkness.

Before we leave, my eyes go to Ryan's lips. It takes every fiber in my being to walk away without a kiss.

He stops next to his car as I'm pulling out, looking at me like he understands.

He gets it, and he fucking hates it, but he isn't giving up.

After tonight, I owe him the same. He's stirred feelings I haven't had in years. They're going to soothe the scars tainting me for the last five years, or turn them into open wounds.

I'm ready for the truth, whatever it may be.

That's what I tell myself, heading for my unhappy home. If I'm honest, before all this is over, the truth might kill me.

* * * *

I don't have the energy to look at the files tonight.

Reg hasn't come home yet, despite the late hour. I slip into bed with a glass of wine and doze, dreaming about deep blue eyes, stubble on my skin, and a man between my legs who fucks me without asking to hoover suck my toes.

I wake up with a start near early morning. There's no one next to me. Wherever he is, he never came home.

Showering quickly, I dress, cursing myself for not setting an alarm. My internal body clock is the only thing that saves me from being late to opening Grounded.

I'm in such a rush I don't give a second thought to when Reg got home, or if he did. It isn't until I'm downstairs, heading into the kitchen for a banana and some yogurt, when I see him.

He's sitting at the counter, the little black stick in his hand, tapping it against the marble. "Who gave you this?"

My feet turn to ice. I'm stuck, staring at my fiance, his polite mask hanging by a thread. It isn't hard to see the anger underneath.

He's seen what's on it. Somehow, he knows.

Gutted doesn't begin to describe the way I'm hollowed out. If I hoped to control my world self-destructing, there's no chance of that now.

He stands, comes toward me, his eyes narrow and dark. "Jesus fucking Christ, Kara. I thought we were getting better. Then you go behind my back, get this thing from some goddamned jackass, and find pictures taken over my shoulder by a stalker psycho? What did you do, hire a detective?"

"Whoa, back up. I haven't even looked at it!" I decide to give him the truth. "Jesus, calm down."

"Calm down?" His voice bristles, the same as his angry, erratic movements. "You're asking me for calm when you won't even say where this came from, bitch?"

New pain rips through my heart. In all our arguments before, he's never called me names, much less a *bitch.*

"To think, you asked me if I was having a goddamned affair the other day," he scoffs, shaking his head. "You hired a PI to trail me, didn't you? Admit it. Some busy little jackoff you dropped money on to tell you you're right? Well, let me tell you something, Kara-bell." That name has never sounded so sinister on his lips.

I'm officially afraid.

He steps up, grabs me, and rips me into his chest. I'm too shocked to scream, afraid he's going to throw me against the counter, or worse.

"There's no fucking affair! I'm too good to sneak around behind your back, and you're too stupid to believe it." He's snarling in my face, continuing to scream, growl, and thunder when my eyes are pinched shut. "This ends here, okay? I'm giving you a choice. We're marching ourselves down to Dr. Evans tomorrow, as planned. You're telling him the truth and asking for help to fix your psychotic paranoia. Otherwise, we end this here. And if we do, I'll make damned sure the whole town knows why."

My ears try to close in disbelief. For the first time since he pushed me against the counter, I'm angry enough to get over the fear. Opening my eyes, I stare at his face. It's incredible how someone you once loved can transform into a demon in front of you once they've done the unthinkable.

"Are you threatening me, Reg?"

"Is that what you think is going on here?" Raw hate gives way to frustration in his tone. He pulls away, muttering to himself, hot shame warming his cheeks. "Jesus. You're really disconnected from reality, you know that? I'm reacting how any sane person should. Any man would be just as pissed as I am if he found out his fiance had him trailed. I told you the truth the other day. You wouldn't believe me."

He's right. I wouldn't. Seeing him standing in front of me, rambling like a madman, doesn't bolster my trust.

"I'm leaving for work. We'll pick this up in the evening," he says, raising his arm.

Our eyes lock as he brings the little thumb drive down against the counter. A second later, it's smashed.

It was my mistake leaving the thing out. I wasn't thinking after coming home so late last night, too emotionally drained by yesterday's events to put it away.

Now, I'll never get that chance. Reg doesn't stop to pick up the pieces laying on the floor. His heavy footsteps plod toward the door, which he slams on his way out.

There's no mistaking the adrenaline flooding my system, my heart beating like a clock out of sync. I'm starting to hate this man. It's incredible how quickly our love has soured, how it's damaged to the point of almost no repair, held together by social pressure more than anything else.

But I've never seen this crazy before. I can't judge what's

on the destroyed drive, but what if he's angry because I misjudged him? Not because he's covering up the awful truth?

I pick up the pieces, no longer worried about getting into the cafe a few minutes late. I reach for the tiny shattered pieces, and push them together absent-mindedly, hating that I can't put Humpty-Dumpy together again.

It takes me a minute before I toss them in the trash. I don't know who to believe, or what's true.

Reg has never been this upset. The glow in his eyes...it was rage.

Pure, unfiltered contempt.

There's only two possibilities: he's the best damned liar in the world and he's completely soulless, or it's Ryan manipulating me.

I hold in the scream building up in my chest until I'm out the door, in my car, and on the way to work. When it comes out, I'm sure several people on the main drag in Split Harbor hear it, out on their morning walks They stop and look toward my vehicle's headlights.

I think back to what went through my head last night, realizing how wrong I really was.

This isn't even close to over, and I'm already dead inside.

Someone's lying to me. Ryan, Reg, or maybe both. I'm just sick of being used.

I won't be anyone's whore, or their trophy wife. We're past the point of anything a psychologist can help with.

I'm not coming home this evening. After I close up Grounded today, I'm getting in my car and going for a long,

long drive. I need to clear my head, search my heart, and forget about the two men pulling me in half.

It's the only way I'll know if I can stay in this town without losing my mind.

VIII: Shocked (Ryan)

It's evening, and she isn't responding to my texts. I'm supposed to work late tonight, but my concentration is blown.

After last night, after I gave her proof she's being fucked over by her cheating fiance, I thought for sure I'd hear more. I haven't heard a word all day.

Something isn't right.

I taste it every time I take a sip of the smooth, black brew my assistant brings me for a late day pick-me-up. It's Grounded coffee, a fresh corporate supply of beans I've dropped a couple thousand on this week, without a second thought.

I'm running through financial reports from accounting, watching the numbers blur together, when I decide I've had enough.

I stuff my laptop into my messenger bag and head out the door. About half a dozen women working late ogle me between the elevator and the receptionist's desk downstairs. They won't say anything, risking their jobs for petty advances, because they know who I am. But there's no mistaking the hunger in their eyes, the way they want to pull me into the nearest office, rip off my Superior blue suit, and offer every inch of their skin to me on a silver platter.

They're lucky I'm the kind of man who's always kept business and pleasure separate. Doubly lucky there's only one woman on my mind, and right now she's driving me fucking loco.

I'm almost through the security gate surrounding the Punch Corp complex when a security truck speeds through, stopping just short of making my right side into a pancake. The man behind it has his window down before mine. His eyes bug out when he recognizes me.

"Mr. Brooks! I'm so sorry."

"I don't know what you're talking about," I lie. "What's the hurry?"

"Police alert for a missing woman, sir. It's the one who owns the coffee shop down at the edge of town. I thought I'd better scour the perimeter. There are plenty of dark little nooks around our property where a vehicle could go if anything nasty happened. Or if a person didn't want to be found."

Shit. The non-response from Kara is more serious than I thought.

Now I'm really worried. I thank him and drive off, roaring down the highway, out toward the lighthouse where I can stop and think, plan what I'm going to do next.

I don't know what the hell happened.

Did she look at the data on Reg? Did she confront him already? Is the cheating sonofabitch a lot crazier than I think?

Fuck, maybe he hurt her? Nothing's impossible, considering the sick, twisted secrets I found hanging over his bastard uncle.

If Kara's gone, there's a good chance Reg is the reason why.

Ten minutes later, I'm sitting on a bench next to my car, a cold wind slapping my face while I work my phone furiously. The dot for the special GPS tracker on his car hasn't moved since this morning, the first time that's happened in days.

He's either been at home all day, or he's found the device, and taken it off. Deep in my gut, I know what's more likely.

I'm running purely on instinct when I climb back in my car. I take the highway toward Marquette. Sure, there's a thousand other places he might have gone, but I go for the most logical, the quickest place he would've went for comfort if he had a falling out with her.

Half an hour later, I know I'm on the right track when I see the asshole's car in the lot. His grey Mercedes melds into half a dozen other fancy vehicles at the high end hotel's valet parking, but not to me.

It stands out, hits me between the eyes, and tells me I need answers.

I'm running to the hotel's front desk. It hurts like hell to stop, give them a friendly smile, and pull out my black card, asking for a room.

Even in a small city, security is an obstacle. The only way I'll get to Reg is if I'm on the inside.

I wait impatiently through the check-in process. Before I go, I ask what room my business associate is in. The woman rattles off a number, and then I'm heading up the elevator, bypassing the floor with the room I'll never bother to look at.

I'm going straight to his. No more wasting time.

A brisk walk down the hall later, I'm there, pressing my ear against the door.

There's laughter. A woman giggles. It's the kind of laugh that means two things.

She's either heard the funniest fucking joke in the world, or she's just finished riding a worm who should be home in his own bed, with the woman he wants to call his wife.

Fuck. I'm furious. Part of me is glad he's here. The chances that I'm going to kick his ass and claim Kara for myself just spiked a thousand percent.

But if he's hurt her, if he's thrown her out of their condo or worse…I'll throw my budding empire away knocking his teeth out. I'll destroy the asshole, right here, in cold blood, becoming the monster everybody back home thinks I am.

I'll make sure he never, ever cheats on a woman again with the crude joke of a face he's got left when I'm through.

My fingers tighten into a fist, and I stand up straight.

This is it.

I don't think about keeping it subtle, hiding what's about to go down from anybody else in the adjacent rooms. The place seems mostly deserted for an autumn weekend. My fist slams into his door like a rock, banging the surface again and again.

It creaks open slowly a small, frightened brunette face peering out at me through the crack. "Can I help you?"

"I need to talk to Reginald Drayton." I don't know what to think of the girl, but my beef isn't with her. Maybe she knows she's fucking around with a taken man. Or maybe she's innocent, one more girl he's wiping his feet on because he thinks he's the biggest swinging dick in town.

Before I showed up, the bastard was in the running, thanks to his money. Not anymore.

"Amy? Who is it?" I hear his voice for the first time. He's coming toward her, and I see him moving over her shoulder.

She turns around, frightened, her hand on the door like she doesn't know if she should push it shut.

I never give them a chance. My hand goes through the crack, rips apart the cheap silver chain, and my foot kicks the base of the door like a charging bull. Asshole shields himself from the noise, backing up into the corner, taking his mistress into his arms.

"Who the fuck are you?! What do you want? This must be some kind of terrible mistake! I swear, I've never seen you before in my –"

I pull her gently out of his arms, flinging the girl onto the nearby bed. With him, my hands forget what gentle means. Slamming him into the wall, I hear his bones creak, knowing I can snap them in half like twigs if I really need to.

"Kara Lilydale, asshole. Where is she?"

"You! You're the detective, aren't you?" He's looking at

me, wide eyed and filled with hate. "I'm going to have your license stripped, you know. If you lay a finger on me, you'll be in jail before the end of the night."

Enough.

My knee goes into his guts, and then my hand is on his throat. Typical Drayton. Always trying to get the last word, thinking the entire Earth wants to hear it.

The stupid fucking cheat still tries to squawk when I press my palm into his windpipe, making words impossible.

I'm done hearing his shit. It's time for him to listen to me.

"Shut up. I'm not a detective, and you don't give a shit about what she does." There's something dangling from his neck. I notice for the first time I don't need my hand to choke him.

This sick, twisted freak is wearing a choke chain attached to a leather collar. Just like a dog. I take it in one hand, eyeballing the ring around his neck to make sure it's still on, and pull. He hits the floor, and I put my foot on his back, cutting off his air while I look at the woman.

"Put the phone down," I tell her. "If you so much as whisper a word to the cops, or the front desk, the man you've been screwing around with dies."

Her eyes are huge, frightened, stunned. She's wearing heels that must be impossible to walk in. They're blood red, a perfect compliment to her candy cane stockings hugging her legs. I can only imagine her walking all over him before I showed up, lifting the pointy heels out to his tongue.

Christ, no wonder Kara-bou's been craving my touch, if

this is what her soon-to-be ex is into.

"You're going to shut up and listen to me, Reg. Nod if you understand," I say, waiting until he shakes his head weakly. I let up on the choke chain, just enough to give him air. "When I let go, you're going to tell me where Kara is. You're also going to finish your business here with Miss Dominatrix, get in your car, go home, and pack your shit. Leave her a note that says you're leaving. She doesn't need to see your lying, cheating ass in the flesh anymore."

He's squirming underneath me. If I weren't so mad, I'd smile.

It gives me a sick pleasure knowing he's helpless, and such a gutless little pissant, he'll do everything I say. And if he doesn't, then we're going to have some *real* fun.

"Do you understand? Nod if you do."

He does it very weakly. My cue to step off his spine, ease back on the chain, and let him breathe. His mistress walks over, gets on the floor, and caresses his face. I let her give him several seconds worth of comfort he doesn't deserve.

I'm not here to torture him, tempting as it is. I just want answers, and then I'm going to make sure he follows through.

"Who...who are you?" he sputters. "Why are you doing this?"

"I'm the one she's supposed to marry. Not you, cheater. Question time is over. You nodded, so I think we have an understanding. Do you remember everything I said?"

"Yes," he says, leaning heavily on the skinny little thing holding him up. "I'll leave tonight. Whatever you want."

"Good. Now, answer my question," I growl, giving the chain a warning pull.

He tenses up, turns toward me, and gives me a glare through his angry, watering eyes. "I don't know where she is. Honest. I'm the one who sent the alert to the police. She didn't come home when she was supposed to a few hours ago, and her phone's completely dead."

My fists are hungry. They're looking for any excuse to make this man bleed, but I don't think he's lying. The brunette digs her fingers into his scalp, pulling his face to his shoulder, protecting him.

It's almost laughable. Her non-existent balls are ten times bigger than his. I can't believe I almost let my woman tie the knot with this dickless animal.

"He's telling you the truth!" she says. "I'm their wedding planner. The woman's impossible to deal with, she always does things without thinking them through. She'll turn up sooner or later. And when she does, I'm refunding her money, telling her to keep the fuck away. She's made his life *hell,* and so have his parents. He doesn't want to be with her. They've put so much pressure on him to do the right thing, to keep their reputation going for another generation in the U.P. He deserves better than a bad wife and a family who'll never understand."

Is she joking? Does she think I'm going to stand by idly while she gives me his life's story?

"Stay right there," I say, reaching for my phone.

She covers her face, flushing bright red, while I snap several pics. I don't give a damn what kind of excuses she's trying to make for this pathetic creep wrapped up in her arms.

I only care about getting new damning evidence for Kara. She deserves to see this, and know beyond any doubt who he's left her for.

"What else have you got in your stack of toys over there?" I ask, nodding toward the bed. "Handcuffs?"

She gives me an uneasy look. Yeah, of course there's handcuffs.

I don't say a word. Just march over, pull out the small silver pair, plus a black cord that feels like a jumprope. I order them down into two leather chairs with the thick wooden legs.

First, I cuff the asshole's hands behind his back, making them tighter than I really need to. With her, I'm more gentle, though I've got an ugly feeling I shouldn't be.

She knows she's fucking around with a man who's engaged. He's probably fed her a sob story, but the one thing missing from her little account was any regret.

They won't be tied down long with the job I did. But it's all I need to walk out of that room, head down the hall, and get to my car. I tell the woman at the front desk I had a family emergency, and check out with the room on my tab for a grand total of thirty minutes.

I have to find Kara, and this time it's for good. I won't stop until I have her lips on mine, haul her into bed, and make up for all the nights we lost since I fled town.

This time, I'm back. I've said my apologies and I'm ready to move on. I'm going to give her the life she deserves, the one I promised her. It's the life I've always meant to deliver after five brutal years apart.

Never again.

"Baby, I'm coming," I whisper to myself, pulling onto the highway, stabbing my foot down on the accelerator. My car goes from ten miles an hour to seventy in two seconds flat. The average Tesla has some nice perks.

It isn't fast enough. Five years without her is too much time to lose, and after tonight, I'm not wasting another second.

I'm putting us back together. Taking her to bed, shoving my ring back on her finger, and fucking her like the sad, strange bastard at the hotel never could.

She isn't his anymore. Hell, she never was.

I don't care if she isn't sure about second chances yet, I'm going to tell her the truth, show her, make her believe. There's nothing clearer beating in my heart, and I hear the truth in every booming thud. I feel it spike into my blood, feed my veins, fill my soul with one voice screaming *mine, mine, mine* a hundred times.

Honest to God. That's all she'll ever be, all she's meant to be, however much the universe tries to hold us apart.

My Kara's coming home. Her forever is my own.

Entangled. Beautiful. Inseparable.

IX: Reset (Kara)

Several Hours Earlier

I closed down Grounded a few hours ago, telling my assistant manager I won't be in tomorrow. I packed a few waters and sandwiches, ready to make the trip to Sault Ste. Marie. It's a quiet town at the end of the U.P. on Canada's border.

Perfect for the introspection and time alone I need the next few days. I'm about twenty minutes outside town, passing through the edge of Marquette, when my phone rings.

I have to talk to Matt, however much it's bound to upset me right now.

"Sis? Where are you? We need to talk," he says, little Holden laughing in the background. I hear another voice, mom's, which tells me he's home. He's probably also dropped the news about Ryan.

"We're talking now, Matt. You must be calling me because you've decided what you're going to do. Just tell me."

There's a pause, and then a heavy sigh. "I haven't turned the asshole in. Not yet. He's dangerous, and he shouldn't be out on the streets, much less in your coffee shop late at night. I want you to tell me why he came back. What does he want with you?"

I think about his arms, his heat, the truth he promised last night. I remember Reg this morning, the bitter, violent edge in his voice, how he flung me around our kitchen and smashed his secrets – if that's what they really were – into a dozen pieces.

"He's trying to prevent me from making a mistake," I say, as close to the truth as I can get. It's also the closest I think he'll come to understanding, since he's convinced I'm dealing with a monster.

"Mistake – what? Surely you don't mean marrying Reg?"

"I don't know, Matt. He told me some things. Even gave me what he said was proof of things Reg has been doing behind my back."

"Kara, fuck, come on! You don't really believe that, do you? He's putting ideas in your head. You're happy together. Ain't like me and Maggie."

He's so sure it hurts. I guess that's what I get for keeping the strain in our relationship to myself, hiding it from everyone. It was mostly his idea. God forbid his parents and their rich friends find out there might not be a wedding to deal with, when they've spent so much time and money planning it.

Well, there won't be now.

I'm still trying to form an answer when Matt swears

again, his frustration boiling over.

"Look, I don't have time for this crap. Here's ma, I'll let her try to talk some sense into you."

Great. I can't follow the road safely anymore with everything going to hell. So, I pull over, into a small scenic overlook. Down below, Superior's dark waters slap the rocky shore, mirroring the feelings kicked up inside me.

"Kara? Your brother told me everything. Listen, I know how much it hurt when he walked out. I saw the damage he did to you – we all did – but no one like me, first-hand. If you want him gone, honey, and you can't do it yourself, then let us take care of him. We can talk to Sheriff Dixon, make sure he's apprehended before he has a chance to play more games. We're here for you and –"

"Jesus. Fuck." I'm gripping the steering wheel hard, ready to tear it off. "You don't get it, do you, mom? Neither of you. I'm the one who agreed to meet with him last night. I've known about him being back in town for almost a week. He isn't here to hurt anymore."

"Kara." She says my name in a tone that lets me see her holding up a finger. "You don't know what he's here to do. He's an awful man. You shouldn't trust him with anything. Honey, I've heard you might be having some issues with Reg. You're vulnerable. Ryan probably knows it, which is why he's come back here to mess with you again. Don't believe a word he says. Don't –"

"I don't know what to believe, but the only one who can sort it out is me. Nobody else," I say, jabbing my finger against the dashboard. The pain gives me a nice distraction.

"What is it he's done, anyway? Why won't anyone be honest about it? It seems like you know more than I do, as much as daddy took to the grave a couple years ago."

She's quiet. No different than the other times I've asked her about what really happened that night, whatever they know that goes beyond old articles and rumors.

"Kara, your father wanted you to move past Ryan. Forget him. Pretend he never existed," she whispers. "We don't need to relive his betrayal. He stabbed us all in the back when we least expected it. Maybe we failed to recognize the mental issues a boy like him had, coming from those foster homes that didn't take good care of him. It isn't our problem anymore, honey, and it isn't yours. He needs to be locked up so he can finally get some help."

"Locked up *why?* Because you think he really killed Nelson Drayton? I've never understood why everyone is so fucking insistent. He sat at our table almost every night, mom. He was like family. I loved him. If he had a dark side, I would've seen it. He's *not* a murderer."

I'm so sure of my own words I almost believe them. *Almost.*

What I really want is to get off the phone, forget about going east, and find Ryan. I want him to clear his name. I want to believe I'm not falling for another dangerous liar, when Reg has shown me that's all he really is.

"You don't know that. Kara, please come home," she says, snapping at first and then softening her tone. "Please. We can sit down, talk about this, sort out what we're going to do. I'll leave a light on for you. We'll figure this out as a family, together. We won't do anything until I let you have your say, if that's what you want. You've seen him last, so you might know how to deal with him without anyone else getting hurt."

I'm not going to change her mind, no matter how many much time I burn talking. She clearly isn't opening up, and isn't going to tell me any new big, ugly secrets.

I hang up. Turn off my phone. Ignoring another text from Ryan while I do it. I can't let them trace his last communications to me if mom and Matt decide to turn him in, and it turns into a manhunt.

I need to find him, before the wolves close in, and rip him away from me forever. Whipping my car around, I peel back onto the highway, watching my headlights stab into the night.

* * * *

My first mistake of the night is stopping at home, before I try to get in touch with Ryan. I'm surprised to see Reg's car there when it isn't even midnight. After what happened, I thought for sure he'd be gone.

As soon as I step inside, I hear something being thrown around upstairs, bounding loudly across the floor.

I take each step up cautiously. When I reach the hall, I look into our bedroom. It's a total mess. Clothes everywhere, drawers ripped open, debris from the master bathroom strewn around in the clothes. I've never seen Mr. Clean in such a chaotic frenzy, and it sends a chill up my back.

"Reg? What's going on?"

"Kara." He stops, turns around, his eyes wide like I've just caught him pulling money from the safe. Thankfully, that seems to be untouched. There isn't a single fingerprint reflecting on the shiny metal buttons at the bottom of our closet. "I was going to leave a note, but…I'm leaving."

"Leaving? What do you mean?" I say, folding my arms. "Another work trip?"

I'm so sick of his excuses. The only thing that stops me from walking away is the mess he's made, which tells me he's in a hurry to get the hell out. I'd like to know why.

"No, not work." He shifts uncomfortably, stress lining his face. "Look, I'm sorry it has to go down this way. I'll be gone for the rest of the week, and I expect you to be out of my condo by the end of the week. Wedding's off, and we're done."

My heart shouldn't hurt anymore. It's irrational. But it does, bleeding into itself, pain throbbing at the grim finality. I told myself I was ready for this. Hearing it is another story.

"So, it's over…just like that?" Anger invades my voice. I step into the room, kicking aside my dresses, which he's flung all over the floor. I'd say it's a disrespectful way to end, but it's no different from the way things have been the last six months.

He doesn't care. He never did. Never will.

I draw in a breath. "You know what? Fine. I'll be the bigger person and leave, since that's what you want. You've already turned my life upside down, wasted years, so what's another week?"

He doesn't say anything. For some reason, that's more infuriating than watching him stoop down like a scolded animal, tuck his toothbrush into his leather suitcase, and scurry past me.

He's halfway down the staircase when I lose it. I'll take his abuse, his nastiness, and his cold, but I can't stand this vicious silence.

I'm snatching at everything I can find, throwing it after him. A bottle of dry shampoo hits him in the back of his head, causing a satisfying echo.

"Fuck!" He stops, turns around, and looks at me, waiting near the door. "Your boyfriend is fucking insane, Kara, and so are you. You're lucky I don't turn you both in, and tell them everything right now. There's a police bulletin out for you. Call the cops and tell them you're safe before I do. It's the last favor you're ever getting from me."

I'm looking at him, trying to take in the insane things he's saying, one at a time. It's like my brain has reached its limit on crazy today.

Before he walks out, he stops, and gives me the most hateful look I've ever seen on his princely face. "This is the last time you'll ever see me, but we're not done yet. Nobody assaults a Drayton and walks away. Your boyfriend isn't either."

Boyfriend? What the *hell* is he talking about?

The door slams behind him, and I walk to the nearest window, overlooking the garage. His grey, freshly washed Mercedes screams out a second later. I know in the pit of my gut it's the last time I'm ever going to watch him leaving our home.

There's no time for tears, wine, or a lavender scented soak in the tub to calm me down. I'm going to go ballistic if I can't get answers.

Before, I needed to see Ryan. Now, I'm going to lose my mind by the end of the night if I can't find him. Hell has broken loose, spilling out a little more by the second, and I *need* answers.

* * * *

His offices are dark. The security gate is locked up tight. A couple vehicles roam the lot, but I know they're mostly guards working night shift. I seriously doubt he's at work, especially if he's learned the police were trying to chase me down just a few hours ago.

If he couldn't find me, where would he go? It takes me a few minutes before I think I have an answer.

I drive on, leaving Punch Corp behind, heading for the spot where I believe he's likeliest to find me.

When I pull into the lighthouse parking lot, I see his lonely Tesla, and start to smile. How fitting.

He's upstairs, staring across the wide, dark sea. He doesn't wait for me to come up and join him. As soon as he sees my light, his solitary figure takes off, heading inside and racing downstairs. He bursts out the doors a second later. His big beautiful arms are around me before I've even had a chance to close my door.

"Are you okay, babe? Did he hurt you?" His voice scratches my ears. Low and rough, delicious as the drag of his stubble on my skin.

"Only a few bruises to the heart." I sigh, pausing to breathe him in, the only man who's ever felt right.

Ryan's blue eyes are dark and beautiful in the night. He takes my face in one hand, tilts it up, forcing me to hold his gaze. After all the hell I've been through tonight, I love it.

"That's over," he whispers, low as distant thunder. "I'm here, Kara-bou. Never letting go as long as I've got a pulse. You're spending the rest of your days with a smile on those precious lips."

"I want to believe you," I tell him, nestling into his chest. His hands roll down my back, lower, warming the chills running up my spine. "It's hard, after all this."

"It's not." His hand cups my cheek again, and his forehead touches mine. "This is our reset, Kara. The pain, the hurt, the regret, that's all over. I'll mend fences with you and my family. I'll throw him out of your life if he ever comes back to give you hell again."

"Like it's so easy." Sarcasm creeps into my voice.

"I never ran away from a challenge," he says, flashing me his mysterious smile. "You're the best one of my life. It's easy, because I say so, babe. I told you what this is – reset. Whether it's easy or hard doesn't matter because I just pushed the fucking button, and this ride doesn't stop until you're happy, living under my roof, and curled up with me every single night. We've lost too many nights. It'll take a whole army of assholes like Reg to keep me away from you even one more time, and I'll still go down swinging to keep you."

No more talk. I lean into him, and let his lips take what they've wanted.

Our kiss ignites the fireball building in my belly. Rampant, scorching heat runs through my veins. His tongue presses into my mouth. Mine dances against his in hot, furious ripples. I'm actually swooning in his arms, losing support in my knees, falling into an embrace that's just like home.

"Your ex is gone tonight, yeah?" he asks.

I can't help but laugh. He calls him my ex like it's already official, and I don't have a hundred loose ends to wrap up, getting Reg out of my life for good. Finally, I nod.

"Good. Then let's take this to your place. I'll get the movers in the morning to grab your stuff as soon we've had our fun. They'll strip down everything that isn't his in that damned condo except the sheets we're about to ruin. I want him to rub his face in our love after everything he did to you."

Sweet Jesus, he's insane.

But I have to admit, the idea has a certain wild charm to it. It satisfies my jealousy, my anger, and my hurt all at once. More than anything, I just want Ryan again, the sex I've craved for half a decade, suffering through abstinence and then the awkward encounters with Reg that weren't much better.

I hate him for lying, walking out, and wasting my time.

Unfortunately, there's also no telling what's true, and what isn't, since he wrecked the evidence on the thumb drive. What if I'm wrong about his affair, however suspicious he's been acting, and he's decided to dump me over something else?

He's a bastard for doing it, yeah. But does he deserve to be humiliated?

"Ryan...I don't know," I say, pushing against his broad, incredible chest. "It's happening so fast. He never even admitted to cheating on me. I didn't see the data – he broke it before I could. Don't worry. I'm not taking him back, not after what he said to me today, or the way he walked out."

"You need to see this." His strong, square jaw smooths his smile. Ryan's expression turns deadly serious as he reaches into his pocket, flips through some keys on his phone, and then holds it in front of me.

It takes several seconds to recognize what I'm looking at. It's Reg on the screen. Nearly naked, red faced, looking like he's about to rip someone's head off.

He's cuffed to a leather chair, staring hatefully into the lens. The bastard's erection is still straining in his boxers, despite his gross humiliation. It's one dick I'm never going to miss.

Ryan flips through several more pics of my ex tied down. Then there's another one with a woman I don't recognize at first. She's wearing the tallest candy colored heels in the world, her ankles splayed, legs pressed defensively together at the knees.

Her face hits me through the makeup. Wedding planner Amy stares at me like a helpless animal. Frustrated, ashamed, and maybe a little afraid.

Really? Is there any low he won't sink to?

I can't stop shaking. I thought I'd braced myself, prepared to see undeniable proof of him being a cheating asshole. But doing it with the woman we sat with yesterday? The one who was supposed to help craft the happiest day of our lives?

I shove his arm away, threatening to knock the phone from his hand. "Sorry," I mutter, turning my back, facing Superior's loud, steady churn.

"No, babe. Don't apologize," he says, wrapping a protective arm around my waist. "It's a lot for you to take in, and there's not much time to do it. We're moving like the wind, but hell, we always did. We've lost time. That's the real tragedy here. Too many years robbed away by my mistakes and this asshole. Now, we're taking them back. Fixing everything."

I turn, facing him, hot new tears rolling down my cheeks. His confidence comforts me. So does the inferno rising in his eyes, wide as open skies, ready to lift me up to a higher, better place.

"We're fixing it all," he says again. "Kara, I love you. I never stopped. When I look at you, it's like the time we've lost doesn't even matter. Nailing that cheating fucker's coffin shut, making sure you're safe and loved against me tonight and every night after…that's all we've got to worry about. When I look at you, I see the sexiest, smartest, and most gorgeous woman in the whole damned universe. Same woman who said 'yes' to me all those years ago, who I'm hoping will say it again."

My heart hits meltdown. It's not made to take this much happiness and pain, to be tossed from heaven to hell and back to earth again in a matter of days.

Before I can say anything, he pushes his finger softly over my lips. "Don't say it now. There's a time and place for that, love. I proposed to you once like a little boy, and when it happens again, it's going to be a man asking to put a ring on your hand."

He's growling when he lifts my arm, lacing my fingers into his. God, they feel so right.

So perfectly, undeniably, impossibly right that I'd probably overrule my sane side and agree to marry him tonight if he just said the words.

Instead, he starts leading me to his car. "You okay with leaving your ride parked here tonight? I'll send for someone from the company to get it in the morning."

"Of course." Saying it is the last little thing I remember before I'm tucked into the warm leather seat next to him, the instrument panels lighting our faces in dull blue light, taking the winding roads into town.

It's really happening.

Holy shit!

It starts to sink in when Ryan's hand goes to my thigh just as we're getting into Split Harbor. He rubs circles there, each lap like a shock to my core, obliterating the night's emotional storm in rays of sweltering heat, want, and need.

I don't bother directing him to the guest parking. He pulls along the curb, parks, and several seconds later, he's opening the passenger door and lifting me into his arms.

He carries me all the way through the door, and then straight up. Jacob isn't at the front desk to see us, thankfully. He respects the Draytons too much, just like everyone else in town. I'm sure he'd start dialing Reg right away if he saw another man leading me to the elevator, which has had a lot of work done lately because some mad man laid his fists to it, breaking the mirrors on the walls.

Upstairs, I reach for my keys, but I fumble several times. He's insatiable. Ryan slams me against the door, his mouth crushing mine. We're feeding a lust neither of us can handle with every kiss, surrendering ourselves to a greater power that won't be satisfied until we're naked, sweating, and totally spent.

He snatches me up in his arms again as soon as I get the door unlocked. I'm laughing when he carries me over the threshold.

It's everything I imagined five years ago, on what should've been our wedding night, entering our first place alone as man and wife.

"Upstairs," I say, guiding him through our place. He doesn't stop to inspect anything.

His hands are all over my ass. Cupping, squeezing, forcing me to imagine everything that's coming next. I feel like it's a hundred and ten degrees when I think about his big, rough hands ripping off my clothes, rolling my nipples, bending me over.

His palms, slapping both cheeks if I don't ride him hard enough. *God.*

Not that I think I'll need any help in that department. After months – hell, *years* – of sub-par sex or nothing at all, I'm starving.

My purse drops as soon as we're next to the bed. Ryan

starts tearing at my clothes, and I don't resist, moaning when he pulls one breast from my blouse, pushes down my bra, and bends me over the bed while his teeth pull on my nipple.

Oh, shit. Yes!

He sucks and licks for one outstanding minute. It's so good and hot and sudden I swear I'm about to come on the spot. But he pulls away before I can, pins my shoulders against the bed, watching me while I pant and writhe. My entire body begs for more.

"I'm clean, babe, in case you wondered," he says.

I smile. It's sweet that he still cares. It also makes me a little jealous.

No, I don't hold it against him that he's been with other women – he's only human. I've been busy with Reg, deep in more kink than I ever wanted, and the wrong kind, too. But imagining him fucking anyone except me right now makes me want it more.

"I'm on the pill," I say. Thinking about taking him skin-on-skin, feeling him erupt deep inside me, sends a delicious tingle through every nerve.

That hot, sly smile hanging on his lips gets wider. He doesn't say another word. I watch in awe as he starts pulling off his suit, piece by piece.

First the jacket, then the tie around his neck. His fingers work each button loose. When he throws his shirt off his chest and lets it drop to the floor, I gasp.

The tapestry covering his rock hard muscles wasn't there before. It's rich, dark, fiery ink. What looks like dark skies spewing lightning through clouds, and a tiny boat rowing out to stormy seas, where a dragon pokes its head up with a ferocious smile.

The lightning ripples outward, tapering into stripes that go down his arms. Each one looks like a band stretched across his massive biceps, down to his wrists.

Now, I know why he needs to wear full suits everyday. Anything cut low, too business casual, and the whole world will know what a freak lurks underneath the whiz entrepreneur.

"When did you get that?" I ask him, sitting up on the bed so I can touch it. His skin feels warm, smooth, delightful beneath my fingertips.

"Been a work-in-progress since I set up shop in Seattle. A little of my sub-conscious working its way out on my skin, I guess."

"A little?" I wrinkle my nose and smile. "It's amazing, Ryan. Whoever did this work has crazy talent. Not like the amateurs here."

"Here?" He raises an eyebrow. "Are you telling me you're hiding something on that beautiful skin?"

I blush, and don't say anything. It's his job to find out.

He moves faster, drawing off his belt, kicking down his trousers. He leaves the huge, throbbing bulge underneath his boxers to taunt me while he rips me up in his arms, pushes one hand below my waist, and starts undressing me.

He isn't finished until I'm down to just my panties and the stockings underneath my long dress. They're sexy for an autumn outfit. He growls his agreement into my ear, kissing at my neck, fisting my blond hair in his hands and pulling. *Hard.*

When his free hand starts plumping my breasts, I'm done.

My knees buckle. I have to lean back into the bed for support. Beyond ready for him to throw me down, rip away the sopping wet mess between my legs, and fuck me like I've missed for too many years.

He's rougher than I remember. His hands move with the confidence of a man who's learned a few things over our absence. His touch, his lips, his teeth all coax different points on my body into one steaming, sensual pulse.

I need this. Fuck, do I ever.

Everything he does starts so delicate, and quickly turns wild. His soft, teasing lips take mine when he twists my head. His tongue conquers, slipping in and out of my mouth, a crude promise hinting everything to come.

"Ohhh," I sputter when his hand glides down my belly, brushing my side, pushing below the waistband to my panties. "Oh, yeah."

Yeah. Everything I've ever wanted oozes in that word when his fingers find my slick folds, run up and down them like he's teasing me with the head of his cock. He spreads his hand to cup the warm, dripping mound dying for his heat.

"I see it" he growls, distracting me with his fingers when he finds the tattoo along my side, hugging my right hip. "It's beautiful, babe. Even if it's a little sad."

It's a pitch black heart, split in two pieces, melting like

it's wax over fire. For a second, I ignore the pulse between my legs to marvel at how I've had it for almost four years. I got it during the dark days when I'd just flunked school and moved home, empty and rudderless.

"You know, you're the first one who's ever seen it and given a damn," I say, wrapping my hands around his handsome neck. "I've almost had it for four years. Not once did Reg ever ask."

His eyes narrow, and he silences me with a kiss. When he pulls away, his hand is back in my hair, pulling harder than before. "Fuck him, and fuck everything he did, too, baby girl. You can tell me all about your ink after you're done coming, dripping my seed."

"Shit, that sounds –"

Amazing never gets out. His fingers press back into my panties, and this time they're coming off. One hot, angry jerk shoves them down my legs. He drops to his knees, kissing his way back up my thighs.

His breath teases, entices, quickening the tremor in my leg. I swear to God, if he doesn't put his face there right now, I'm going to –

Ryan grabs my legs, holding them apart. His lips taste my pussy for the first time in forever, and it's hard to even stand.

The tongue I've missed for an eternity goes to work.

Licking. Sucking. Vibrating his growl each time he runs its tip through my folds, devouring me like he can't get enough.

He inhales my scent. I struggle to breathe at all. I flop

over at the waist, grabbing the edge of the bed, fighting the urge in my legs to close, to soften the merciless wave crashing through me each time he brings me closer to completion.

His hands won't let me go anywhere. I'm his willing prisoner, captive to his mouth, and it gives me the most exquisite torture a woman can experience.

There's ripples in my thighs by the time he brings his attention to my clit. I'm panting, moaning each time his tongue flicks my hot little bud. One hand climbs higher up my leg; up, up, up, until his fingers stop near my ass, grazing the very center.

"God, yes!" I pant, my eyes clenching shut. I'm bracing for a firestorm. "Ryan, don't stop. Ryan, fuck! I'm about to –"

He preempts me. Two stiff fingers push gently into my ass while his teeth pull my clit. He holds it, smothers it, flogs it like it needs to be punished for missing his mouth for this many years.

Maybe, just maybe, it does. Before I can reconcile anything in my brain, my muscles coil up and everything goes blinding white.

Coming!

I come on his mouth with my ass clenching his fingers, my body still hungry to take more of him inside it. Dragging my nipples into the blanket strewn over the bed, I'm screaming, loving the roughness coursing through every part of me.

This is what I missed, what I've only had a taste of my entire life.

I need my sex wild, spontaneous, with no apologies. Ryan delivers, tongue-fucking me straight through my convulsions, making me ride his beautiful face for every sweet spasm.

I'm in the ether for what seems like an eternity. When I start coming down from it, he eases me onto the bed, ass up as he backs off my pussy, kissing up my back.

"How long as it been since you've come like that?" he whispers, threading his fingers through my hair. "Be honest."

"Too long. Not since the night we got engaged." I pause, hit by the enormity of what I've just said. "Jesus. I wasted a lot of time with the wrong man, didn't I?"

"He kept you waiting for me," Ryan says, turning me around, stopping to brush his lips against mine. "I've missed your taste, Kara-bou. Missed it like my own damn reflection. I've had to see Tanner Brooks staring back for the last five years, living a lie I never wanted. When you're naked in front of me, screaming my name, I see the man I used to be. I see Ryan, and I want to bring him back."

"You will," I whisper.

My legs keep shimmying against his boxers. I want to return the favor.

He couldn't have missed my taste more than I've yearned to have his cock in my mouth again. I want to bear down deep on every inch, rub my tongue on his swollen tip until he floods my mouth.

I want him grunting, grinding, clenching the sheets like he's about to explode.

Because once he does, the mistakes we made die a little more. Every time we come is a little more assurance this bitter road ends here, and a new one opens.

We're staying here, entangled, right where we belong.

"Does Tanner like to fuck, or make love gently?" I ask, pursing my lips, desperate to see his cock again.

He smiles. "Ryan fucks both ways, and that's who you're with tonight, Kara-bou."

He straightens, hooking his thumbs against his boxers. They come down too slowly for my liking. His cock springs out, into his fist. He kicks his boxers off behind him, and then he's crouched on the bed, giving me a magnificent view.

It's just as glorious as I remembered. Huge, thick, throbbing and – what the hell? – *pierced?*

"No way," I say softly, sitting up so I can get a better look. "You're just full of surprises, aren't you?"

"Only the best kind," he whispers, taking my hand. He opens it, pulls my fingers apart, and wraps it around his seething length. "Come closer. Get a better look. You ought to see what you're dealing with before it's in you, babe, making you come harder than you've ever come in your life."

Holy shit. I don't think he's lying.

No, I know he's telling the truth when I run my fist up, edging the tip with my thumb. Thick, hot pre-come spills out his little slit. I lean in, hovering over the silver bead in his dick, and give it a quick kiss.

"It's warm."

"Just like the rest of it," he says, taking my wrist again. He grabs both arms, laying me back, spreading me apart to make way for him as he moves between my legs. "Much as I want your lips wrapped around me again, I have to see your face when I fuck you, Kara. Need to see every muscle twitch when I'm balls deep, scratching that five year itch, spilling everything I've got inside you."

How could I possibly argue?

My legs open for him automatically. He takes his sweet time, rolling his eager dick across my folds, tormenting me with just the tip. It brushes my clit, sending lightning through my blood.

The beautiful bastard's going to make me beg, isn't he?

"Please," I whimper, moaning when he edges his dick lower, pressing its head against my entrance.

I'm soaked. Crazed. Dying to feel him inside me already.

"Louder," he says, flicking his cock against my pussy faster. "I've waited so long to hear how bad you want this."

"Please. Ryan – oh, God!" My legs can't stop brushing his, and my hips are trying to bring me closer. I'd be grinding against his cock, if only he weren't holding me down. "Fuck me. Please."

Please.

His smile grows. It's an evil one now. I'm rolling my head, thrashing back and forth, animal need taking over.

"Please!" I say it once more, the last time before I'm going to bite him in the face.

His hips move. They roll forward, sinking his dick into me, good and deep.

Five fucking years. I can't believe I'm having him again, taking every inch to my womb, anchoring him in me with my legs draped over his, panting like mad.

I can't hold back. He only thrusts for half a minute before I'm coming. I've barely sampled what he offers, and I'm already losing it. Giving up my pleasure to his lips, his thrusts, my eyes fluttering every time he plows deep.

He's stretching me open. He's massaging me in places I've never felt before each time he moves near my womb, owning my pussy with the smooth, hot bead in his tip.

"Yes, yes! Ryan – *yes!*" He fucks me faster when I start convulsing.

Oh, this man. This wonderful fucking fire.

More, more.

Yes!

My pussy clenches around him so hard I think we're melting into each other. He rumbles his delight, slamming into me faster, fucking straight through my first release like a train without brakes.

Fingers, toes, everything curls. Bending to the pleasure, the heat, the love I've missed for so long.

He stops to kiss me alive again when the maelstrom stops. His dick is still moving, deep inside me, making slow, hard strokes. Stretching my walls apart for the only man worthy of owning them.

"Yeah, fuck yeah, babe. This is our night," he says, whispering while he takes my earlobe with his teeth. "I'm going to turn you over. Fuck it all out on my dick. All of it, Kara. Every time you've missed me, every time you've dreamed about us, every time you knew he was wrong for you. We don't stop until we've torn these sheets. I want you to squirt all over them, and I'll bury every hot load I've got in your sweet cunt."

I'm almost squirting with every rough, dirty sentence rolling out of his mouth.

Ryan's strong hands lift me up, put me on my knees, and guide me down. I'm stuck for a breathless second, burying my face into the sheets Reg and I shared for the last time.

Behind me, he tilts my ass up. His cock mounts me from behind, sinking into me again, fisting my hair.

His thrusts come quicker this time. I fuck back against him slowly, slamming my ass into his lower abs.

It's love. It's hate. It's everything I missed and everything I thought I'd lost, everything I secretly wanted when Reg would try to fuck me like a man, and failed miserably.

I was blind, or just put to sleep by his bedroom antics, plus wishful thinking. But I'm awake now, electric and alive, moving my hips to the savage thud in my heart.

"Fuck me!" I scream it, beating my hips into his, hair flying everywhere that isn't collected in his fist.

His fingers catch, pulling me back, making it hurt so good.

The entire bed shakes like never before. I don't even know if this hand-crafted wood can hold up to the beating it's getting. I'll break it before I slide off his cock.

"Are you ready, beautiful?" he growls, slamming his hand into my ass.

The sharp, brusk heat catches me by surprise. My pussy blazes again on his cock, close to overload.

"Are you fucking ready?" he asks again, his last words snarling out.

The frantic twitch in his hips as his cock stabs into me tells me exactly what he means. He's about to come inside me, marking me again from the inside out.

"Come!" I whisper, voice trembling. I never knew it would be so hard to wish for something I want this much. "Come inside me, Ryan. *Please.*"

He lunges. Burying his cock in me to the hilt, he rips at my hair, grabbing my hips with his free hand to hold me onto his length.

Then there's nothing but hellfire.

His heat picks me up, slams me down.

He fucks me, fills me, pours himself in, bathing my pussy in molten, satisfying warmth.

I'm undone. Lost. Coming, coming, coming like a lake storm, sudden and fierce.

His cock drills deeper, flinging my body against him like a doll, grinding his roar through his teeth. Swelling, shooting, exploding, he empties himself several times over, digging his fingers into the red burn he's left on my ass cheek the whole way through.

When it's over, he pulls out. His heat runs down my thigh, liquid fire making me shudder.

I collapse in his arms. We breathe, we gaze into each other's eyes, but we don't speak.

I don't know what happens next, except that he's going

to fuck me many more times before the night is through.

He turns to me when we've both replenished the air in our lungs. "I'm heading back to Seattle for a few days next week. Come with me."

He doesn't ask. I smile because we both know he doesn't need to.

There's no need to answer him with anything besides another kiss. Hot, sticky, and full of new love.

"Is that a yes?" he says, smiling because he knows it is. I give him another kiss, hotter than before, lowering my hand to his cock.

What we've kindled tonight is precious. There's so much more to fix before we can just be, and all our problems will be here when we get back, if we can put them on hold at all.

After tonight, they don't matter. I'll follow him to the ends of the Earth.

Anything, everything, and always to hold onto this second chance.

X: Morning, Noon, and Night (Ryan)

She wakes up with my hand between her legs. Doesn't take her long to moan when I press my thumb against her clit, pushing my fingers through the sweet, hot wetness I fucked long and hard last night.

"Ryan?" she murmurs, smiling, as if she has to remind herself it's really happening.

"Say my name louder," I tell her, pushing my fingers into her harder, teasing the spot along her inner wall that makes her legs to tremble. "I want everybody in these condos to know who's fucking you, babe."

Her body ripples, unsure, the last shred of reason on her brain trying to pull her away from me. I grab her by the waist, jerk her back, and rub her pussy until the next few moans off her lips flow like honey.

"You love it, and you love me, too. I'm done hiding, Kara-bou. Done holding anything back. We're waking up fresh and alive. Today's the last day this town ever thinks you're with him. Ruining this bed is just the beginning."

Her lips form a circle when she hears it. My ears prickle, listening as she sucks in a fierce little breath, turning me to granite.

I need to be inside her.

Can't get enough since we started last night. I barely backed off fucking for a few hours so we could get some sleep. My jet leaves in a few hours, ready to bring us out to Seattle, just like I promised. I intend to spend every waking minute we're left in this town naked, joined, and making up for every lost night I wasn't with my wife.

Still feels like I haven't made up one one-thousandth of the time we've been apart.

My dick swells, bulging against her ass. Kara wiggles into me, urged on by lust, but also the chill in the air. Didn't allow her any clothes, not when I've waited five years to have her naked next to me again.

My heat will do. So will the friction of my frantic cock when it's buried deep inside her, promising to make her moan, scream, and sweat through the whole winter.

Her thighs twitch around my hand. She's fighting me, the little minx, so overcome with pleasure she can't stand it.

Growling, I pull her legs apart. My fingers go harder, faster, and I bring my mouth down on hers, letting my tongue mimic my hands.

In. Out. In. Out.

Fuck, yes.

We suck hungrily. She whimpers each time her throbbing clit grazes my thumb. I'm going to go insane if I can't own every hole in her body over and over and over again. My dick presses against her tight ass, and soon, I can't control myself a second longer.

I move away. Her face looks pleading and infuriated.

"Climb on top of me, baby," I growl, reaching for her ass, helping her straddle me. "I want your beautiful tits in my face when you're coming on every inch."

She blushes. I move my hands on her faster, aggressively, pushing her slick pussy down on my aching length.

I can't believe this. It's incredible that she fucks like a virgin after all these years.

Part of me feels touched, like I've been handed more than a second chance. It's a fresh opportunity to do everything I always wanted, but better because I've become a man.

The other part is pissed.

I *hate* the worm who's been laying in her bed for the past year and a half. It enrages me to know he left her wanting like this, grinding her hips in desperation as soon as she sinks down onto me, wrapping her arms around my neck and pursing her lips for another kiss.

It's like she hasn't been fucked good in all five years. She's starving, and the maggot I roughed up is responsible.

No more. She's never rolling out of bed unsatisfied again.

My lips take hers. I give her everything. My hips crash into hers with twice the fury, running my public bone against her clit.

Her head goes back, she moans, and everything gets hotter and wetter around my dick. I'm going to turn this woman into a permanent squirter. It's the least she deserves after being robbed of real sex, chained to a boy who never had the strength or heart to fuck her like a man.

"I love you, Kara." I whisper the words right before I take her nipple between my teeth.

She whimpers, rocking into me faster, sweet and close to coming. It's not enough to pluck every nerve in her gorgeous body, even though that's what makes my cock howl for release.

I want her heart. I want it back. I want it bound to me like we always promised, and I won't stop saying everything I've locked up for years.

"Come, baby, come." I grab her hair, fisting it in my palm. Then my hips pound hers, bringing her over, forcing her nails into my shoulders when she clenches them.

Rolling her head back, she screams. "Ryan – fuck!"

Her pussy squeezes my entire cock for what feels like forever. The heat in my balls becomes a second sun. We fuck like no tomorrow. Fucking to wipe away yesterday. She's barely coming down from the high when I'm snarling, quickening my speed, crashing into her so hard the bed beneath us rattles like sticks in the wind.

"Good goddamn, you're tight, baby. Only pussy in the world that was ever made to fit me like a glove. You were mine for good the first night we fucked, baby girl. No years apart will ever change that." I'm pulling on her hair faster, slowing my strokes until she looks at me, her green eyes flashing lust and need. "You knew I'd come back, didn't you?"

She bites her lip. For a second, I'm worried I'm going to ruin the mood, but she moans when I drive myself deep into her again.

"I knew," she whispers. "I always believed, even when I wanted to quit. When you showed up, you saved me from the biggest mistake of my life."

"Guess it's your lucky day. I'm about to save you from the second biggest, too," I say, pressing my forehead to hers, my free hand palming one breast as it pulses in my hand, her lungs trying to make up so much lost breath.

"Not that." She looks at me and my hips twitch, picking up speed again, until I see her eyelids flutter. "Jesus. I don't know if I can come again, Ryan. I –"

Bullshit. I own her now. I always did, and I'll tell her when, where, and how many times to come.

My lips meet hers, more of a love bite than a true kiss. "You're dead wrong. I won't stop taking your sweet cunt until you give it up to me one more time. You're mine, Kara-bou. Morning, noon, and night. You were mine yesterday, and you'll be mine tomorrow, sharing every last, best part of me. When I tell you to come in and see my soul, you do it. When I tell you to just come, you're going to fucking do it. Come for me, beautiful. Come like you always wanted every night you were with him, hoping it was me. We're not leaving this bed unless it's broke."

I'm thrusting like a madman now. She bounces every time my dick plunges in to the hilt. My balls fly up, spanking her skin. There's no doubt she's heard me because her eyes are closed.

She's soaking in every last word, every sensation as I take both her hands, hold them in mine, and power fuck through every doubt she's ever had.

It doesn't take long for her pussy to tighten on my dick. The feverish sound slipping out through her teeth when she comes again gives me a rush. I fuck harder, ready to go over the edge with her.

There's a spring of fire coiling up in my balls, running up my spine, igniting my brain. When it hits the base of my dick, everything I've felt for this woman wells up in half a second, and then it ruptures.

I'm coming.

Snarling, grunting, growling like an animal who's taken control of its mate. I'm not afraid to admit that's what I've become, and I'm not letting her go, no matter how much this town wants to skin me alive when they find out who I am and what I've done.

My seed pours out in hot, dense ropes. Her mouth falls open, but she's too overwhelmed with my heat to even scream, breathlessly caught in her pleasure.

My beautiful, beloved captive. The only one I've ever wanted and ever will want for the rest of my days, and at least half of those days are going to be filled with her convulsing all over my cock, both of us crying out when my seed fills her belly again.

One day soon, my load is giving her a kid. It won't be the last one I put in her either. I'm not stopping until we've got everything we always wanted. The love, the ring, the family.

All of it.

Desire runs hot, especially when I think about her soft belly swelling with our child, her pert breasts turning full and dark.

I can't stop fucking her now. My body moves like a machine, programmed to fuck and nothing else.

I'm not exaggerating. I've just come my brains out, and I'm still hard for her.

My orgasm only weakens when I start thrusting again, ready to see if I can bring her off a third time in the same half hour.

I'll carry her onto my private jet if I have to. Spent, satisfied, and wearing a *just fucked* smile on her lips.

We never get that far though. Several more furious strokes in, something gives way when she crashes down on me, engulfing my cock.

There's a loud *snap!* Next thing I know, we're flat on the floor. The mattress bangs the designer rug underneath the bed like a bowling ball dropping on the Brazilian cherrywood.

I'm still buried in her when she starts laughing. It takes me a several seconds to shake off the surprise, and then I'm grinning like a fool, chuckling alongside her.

"See that? When I told you we'd break this bed, I wasn't kidding."

"You're insane!" she says, scolding me with a finger tapping on the lightning bolts tattooed on my chest. "He's going to kill me when he sees this, you know. We'll both catch hell for it. This rug belonged to his rich parents. They gave it to us as a housewarming present."

"Fuck the Draytons," I tell her. Honestly, truthfully, carelessly perhaps, I'm done holding anything back. "He deserves a lot worse for what he did to you. Whenever he gets home, he's going to find all your stuff gone, and every sheet left on this fucked up bed stained with us."

"You're really evil," she says, but the smile on her face tells me there's no warmth left in her heart for the cheating bastard who nearly screwed her in all the worst ways. "Luckily, I kind of like it."

"Kind of?" I say, cupping her face in my hand, bringing it in for another kiss. "Kara-bou, you've got my whole heart, the dark and the light. Let me see everything in yours. We've got time before the jet takes off."

She smiles. "That's what? A couple more hours?"

"Yeah, and I'm still hard."

I roll her over, planting her hands above her head as she bends over, taking her ass in both of my hands. I mount her from behind and take her pussy to heaven once again.

She comes a few more times, and so do I, before we hit the shower together.

* * * *

When I come upstairs, bringing a thermos of coffee like she asked, she's in a robe. Her face is turned to the window, and she's sitting on the chaise next to the fallen mattress, the sheets still tangled and torn in a few places from our savage loving.

"You ready?" I ask, handing her the coffee, about to head to the opposite corner where I dropped my clothes last night. "I told my assistant to get some movers out here tomorrow. Just need to drop the keys at the office when we're on our way to the airport, and they'll take care of everything. Should have your stuff in storage this time tomorrow, until we decide where it goes next."

"I can't go with you," she says, folding her arms. "Not unless you're ready to tell me the truth about what happened. I need to know why you left, and why you killed a man, assuming that's what really happened."

My heart relaxes for half a second before it starts banging my ribs like mad. I'd been ready to give her the full truth the other night, before her brother interrupted us, but now I'm taken aback.

"It's a long story," I say, moving to the chair across from her, wondering where the hell I should begin. Not that there's ever a good starting point with something this twisted. "I can give you the abbreviated version. Plane leaves in less than an hour."

"I don't care what version you give me, as long as it's the truth. I need to know why, Ryan. Believe me, I *want* to go. I want to trust you. I want to rebuild what we had before. But we can't do any of that as long as it's hanging over us" She folds her hands, leans forward, and looks me in the eyes. "Please. Just tell me why you ran."

"Okay." Now, I know what a man under an interrogation feels like, and the stakes are just as high here.

What if the story I'm about to tell her frightens her to death?

What if she won't go? Won't look at me after she knows?

What if she can't forgive the blood on my hands, or the lies?

"I'm waiting," she insists, unclasping her hands. They come out, reaching for mine, and I look into her eyes.

No, fuck, I can't lie to her again. I won't run away a second time when I'm one step away from having her back in my life.

"You can't hate anyone who's already dead," I say. "That's the only thing I want you remembering before I tell you the rest."

She blinks, confusion clouding her eyes. I don't say anything until she nods, agreeing to my terms. Then I launch into the cruelest night of my life, the one that fucked up everything.

* * * *

Five Years Ago

You know about Nelson Drayton. How I buffed out the scratches on his car, made his baby just like new again, all while the dinosaur with the lifelong silver spoon in his mouth expected miracles without any time to work them.

He asked me to clean up the interior after I'd finished the main job. I was happy to do it quick and clean, just to get him the hell out of there.

I'm on my hands and knees, jabbing the vacuum in hard to reach places. There's a lot of ash everywhere, like the pig spills it all over his car, carelessly flinging ash from his cigars everywhere. If I miss a speck, I'm sure I'll catch hell, so I do several sweeps.

There's something in the way underneath his driver's seat when I reach down. I have to turn off the vacuum and pull with both hands just to move it.

It's a thick black leather folio, bloated with so much material stuffed inside it's barely held together by the metal clasp.

If only I'd been more careful pulling it out, I'd have saved everyone so much grief.

Didn't work that way. My hand catches against the steering wheel when I lift it up, banging the leather binder so hard it comes apart. A hundred papers go flying out.

"Shit!" I swear, hit the ground, and begin reaching for the material strewn everywhere, escaping underneath his car.

Halfway through gathering it up, I get a good look at what's on those pages. My brain freezes, realizing what I'm seeing.

Maybe a third of the mess are ordinary papers, lists of names and numbers. The rest, the other two thirds…

They're pictures. Violent, sadistic, unspeakable photographs burned forever in my head. And the poor women in them, the girls, they're all too young.

I swear I recognize a couple faces from the orphanage. The place was tied to his charity, which he used to bring me to a foster home in Split Harbor. Apparently, I wasn't the only one he freed, but nobody's seen the girls since.

Certainly not around town.

While I left hell, got on my feet, and found a life here, they've been God knows where, serving this animal and the other brutes in his hideous photos.

My first instinct is to vomit. The second is to race for the phone, call Bart, and ask for advice because I don't know what the hell to do.

I can't just call the cops on a Drayton. Nelson has everyone in this town in his back pocket, and its his word against mine.

These sick, gruesome pictures are the only evidence I have that this man – this fucking monster – isn't the paragon of respect and charity everyone believes him to be.

There's no other explanation. It's him the photographs, leering at the girls. A decent man wouldn't be caught dead with what I've got tucked under my shaking arm.

I have to get out of here. Need to bring it to someone, anyone who knows what to do with it. There's got to be some way to get Nelson Drayton, bring him to trial, and lock this vampire away where he'll never hurt anyone again.

I'm pacing, trying not to let the panic win. I can't freeze up, damn it.

Absent-mindedly, I crinkle up one page with names and numbers – probably other criminals involved in bringing him fresh victims – and stuff it in my pocket.

There's no time to spare.

I'm heading for the office, wracking my brain for options, when the asshole himself walks through the back door. He stops near the wall, stubbing his cigar out. He doesn't see me at first.

Too bad I have to walk by him to get where I'm going. I try to make it, but he hears my footsteps, whips his head around, and stares at me like a wolf.

"You done yet, kid?" he asks, taking a full second to notice the mess tucked under my arm. Then his old, evil eyes go wide. They darken, black holes full of fury, desperate to swallow me up. "Christ. That doesn't belong to you."

No shit. He's coming toward me, and he's pissed.

I've been in bad places before in foster homes and orphanages, thrown in with unsavory characters from every corner of the Midwest. This is the first time my heart leaps in my throat, and beats so hard I freeze.

He's almost got his hands on me when I start backing up. I hit the corner and I look around, shaking because there's nowhere else to run. Nelson stops in front of me, quietly seething.

He's still trying to keep his composure. It's like watching a wild animal wearing a person's mask, the illusion hanging by a thread.

"That isn't yours, boy. You took it from my car. Need you to give it back." His voice is like ice. "Give it the fuck back to me. *Now.*"

"No," I tell him, standing up taller and straighter than I ever have in my life. Maybe if I can scare him, he'll back off, retreat, buy me some precious time. "You're not getting it again. I saw what's in here, Mr. Drayton…the girls…torture. You're seriously asking me to give it back, look the other way, pretend I never saw it?"

"That's what I'm *telling* you to do, you stupid little shit." Anger curls his lips into a wretched smile. He cocks his head, the blackness in his eyes deepening. "What do you think you're going to do with it, anyway? Run to the police?

The FBI? I swear to God, I'll pay them whatever it takes to let me off the hook. I'll burn my treasures in front of their eyes. You've got a lot to learn about how this world works, kid, but let me give you a primer. I'm on top. You aren't. I can get away with shit that'll curdle your stomach. Don't make this a fight, or you'll find out what kind of damage money and a name can do."

I don't say anything. I look him in his wicked, beady eyes, clutching the leather folio tighter, my eyes scanning everything around us.

There's Mickey's tall, messy toolbox, just a few feet away. All sorts of blunt objects laying out on top of it, right above the Playboy bunny sticker he's got slapped on the side.

"I don't want to fight you," I tell him. My voice crinkles in my throat, harsh and dry as autumn leaves. "But I can't give this up, Mr. Drayton. I won't."

"I'm not asking your permission, fuckwipe," he growls, two vicious fists forming his sides. "It seems you're confused. Let me help you out. You want to give me my property, go home, and pretend we never had this conversation. Only chance I'm going to give. Go ahead and stick your nose where it doesn't belong, I'll damned sure bite it off, boy. I'll burn you to the ground, and that'll just be the start."

He pauses, doing a slow turn, looking around the garage before he's facing me again. "I can, and I will, make everything go up in a puff of smoke. I'll close Bart's Auto. Ruin this place with liens and lawsuits so fast your stupid, righteous head will spin. Believe me, I'll make sure that you and everybody who ever worked here are *done* in this town, and their friends and families are done, and you're packed away in a state pen doing time for threatening an old man before your young life's gotten off the goddamned launch pad."

"No. No," I say it again, instinct taking over, ready to fight and kill if I need to just to put this disgusting bastard away. "You don't scare me."

"No?" His feet are moving again, heading toward me, closing the narrow gap between us. "Then you're much stupider and selfish than you look. I'm not asking again. Give me my book!"

He lunges. I have just enough time to whirl out away, race to Mickey's toolbox, and grab the first thing I see.

Nelson charges me, hits me in the spine, and knocks me on the ground before I can turn around. His strength shocks me for a man his age, but the asshole's fighting for his life.

He knows how fucked he is if I get this out. We both do.

His weathered hands go around my throat and squeeze.

There's no second guessing this. No time to find a legal, just way out that doesn't involve someone getting hurt. The look in his eyes tell me he's serious. He's going to kill me if I don't stop him in the next ten seconds.

I hesitate for two more. Everything grows louder, like a violent, throbbing roar in my ears. It's my own blood, seething with adrenaline.

My hand moves automatically, clenching the wrench. I

put everything I've got into the swing, my one and only chance to take him out.

There's a wet crack, like someone tossing a pumpkin on the street. The killing hands wrapped around my throat loosen, just as everything goes hazy and black.

I think he's going down, falling on top of me, but I'm too weak to kick him off me.

I pass out, the wrench falling out of my hand, overwhelmed with everything that's happened. Blackness drowns me.

There's no telling how long I'm out. When I come back, the old demon's body is off me. In fact, he isn't anywhere to be found. There's no sign it ever happened, except for a rusty red stain drying on the ground next to me.

Shit. Did he get away? I stagger to my feet, suddenly noticing the black folio, and all the hell tucked inside, are also gone.

"You're lucky I didn't have to throw water in your face, son. That was going to be Plan B." Bart's voice causes me to jump.

I turn around and see him wiping his hands, cleaning them with some chemical that makes my nostrils pucker. He's watching me sadly, like I've done something irredeemable. It hits me that, Jesus, maybe I have.

Did I kill him? Murder the old man?

I have to explain everything before it's too late. I rush up to the man who's been like a father to me, grab him by the shirt, and stare into his eyes, hoping maybe they'll give me a shred of peace and sanity.

"Where did he go? And the pictures, the wrench…? Please, tell me you didn't let him get away."

"He's finished, Ryan. Doesn't take a genius to put two and two together. I saw the photos. Then I saw the wrench with your fingerprints on it and the blood pouring out of the crease in his skull. I'm looking at the bruises on your neck right now, son. I know you had no choice."

"Is he…dead?"

I honestly don't know what answer I want. Is it worse knowing I've killed a man, or that the sick fuck got away?

Bart's expression turns stone cold. He nods. "Caught him trying to get up when I walked in. We're all very lucky on the timing. You hit him hard, enough to do some serious damage. Just not enough to put him away for good. You don't have to worry about him anymore. I finished what you started."

"Finished?" I realize I'm not looking at my boss or future father-in-law anymore.

I'm staring at a man who used to be special forces more than twenty years ago. Cold blooded, efficient, and always accurate.

Nelson is done. Thank God. That's all I need to know.

I don't need the details, and he isn't offering them.

"What about the folio, Bart? We've got to bring them to someone who knows what to do. I'll tell them how I got them, who was in those pictures with the girls. I don't give a damn if I'm testifying against the mafia. Dead or alive, people need to know. Maybe they can help if his victims who are still out there."

"You're in no condition to throw your life away, son. Frankly, neither am I."

His words make me blink. I don't understand. I'm shaking my head, slowly releasing his shirt, pacing back and forth over the blood stain on the floor.

"What are you saying?"

"You're leaving tonight, Ryan. I've done everything I know how to prep his body to be laid out just the way I want, to take the flak off both of us. But I can't work miracles, son. They're going to think it was one of us who did him in, and if I turn over those pictures, it's going to be pinned on us."

I can't believe I'm hearing this. I'm not sure whether it's the defeat in his words, or the coolness in his voice that turns my stomach the most. "He's dead, man! Gone. There's no way he can come back and twist the truth. Why in the hell *wouldn't* we do the right thing?"

"Because there's plenty more where he came from, Ryan. The Draytons are a powerful family. You don't just kill their head and expect them to take the fall. They'll stomp us like ants with their money and connections. I've lived in this town a lot longer than you, son. Long enough to know people like us don't win when we take them on through the system. We've done the right thing, the only thing we can, taking it onto ourselves and putting him away like this. That's the best case scenario, son. Unfortunately, with everything else, the damage is done."

My head's about to explode. Next time I turn around, stop moving, and plant my feet firmly on the ground, I point my finger. "I can't let it go! It's insanity. You *saw* what was in those pictures, right?"

He nods.

"Then you also know what a sick fucking pervert we're dealing with. I don't care how corrupt he is. We'll go to the Feds. There's got to be *somebody* who'll look at all this, bring it where it matters, and end them all if they're in on it, without costing us our livelihoods!"

"There's nothing to show them, Ryan. I took the entire folio out behind the shed in the back, and burned it. I'll be vacuuming up the ashes later."

"You did…what?!" My ears are ringing.

It's like the world is imploding on itself because I can't comprehend what's happening anymore. Burying my face in my hands, I back into the nearest wall, and start sliding down. It's impossible to stand with the only thing that might save our lives, gone to the seven winds.

"I'm sad that you're going to hate me, son, but I'd rather save your life. Even if we got the evidence into the right hands, the Draytons would have you in the hardest, dirtiest prison they can find." He grabs a mop, and sloshes another acrid chemical over the blood stain on the floor, calmly scrubbing it with a brush.

"I don't care!" I mutter. It's weaker than it should be, words like lead pushed through my teeth.

"Well, I do. I'm not going to let them bring you up on murder charges, Ryan. I'm also not going to throw Bets, Matt, Kara, and all my employees under the goddamned bus. You'll have to trust me on this, son. You're leaving tonight to make a new life for yourself, and that's the way it's got to be."

I'm hunkered down in disbelief, my face buried in my hands. At least a half hour blurs by with Bart cleaning the blood.

When he's finished, there's no sign a man ever died on the floor, and I'm no closer to answers.

"Let me talk to Kara," I tell him, standing, reaching for the landline attached to the wall.

He runs up and tears it out of my hand before I can press a single button. "You still don't get it. When I said you're leaving tonight, son, I meant for good. You're vanishing like a ghost with no goodbyes. I can't allow it."

I don't know if it's the confusion, or the horror of what he's saying. It takes all my strength to lift him up, throw him against the wall, and scream in his face.

"What the fuck are you talking about?! I have to tell her what's happened here! Or, at least, somebody does."

"She'll never know a thing. I'm taking this to my grave, Ryan, and it's the way it has to be." The same green eyes on my beautiful fiance drill into me. They're hard, sad, and determined. "You need to keep quiet, too. The entire town is going to think you killed him, regardless of what we say or do. I told you, I can't work miracles. When I lay his body out, I'm going to tell them I found him like that. The wrench, they'll find in the dumpster out back, but it won't have your fingerprints."

"You're not telling them anything, you selfish, backstabbing sonofabitch. I'll tell them my version."

"Son, please." His eyes turn dark, desperate. "I'm trying to reason with you. Hate me, call me every name in the book if it makes you feel better about what's going to go down. But I'm driving you down to the docks and putting you on the first boat I see. You've been out with the crew enough times to know how to get anything with a motor out on Superior, or near enough."

No, no, no. *Fuck no.*

I'm shaking my head, and then I start shaking him. He never fights back, just stands there and takes it. Hot, crazy tears stream down my face as I'm slamming the only man I loved like family into the wall, raging because he's telling me everything I'll never accept.

I don't care about the truth.

I care about seeing her, fulfilling our promise, making her my wife. One brutal, but justified murder shouldn't fucking change that.

"Please," he repeats, when I've lost the will to throw him into the brick again. "If you go behind my back, you refuse to listen, I can't stop you. But you'll do it knowing you're ruining your life, and Kara's too. You'll wreck the whole family's."

"We can all leave. Find another town. They can't keep me in prison forever, and I'll send every damned dime straight to you, if that's what it takes to support the family. I'm supposed to be a part of it, remember?" My eyes search his, looking for the same acceptance I saw the day he gave me his blessing to date his daughter.

"And you always will be. I love you, son, because you're

always willing to do the right thing, after all the shit you've suffered. You've got a good heart. There's no man I'd rather hand Kara off to. If it'd been anything but this, you know, I would've walked her straight down the aisle, into your arms."

I see the familiar spark in his eyes, behind the sadness. It hasn't changed. He puts his hands against my chest, gently pushing me away, and gives me the saddest smile in the world.

"Think about her for a second. She'd want you to be happy and *alive,* Ryan. Not stabbed to death by some punk in the shower because he's pissed you won't join his gang for protection. You're too good a man for prison. You'll wind up dead if you go there. I don't care if we ever clear everybody's name, including yours. It's no good if you're gone, and my girl will never forgive me if I had a way to stop it. Well, I do. If you come to your senses, we'll get in my truck and go right now. I'll hand you all the money I can spare, and make it up to whoever's boat we steal later, one way or another."

He won't stop stabbing me in the chest. I've stopped resisting because he's *right,* damn it, he's so right it's killing me worse than Nelson's evil hands ever did.

There's a boom in the distance. Loud and mournful, dense enough to shake the ceiling. Bart puts his hand on my shoulder, giving me the most fatherly squeeze I'll ever get.

"Go, son. Leave the rest to me. You have to get on that ship and go now. It's your only chance. Remember – and it's going to be an absolute bitch – you can't come back.

You can't call her. You can't write, phone, email, or send a note by fucking pigeon to anyone here. Because if you do, and they realize where you are…"

I get it. Fuck, do I understand, like a blow to the face.

Defeated, I follow him out to the truck. It's raining by the time we get to the marina. He leads me over to the best boat docked there, the new thirty foot baby with the little cabin old man McCoy bought when he sold his land in Wisconsin last year.

He's trusting, like most people still are in this little town. It doesn't take us long to find the spare keys he's tucked into the ship's rear storage.

It's bigger than anything I've ever piloted before, but the controls seem familiar. Bart stands over my shoulder in the cabin. He doesn't leave until I've started her up, done a few checks, and taken down the tether from the dock. Then he takes an envelope and shoves it into my hand.

There must be two thousand dollars stuffed inside, maybe more.

I look at him, nodding glumly, hating how it feels when I jam it into my pocket. The money is a curse, a one-way ticket to a lonely new hell. I already want out.

"Take care of her," I say, throwing my arms around him for the last time. "She's going to need everything to make it through the heartbreak. If you won't let me give her the life she deserves, I'm counting on you to do it. Make it right. Make her happy."

"That's all I ever meant to do, son. Curse me when you're on the other side of the country if it helps. Best thing you can do is forget. It'll take time, but you can make it happen. Just forget about this town, about Nelson, about the family, and me. Forget her. Forget everything, and live your life." Every time he says *forget* it's like another rusty blade digging through my ribs. "Because if you don't, if you ever come back, and you get busted…"

He doesn't finish his last thought. I push him away, turning back to the ship's controls, watching a bolt of lightning crackle through the sky.

"I'm sorry it has to be this way, Ryan," he says, stopping one more time on his way out. "You deserve a second chance, and so does she. I'll fall all over myself to give it to you. I'll die, if that's what it takes."

By the time I watch his dark shape climb onto the dock through the rain, he's already dead to me. I'll never have as much love and hate warped together as I do him in this moment.

Soon, I can't think about anything at all, except how much the ship is about to break apart. It's dark and terrifying among the high waves. They kick me around, tip the entire ship, barely let me stay on the GPS course.

I'd be scared, if I weren't numb to everything. I'm drifting further into the night, remembering the last flash of lightning over Armitage Lighthouse, as brief and harsh as seeing Kara herself ripped away from me.

I can't remember how I made it near Superior in one piece, grounding the ship on rocky northern shore sometime before sunrise, or how I hitchhiked all the way to Saint Paul to get on the train going west a few days later.

Somehow, I made it. I got to Seattle through the horror, the fury, the loss, and then I broke my promise to Bart on the first day. Standing there by the ferry terminal, looking out across the Puget Sound, I swore I'd see familiar waters again.

I wouldn't let her go, or Split Harbor.

I'd come back someday. Bigger, stronger, and better equipped to marry the only woman I ever loved. I'd find a way to erase the nightmare that went down that night, even if it meant stopping Bart from taking the dirty secret to his grave.

* * * *

"I'm going to be sick," Kara says, arms pressed tight, clutching her belly. "I can't stop thinking about the Draytons. Jesus, I was going to fucking *marry* one of them!"

"You aren't anymore," I say, pulling her onto my lap, running my fingers softly through her hair. "That's all that matters, babe. You didn't know. Your father was hellbent on making sure you'd never find out."

"I'm not sure that's true." It takes her a moment to look at me. "I knew something didn't add up. He always walked away whenever I tried asking questions, told me he wouldn't talk about it. But the night he died, before he slipped into his coma for the last time…he wanted to tell me the truth, Ryan. I know he did. He regretted it. Knew he made a mistake. He knew I never stopped loving you."

I've forgiven Bart for what happened over the years. He saved my life, even if he had to become one of the biggest bastards in the world to do it.

But hearing her tell me he cracked, almost confessed… I'm floored.

It's too much to take in all at once. There are no words.

So, I just sit there with her wrapped my arms, rocking her on the chair next to the bed we just crashed. Entire worlds split apart, burn, and start to make sense.

The alarm on my phone goes off, the last warning I set to get going to the airport, jarring us out of our emotional trance. She throws her arms around me, wiping the tears that have already begun falling, burying her face in my chest.

I kiss her, hold her, rock her like the miracle she is.

Christ, I've taken her back, against the odds, and I'll never, ever let her go.

"You have to come clean," she says, looking up. "Jesus, Ryan. We have to find the right authorities, clear your name, tell them what really happened. There *has* to be some kind of statement we can make, something to lead them in the right direction, even if there's no evidence."

I nod, knowing there's only one way we've got a chance. She's still shaking, and it takes me a minute to calm her, folding my embrace tighter.

"God, what was he thinking?" she snarls, banging her fists on her knees. "I can't believe daddy burned the creep's book."

"Not everything," I say, smiling when I see the hope sparking in her eyes. "I stuffed a single page in my pocket. Forgot about it until the first driver gave me a break the next morning, taking me out of Wisconsin. I've kept it after all these years, and had a P.I. take a look at several of those names.

"And?" I can tell she's holding her breath.

"One's behind bars, busted for sex trafficking in Chicago a couple years back. The others are like him – entitled, heartless bastards who believe they can do the sickest shit in the world and never get caught. One good lead will bring them down, soon as we bring it to the right place. I would've done it already, but bringing you back into my life was more important. Plus the town might've beat me alive if they realized who I was the day I came in to cut the banner, opening Punch Corp here."

"We shouldn't wait," she says, standing up, her hand still grabbing at mine. "We should go now, or as soon as we land in Seattle. If we talk to the police there, surely they won't be corrupted by the Draytons."

"It's time to go, Kara-bou," I tell her, planting one more kiss on the forehead. "I have a few ideas, and we're going to discuss everything on the flight out there. Then we're going to forget all this, enjoy some alone time, and remember why every fucking punch we've taken is absolutely worth it."

When we're finished dressing, I take her hand. There's hardly a moment her fingers leave mine the whole way to the airport.

XI: Rekindled (Kara)

It's a big blue Gulfstream jet that takes us to heaven, emblazoned with the Punch Corp logo on the tail. I've never been on a private plane before. Ryan teases me the whole way to Seattle. We share wine and coffee. I curl up next to him on the ivory sofa, only looking up when someone from the crew comes by to ask us if there's anything else we need.

The next three days are just as much a whirlwind. He shuttles me around to the city's best restaurants, the art museum, and half a dozen awesome coffeehouses. I'm going to go home bursting with new ideas for Grounded.

He also shows me the places where he started his company, built it from the ground up with long hours, a little luck, and lots of networking with the right people. It's incredible to see what he's accomplished since his time in the garage. I wish daddy were here to see everything.

We've both forgiven daddy, now that the hard truth is out. He lied to me, left my heart in pieces, but there's no telling what I would've become if I'd known what happened sooner.

We've lost too much time looking back. Moving forward, that's what counts. There's a spring in my step every time I think about going home, clearing his name, and starting over.

The last day, we're coming back from Bainbridge Island, watching several kids chasing each other playfully on the deck of our ferry. I'm exhausted, but I can't remember the last time I was ever this happy.

Ryan clasps my hand as I lean into him. "Well, Karabou, what do you think?"

I give him a smile broader than the distant mountains. "It's a lot to take in, but I like it. Only thing that's missing out here is a lighthouse."

"Armitage would be a great end to the day, no doubt. Lucky for you, I've got something better planned."

Better? He won't tell me, won't even drop a hint, no matter how many times I beg between disembarking from the ship and getting into the car with our driver. He takes us across town, now dark and lit with a thousand tinsel lights. I still don't have a clue where we're going until the Space Needle looms large above us.

I'm excited. It's nothing compared to following him quickly through the park and taking the elevator up. In less than a minute, we're at the top of the world, staring down into the dark lights, and very alone.

"Who'd you shakedown to arrange this?" I ask, when we're standing out on the observation deck, me sinking into his embrace.

"I made a lot of donations in the right places last year.

Consider this one of the perks. It's just you, me, the city, and a whole lot of night, babe. Nowhere else I'd rather be."

We're quiet for a little bit, staring down at the beautiful scenery. I pull my coat tighter, leaning into him, steeling my body against the cold. It's such a spectacular view I forget the numbness fighting its way into my skin.

"God, this is beautiful. I don't want it to end."

"It won't," he growls, running his hand up my side, stopping with his fingers on my face. "I've danced plenty of times with the pretty lights and tall buildings down there. Built a name for myself that seems like it's got no limit. Wined and dined with rich men and women alike, politicians, lawyers, and geniuses who all wanted to shake my hand and welcome me to their world."

His chest vibrates gently against my ear. I love the deep, rich sound of his voice. It's a soothing echo I could listen to forever.

He turns my face up, bathing me in his ocean blue eyes, now reflecting the Seattle night's glories above and below us. "I didn't do any of this for anybody or anything down there, majestic as it is. Right now, I'm looking at the only thing I've ever cherished. This view's so beautiful I'm going to take your lips to remind me I haven't died and gone to heaven."

Neither of us hesitates. He kisses me hard, sucking my bottom lip into his mouth, grazing it with his teeth.

It's salty, possessive, and so fucking hot. It's the kiss I've needed my whole life, the kind of kiss that ruins me, because I'll never accept another that's weaker than this.

I turn in his arms, wrap my hands around his neck, and urge his tongue into mine. Six hundred feet in the air, the wind at my back, and I'm *still* sweating in his rock hard arms. Having him up here in his suit, both of us looking down on the world like royalty, brings me an extra thrill when I imagine the freaky, intricate ink underneath beneath his clothes.

That's the ink I want to be tangled up in forever, especially tonight, when he brings me back to his condo and fucks me senseless.

I think I'm addicted. It only takes a few more furious kisses before I'm moaning into his mouth, spreading my legs and grinding against his knee, aching a little more every second he isn't buried inside me.

It would be perfect, if only it weren't for the hammer hanging over our heads. I think about the mess back home, and my kiss wilts the next time he comes back for more, his hands gliding down my back to cup my ass.

"What's wrong, Kara-bou?" He looks at me, lust and concern churning on his gorgeous face.

"Tell me you've thought about what I suggested last night," I say, gently pulling away from him. "You know, about bringing in Matt?"

"Your brother's got no love for me, and I don't blame him," he says, taking me by the hand. We walk to the other side of the observation deck, where we can see the ocean below, its blackness only broken by stabs of light from the ships streaming across it every few minutes.

"Look, I know it's not his fight. He's got his own

problems, and you don't want to bring him into it when he hates your freaking guts." I sigh, wondering what combination of words I can use to reason with him. "But it's the best chance I think we've got to clear you, Ryan. Do it with him and mom first, and then the whole town will listen. I don't care what kind of influence the Drayton's have. Even Sheriff Dixon won't arrest a decorated Marine for showing him the truth."

"That's what I like about you, babe," he says, after several tense seconds. "You're always cutting straight to the root. If your family hasn't squealed on me yet, then there's something holding them back."

"Damn right," I snap, tightening my fingers in his grip. "I'll invite them to Grounded. We can all sit down in a safe place and talk. Bring the copies you have of the page you saved from Nelson's folder. Matt's a good man, Ryan. He'll stop being a hothead lined up against you as soon as he sees the evidence."

Sighing, he nods. "I'll tape it to my chest before he knocks my teeth out. Don't get me wrong, babe. I'm confident I can take on any man, but I've got no desire to talk to your crazy Marine brother using fists again. Congratulations – you've talked me into the impossible."

"I'll call him as soon as we're on the tarmac back home tomorrow, then." I'm holding him to it. I won't let up for a single second because I can't stand the thought of losing him again, especially if Matt or mom try to turn him in before hearing us out.

"Yeah, and I'll put my statement out to corporate, soon

as it hits the sheriff's office. Everyone in Seattle, Split Harbor, and Marquette is going to want to know why the hell Tanner is suddenly Ryan."

"Won't it feel good to be who you are?" I run my nails against the nape of his neck, loving how his muscles bristle under my fingertips.

"Not half as good as this."

The instant his lips touch mine, I know he's right.

This is explosive. Outrageous. Divine.

When we're alive and electric and touching like this, I don't care what he calls himself. I've known this man by his heart, deeper and truer than any name.

Each flick of his tongue against mine comes like fire, honest and enticing, leaving every nerve in my body begging for more. When I move in to get it, trying to press my mouth against his firm jaw line, he lifts me away, beaming his gaze into mine.

"You've made me happier than I've got any business being," he says, pressing his forehead down on mine. Icy excitement runs up my spine, and it's got nothing to do with the cool night breeze lashing us from the east. "I'm still going to ask you two things."

"Yeah?" I whisper, trembling in his arms. Whatever it is, it's going to be enormous.

Despite my expectations, I'm not prepared for the shock when he reaches into his pocket, plucks something out, and sinks to his knees. His takes one hand in both of his. It's a serious grip, almost painful in its intensity.

"Kara, we're going home tomorrow," he says, lifting one

leg so he's crouching. "We're clearing up the shit I did, setting the record straight, and then I never want to think about it again. I don't want to dream about the five years we lost, or wonder how much worse it could've been if I'd come back too soon, too late, or not at all. I want to live every day with you by my side, babe. I *need* you living, breathing, and loving by mine. All those years ago, I gave you a cheap ring, one it took me two months to save. This one's got a price tag a whole lot higher, but it's the heartbreak and sweat that's the real reason it's expensive. I meant to hold out for this, love, just a little while longer. But hell, deep down...I'd be a fool to wait another day."

The tiny purple box in his hand springs open. My jaw nearly hits the floor. I'm frozen in place, staring at a ring studded with so many rocks it's probably worth more than a small nation.

"Ryan..."

"Marry me, Kara. Marry me again. Truth is, I'm impatient. Can't stand holding your hand around town, or feeling it running down my back when it's bare. Empty. I need to feel this ring where it belongs. Need you loving it, loving me, wearing the finest mark I can put on you forever."

I'm too numb to speak. I just fall down with him, so much like the first time he ever asked, crashing into his arms. We're laughing, rolling on the floor of the Space Needle's observation deck, wind rushing through our hair.

He takes me in his arms, rolling me over, pressing his mouth down on mine while his hand pushes the ring into my palm. My fingers close around it, trying to bend around his. In just a few seconds, the gold warms on my skin, and I *know* this is right.

Call the timing insane. But it couldn't be clearer.

He alternates between my mouth and kissing away the hot, chaotic tears rolling down my cheeks. Ryan's weight presses down, down, his hand brushing up beneath my dress. He groans when his fingers find the spot, feeling how wet I am.

"I need to be in you, wife," he rumbles.

Wife?

God, yes.

"Right here. Right now. That's the second thing I had to tell you tonight." His voice drops an octave, so low it reverberates in my bones. Adding new warmth, an electric energy sweeps through me as surely as it does when his bulge presses on my swollen center through our clothes.

I don't resist when his hands start pulling down my dress. It's gone a few seconds later, and my panties zip down my legs, disappearing in the mess next to us.

His fingers brush my clit, and I'm panting.

Lust hits so fast and hard I barely recognize the sound of his belt coming undone, the shuffle of his trousers coming down to expose his pierced, perfect cock.

Cool air drifts around us. I sit up and grab his length, bending down so I can take him in my mouth.

"Yeah, baby. Sweet fuck." He inhales roughly, making me smile when I push my tongue beneath his pulsing tip. "There. Right *there*."

The soft, warm underside of his cock becomes my target. Pressing my tongue into him, my fist pumps its rhythm, loving the heat in his heavy balls every time the pucker.

He grunts again, drawing another tense breath when he notices my fist. His hand reaches out, wraps around mine, and I suck him harder. He sees the new ring.

"You're wearing it now?" Lust and amusement make his eyes glow. "Fuck, babe, I think you've just shown me the prettiest sight in the world."

I'm smiling inwardly while I'm sucking him. My tongue rolls deep, lips tightening each time I take his length up and down, desperate to make him explode down my throat.

Of course, he's right. I can't imagine anything that gets me hotter than knowing how much he's enjoying my hand on his cock, the brand new gold and diamonds looped around my finger.

His cock brushes my tongue again and again, growing hotter and harder all the time. Growling, his fingers mesh through my hair, shielding them from the wind, adding new heat when he pulls it taut.

"Love you, Kara-bou. So fucking much."

So fucking much. The sweet phrase echoes in my head, heartwarming as it is naughty thanks to the tension in his voice. Not to mention how he bucks up a second later, filling my mouth with as much as I can take, groaning like he's coming undone.

Swelling, overloaded, and lost somewhere between love and lust, he's coming.

His hot, thick essence erupts a second later.

The man I love thrashes, grunts, and spills his seed in my mouth faster than I can swallow it. I take everything I can. The next sixty seconds are more than just a blowjob ending.

I'm worshipping my future husband, the man I was always meant to marry, who's lifted me up over and over again. There's forgiveness and hope, disguised in sweltering heat.

His come is running out the corner of my lips when his fist in my hair softens, turning to loving strokes instead. I'm going to be a mess by the time we get out of here.

My stomach growls, reminding me there's more than desire begging to be satisfied. I guess we're ordering in tonight after this.

I don't care. Nothing else matters except how he holds my face, brushes away the trickle I couldn't swallow with his thumb, and then comes in for a kiss.

His other hand finds mine, takes it, and squeezes the ring he's been dying to put there. We kiss for what seems like forever, until he breaks off, staring at me with fresh hunger in his eyes.

"Stand up, and bend the fuck over," he says, guiding me as he brings me to the railing, lifting my hips. "There's more than half a million people down there, going about their lives. Any one of them might look up, spot us moving in the dim light, and wonder. I want them all to know we're in love, babe. They're going to see how you twitch, flail, and scream when my balls hit your clit."

"Oh, God. Ryan…"

Everything he's suggesting makes me wetter than before, even if my mind is screaming every insecurity I've ever had about sex and good manners.

They're silenced the second he pushes into me from behind. His cock sinks in, drives deep, and anchors with my ass against his warm, hard body.

His heavy breath falls against my ear before he speaks. "First time we're fucking in front of an entire city. Take a good, long look out there when I'm owning every inch of your sweet pussy, love."

I obey, his willing slave as his hands grip my ass, and his cock starts slamming into me.

Several thrusts in, I forget all about the people down below. It's an incredible sight, the vast cityscape blurring before my eyes, melding with the rush, the heat, the ecstasy.

His teeth graze my neck, sink down to my shoulder, and take hold. It causes me to straighten, an angle which takes him deeper. Each thrust slaps my body again and again, pushing me a little closer to bliss.

Ryan's hand takes my breast, finds my nipple underneath my blouse, and squeezes it hard. I'm going over his cock again and again, taking him, losing my mind when that bead planted in his tip rubs the right places.

I won't last long.

I can't.

Fireworks explode in my brain when I go over. He fucks me harder when he feels my pussy clenching, and then he's grunting in tune to my moans, swelling and spilling his come.

We go off together, two shadows moving in the night. Our love, our sex, stands against the blackness, the cold, and every inhibition.

There could be dozens of eyes on us now, maybe someone with a telescope who can see everything, and it doesn't fucking matter.

Nothing else does in this moment except having him fused to me, emptying his fire, pinching the finger with his ring a little harder each time his hips crash against mine.

I come down from the insane high shaking. He turns me around, drags my hands around him, and makes me open my eyes with another kiss.

"We're picking this up at my place," he says, running the stubble on his cheek against my skin. "Then we're crashing until morning. Come light, we're heading home, handling everything we need to, and finding a place to settle down. Soon as my name's cleared, I want our wedding date in all the local papers."

No words can adequately tell him how bad I want everything he's promised.

So, I just press my mouth on his instead, huddling against him for warmth, hating that I have to get dressed before he rips my clothes off all over again.

* * * *

Another magic night passes. We end our time in Seattle with sex, sleep, and coffee, watching the sunrise peek through thick clouds threatening rain.

It's been a marvelous time, but I'm ready to go home.

Ready to get back to my business, fix everything that's kept us apart, and start planning a future with the man I love.

We're both tired from last night. Huddling underneath a blanket, we doze on the jet ride, sleeping through most of the three and a half hour trip to Michigan. When I open my eyes, he's got his face propped up with one hand, looking at me through the golden haze coming through the windows.

"Perfect timing, beautiful. We're about to touch down."

Sitting up, I rub my eyes, falling back into him a moment later. Tucking my face into his shoulder, his arm goes around me, and I wish I could stay here forever.

It's him I breathe, inhaling his calming, masculine scent.

He holds me tighter. It's hard to believe we're together again.

I can't believe he held on after all these years. His heart stayed true, even when I gave up, tried like hell to move on with my life because I believed the worst about him.

Next time I open my eyes, the plane is almost on the runway. I'm clenching his hand, staring intently into the eyes I love, the ones that strip me bare to my heart over and over.

"I'm sorry I ever doubted you," I whisper. "The first night you came to me, when I was at home with Holden, I almost turned you in."

"I don't want apologies, Kara-bou," he says, taking my hand warmly in his. "I want to rebuild. Soon as we're on the ground, we're getting to work building the life we always deserved. The one we had robbed away by circumstance, plus one evil bastard."

He's right. There's no sense looking back, holding onto the pain in my heart, whether I'm hurting over something that happened a couple weeks ago, or four years, during my darkest days.

I'm too close to him when the plane hits the ground. We knock heads gently and I pull away, giggling. His hand goes down my thigh, rubbing with a stroke that's teasing and loving. Every time he touches me, there's more complexity than anything with Reg.

How did I do it? How did I nearly marry the wrong man?

It's not just my new found hate that's making me wonder. I haven't heard from the asshole, despite the movers coming through our old place while we were gone.

The town's probably in full gossip mode already, if they've heard the wedding is off. If not, they will be soon. They'll have plenty of red meat when they find out the truth about Ryan and Split Harbor's fallen hero, Nelson Drayton.

An attendant tells us we're about to disembark. Ryan kisses me before helping me stand, leading us to the little staircase they've rolled down to the tarmac.

I'm still smiling, lost in his kiss, and halfway down the stairs when I see the cherry-blue lights. One glance, and I know there's something terribly wrong.

Ryan stops on the last step, his hand clenching the railing tight. There must be half a dozen black security vehicles surrounding the plane, their lights flashing an evil contrast to the morning's gold.

"Ryan Caspian – alias, Tanner Brooks?" A large man with a goatee speaks as he approaches us. He's dressed like a secret service agent.

Ryan nods, ignoring me behind him. He's standing like the entire world is about to come down on his head. The man never stops moving, ignoring the fear building in my eyes. I'm so shocked I can't even scream when he grabs my love, throws him to the ground, and throws handcuffs around his wrists.

"You're under arrest for the murder of Nelson Drayton. You have the right to remain silent. Anything you say can and may be used against you in a court of law…"

No. My brain is on fire. *No, no, no, no, no!*

I stumble back against the railing, catching myself. Clenching the cold steel is the only thing that stops me from keeling over. My knees shake, spreading numbness through my body, watching as he's hauled away in handcuffs.

Several other people move through the special agents ringing the plane. A man steps up, grabs me, pulls me off the last step. I don't start screaming and beating his back with my fists until I recognize his voice.

"Come on, Kara. Let's get you home. Reg told me everything." Matt locks me in his Marine grip, and carries me toward the small gaggle of people waiting below. "Can't believe the motherfucker thought he could brainwash you like this. He's going away for a *long* damned time, don't you worry."

"Reg? He's lying!" My hands pound into my brother's back repeatedly, too weak to dent his hardened frame.

"Matt, don't do this. Please, fuck, you can't. You don't know what he's done. You don't know Reg is lying."

He isn't listening. He just holds me, ignoring every punch and kick, hauling me away from the plane. I stop hitting my brother for a second to look over his shoulder, just in time to see Ryan staring out the tinted window.

He's shaking his head, his eyes narrowed. They're sad, angry, and imploring me to stop. *Don't hurt yourself, baby. This is my fight.*

When the dark SUV pulls away a second later, I'm screaming. My brother releases me slowly, and I slide down to the ground, sobbing. My brain hasn't spinning before I see the familiar, polished black shoes hovering close to me.

I look up slowly, and see the asshole who's twisted my brother into helping him do the unthinkable. Reg stands there, calm and expressionless as ever, staring down at me like the ant I've become.

"I'm sorry it has to come to this, Kara-bell," he says, using an old pet name he has no fucking business speaking ever again. "I couldn't let him get away with it. The lies, the bullying, accusing me of...of cheating. You were hanging out with a murderer, Kara. He killed Uncle Nelson."

His voice cracks on cue. He stumbles. Like he's practiced it about a hundred times in the mirror, no different than one of his speeches to business associates. Staring through my hatred and confusion, I see the bandage conveniently plastered on his cheek, covering the edges of a bruise that looks more like a special effect than a real injury.

"Asshole. You heartless, depraved lunatic!" Words and

fists fly simultaneously, but they don't do anything to soothe the anger ripping out of me. I strike him on the kneecaps several times before he backs away.

He's retreating, just like the coward he is.

I never expect him to lunge when I keep crawling after him. Usually Reg runs when he's under siege, but not this time.

He tackles me to the ground, pinning my wrists down on the pavement. We're face-to-face with a gaggle of people screaming around us.

"Told you I wouldn't walk away, you little idiot," he hisses beneath his breath. "As soon as I found out who he was, I got your family on the line. Had a feeling they'd know exactly where you'd gone with the jackass who wanted to put me in a coma."

I'm too stunned for words. I just look at him, my hatred overflowing, and mouth the only words I ever want to say to this pathetic, spiteful man again.

"Fuck you."

He smiles. "That's all right, Kara-bell. You've fucked yourself over enough for both of us. See, Drayton's do more than cuss and complain: we bury anybody coming after us."

More screaming. Reg has just enough time to change his sinister smile into a sad one as he's jerked up. Arms slide under me, hauling me to my feet, dragging me away from him.

I'm screaming, spitting, cursing him the entire time. I must look totally insane, and I don't care.

"Kara, come on!" Matt wraps me in a bear hug so tight

it's hard to speak, squeezing me until my fight runs out. "Have you lost your mind? I know you're mad at him because Ryan told you some shit he shouldn't have. He was lying, Kara. You need to calm down. Clear your head. Then we can all sit down, talk about this, and set the record straight. We'll bring in the shrink you two've been seeing. I love you, sis. I'm here for you. God knows, we all are. However long it takes to get you through this."

How about forever, jackass? I can't do more than think it.

I'm too tired to fight more, much less scream. My brother holds me, rubbing my back, doing his damnedest to calm me down.

Mom appears at his side a second later. She's whispering in my ear, squeezing my other shoulder, telling me what a monster Ryan is for coming back to this town after all these years to play with me. He thought he could get away with his lies, as if he wouldn't get caught. He was wrong, she says.

Wrong. The same bitter word, echoing in my ears. False by its own definition.

How can they be so blind? They don't even know they've made a deal with the devil.

I have to fight my way out of my family's consoling grip to face the asshole who's turning his back on me, hiding a faint smile. "We're going to bring you down! If I have to testify myself against you, bankrupt every business with your family's name on it, God help me, I will. You're a fucking monster, Reg."

"Honey, please." Mom's hold tightens. "Matthew, get her to the car. We'll call him later."

They're murdering me. Driving every knife I've always feared in deep, bleeding me out as they pull me away and push me into Matt's big truck. It's their fault this is happening, and they don't even know it.

Little Holden isn't even waiting in the truck to soften the blow. Probably a good thing, since I wouldn't want my nephew seeing me like this.

I lay against the seat and cover my eyes. The soft yellow sun that seemed so nice when we first stepped off the plane blinds me now.

There's a million questions gouging me inside. A million and one things I want to do to set him free, and make my soulless ex pay for ruining my ruining my life a second time.

But I can't think anything coherent. The thing I see when I close my eyes – the only thing – is Ryan's tormented face behind the tinted glass.

Betrayed, tortured, but still dead set on keeping me out of his mess.

* * * *

I don't say anything for several hours. Mom guides me to my old room, now one they only use for guests. Matt sits outside it in the kitchen, playing guard dog, while I hear her make several calls across town.

She's talking to the police, giving them some kind of statement. It doesn't bother me until her voice fades out later. She's whispering in her lowest tone, talking to the man who lied, cheated, and ripped me away from the one I really wanted.

Reg, I'm going to kill you, I vow, folding my hands.

Actually, I don't want his blood anywhere on my hands. I don't even want to look at him again, but not half as much as I just want to end him. I'll settle for getting Ryan free, running his twisted family out of this town, and never having to see his manipulative face again.

"Sis, you need anything?" Matt knocks gently on the door. "Water? Sandwich? We want to bring you out to talk to us shortly. It's time to clear the air."

He's on guard, but he's talking to me like a brother again, rather than a soldier barking orders. The knot in my stomach doubles when I think about him believing he's doing the right thing. Both of them. They believe they're saving me from a murderer, a liar, and they're completely clueless about the real ones hiding in plain sight.

"I'm ready," I say weakly through the door.

I open it a second later, and my big brother lays his hand on my shoulder, guiding me down the hall to our old kitchen. The table used to be so full and happy. It's the same one we sat at with daddy and Ryan in the old days, before the hate and the lies, before I had the world ripped out under me several times over.

It's a miracle there's anything left of my mind to sit down with them today. I don't know how I can bring them around, make them believe Reg cheated, lied, and it's the dead Drayton patriarch who's responsible for everything bad.

I don't have a clue, but I have to try.

"Honey, before we say anything, I want you to know

we're not here to put you on trial. We've seen firsthand how much he hurt you over the years, how hard it was for you to believe the truth about him leaving. You didn't do anything wrong. He came to you when you were weak, pretending to be someone new. We don't blame you for thinking he was more than a murderer, or the man who broke your heart." She reaches across the table, grabbing my hand. "Look, it hurts us, too. We hate having to relive everything, him putting our family through this all over again."

"Ryan deserves to be locked the fuck up, and I'm going to make it happen," Matt growls next to me, banging his fist on the table.

Mom flashes him a disapproving look. "It took us several days to tie it all together after your brother saw him with you that night. Honestly, it's *insane* that he's built this wealth and fame, after everything he's done. When we realized who Tanner really was, and knew you were missing…we called the sheriff's office last night. Told him everything we knew. I think there's a lot more we can offer, several missing pieces we got from Reg, but we want to hear the rest from you. We want your side of what happened, Kara."

Bull. They're both going to hate the truth, and start to hate me for denying what they think he really is.

I've had enough with words. They haven't done anything to protect me, push Reg away, or banish the endless nightmare Ryan and me tried so hard to run away from.

They're staring when I pull out my phone. I'd almost forgotten I asked him to send me the pictures halfway through our Seattle trip, when we were knocking around ideas to fix this.

Thankfully, I didn't.

"You should both take a look at this, and tell me what you see." I slide the phone across as soon as I pull it up.

Mom's eyes go huge and dark when she sees the screen.

Showing my own family the disgusting pictures of my ex in those compromising positions with his little mistress is the last thing I want. But it's the last, best option that might make them believe there's more to this than they think.

"Is that...*Jesus.*" She can't even say the name. She's looking at Amy, the double crossing bitch of a wedding planner, strapped to the chair half-naked. She flips forward. When she sees King Asshole, Reg himself, she gasps, dropping the phone against the table's surface with a clatter.

Matt doesn't wait for her to pass the phone. He reaches out, snatches it, and eyeballs everything. Hatred, then confusion, fills his eyes.

"No fucking way," he whispers, turning it over and slamming it down a moment later. "Where did these come from?"

"Ryan. He caught them cheating himself, at a hotel in Marquette. I wasn't sure either, until I saw the pictures." I give Matt a sharp look. "These aren't staged. Yes, he burst in and roughed them up a little. Reg deserved it after everything he did to me. I don't feel bad for him, and I never will. Now that you've seen the truth…are you still going to call me crazy? Pretend I'm just 'brainwashed' by a man I'll never get over?"

Matt hardens his look, and swallows something heavy in his throat. "Sis, you and Reg got serious problems, and it's not all bullshit. I'll give you that. Still doesn't let him off the hook for everything else."

"No, it doesn't. And he explained to me exactly what happened that night." Their eyes glue to me, waiting for my story. "He didn't kill Nelson Drayton. Not by himself, anyway…"

I spend the next ten minutes recounting Ryan's story as best I can. It probably doesn't have the emotional impact, or all the details, because I feel like I'm about to melt into a puddle.

I hate having to face them like this, explain how daddy forced himself into something so heinous because he had no choice. He thought he was protecting me, protecting us, even protecting Ryan.

Ryan didn't have a choice either. That's the point I keep trying to make, when I tell them how Nelson backed him into a corner, demanded he turn over those disgusting pictures he found, threatened to bring down our family.

"You know that happened anyway," Matt says, shaking his head in disbelief. "You've bought into a sick goddamned joke, Kara. He'll say anything to have you back, make you think he's really on your side. Dad told me he burned a bunch of rough nudie magazines he found shortly after stumbling over Nelson's body. Said he thought Ryan left them out, and Nelson stumbled across them. Probably threatened his job since the man was a total prude. Dad threw the evidence on the fire because he didn't want the police coming after the other employees, thinking they had a beef with the old man."

"Jesus, Matt, can't you see he lied?" Tears come hot and merciless when I say it, slapping my hands against the table. There's no worse truth than knowing what a liar daddy was. "He lied to us all. And he didn't have a choice, not when he knew better than anybody how much the Draytons own this town. He didn't burn any magazines. You're insane if you think Ryan killed a man over finding his porn stash. Ryan found *Nelson's* dirt, and there's no way on earth that man was any kind of prude. Drayton wanted to hide it. They're good at that, burying their secrets, and then threatening anyone who gets in their way."

I'm still fuming over Reg kicking me straight in the ass one more time. The look he gave me as my family dragged me away, smug and self-assured...it was *gotcha* personified. He fed them a story about how he loved me, wanted to bring me back to my senses, knowing they'd find out the truth.

He used them, abused their trust, thinking he'd just walk away quietly after his humiliation.

Matt shakes his head again, grumbling to himself. "Look, sis, you convinced me on Reg because you've got evidence. Ryan...that's another story. Unless you've got something proving what you said, it's your word against dad's."

My brother looks at me, hurt swelling in his expression. "Dad wasn't in love with the fuck who left you out in the cold for half a decade. He saw Ryan as he really was, the orphan kid, knew he had problems none of us saw before they hit us in the face. You aren't telling me anything different, unless you're going to magically dig up whatever got burned in the fire pit."

Sighing, I pick up my phone. I flip through my gallery again, and come to the snapshot I took of the rumpled page Ryan showed me last week, the one with the names and contacts.

"There's a man on there, Edgar Wollenshem. Look him up. You'll find out he's already doing time for getting busted in the sex trade. The others, I don't know, but I believe they're traceable. Ryan certainly did. He's been waiting years to go after them, whatever it takes to clear his name, and bring the Draytons down."

Matt's face twitches. He averts his eyes, looking away from the image I'm pushing in his face. "Wishful thinking, Kara. He could've done the research and typed this list up himself. Doesn't prove a damned thing. Hell, I've been in rooms with men overseas who've always got the best excuses in the world for killing our troops, plus men, women, and children in cold blood. They're never responsible for the bombings – oh, no. It's always some neighbor, the merchant down the street from a rival clan, anyone they think they can frame and pin the fucking blame on."

"Matthew..." Mom speaks up, eerily quiet up until now. "You can't write it off that easy."

We both do a slow turn, fixing our gaze on her.

"Why?" My brother rumbles.

"Because I lied." Her lips twist like she's bitten into something bitter. "Bart told me he helped Ryan escape. It was about the time he was diagnosed, when he came home from the hospital that cold, snowy winter."

She pauses, closing her eyes. "He knew his outlook wasn't good. There was something on his chest. One night we stayed up late, drinking cherry wine, talking about the old times, good and bad. We were laughing, remembering how big and beautiful our family used to be, before the ugliness with Ryan. He got real quiet, teared up a little, and looked at me, said he had something important to say."

Something dark, thick, and angry wells up inside me. I want to believe she's lying, missing details, or didn't have the whole truth from dad.

Because if both my parents *knew*, all these years...

My hands form fists on my lap, tightening as we listen to her talk. "Kara, it's my fault. Not his. He made me *promise* on his life not to say anything. What he burned in that pit wasn't ordinary porn. It was everything you said...dark, demented, evil stuff that shouldn't have ever see the light of day. He talked about how he found Ryan passed out, Nelson struggling to his feet, a horrible wound on his head...he did what he had to. He put a sick, wretched man out of his misery. And then yes, Jesus, he helped our Ryan escape."

I'm going to be sick. I'm about to heave up what little is left in my stomach from a whole day not eating, but not before I stand up, gripping the back of my chair, and look her in the eye. "Why, mom...why the fuck did you lie?"

A single, painful tear rolls down her cheek. "He told me there wasn't any way to bring the boy back, and frankly, I agreed. I understood the danger, imagined the ways it would ruin our family, worse than it already has, messing with the Draytons. I swore I'd protect you from Ryan Caspian, honey, and that's all I've tried to do, even today. It hurt to turn him in. I didn't know about the cheating. I wanted to believe Reg was different, good for you, that you'd moved on with your life and wanted to marry him. He told me how Ryan burst in, beat him up, said he should never, ever come near you again. Honey, he cried..."

Fire scorches my veins, imagining how the manipulative piece of shit I almost married twisted the knife deep in all our backs.

"And you listened to his tears? The same ones from a man whose family fortune should be going *straight* to his Great Uncle's victims?"

"I-I'm sorry. I thought he was better. I thought maybe your father was wrong, that Ryan was bad for you, too damaged by everything that happened. Reg was going to be the one to make you happy." She looks down, crushed. I can practically see the gaping hole ripped in her by the truth – all of it. "I just wanted to protect you. Never wanted to see you ruining this family, or ruining yourself a second time, chasing after a man who's always going to be a walking target. They'll put him away for good when they find out. It breaks my heart, falling for Reg's story, knowing that poor young man is going to jail."

I hear the pain in her voice, but I don't have any sympathy. "He's a *billionaire,* mom. Richer than the Draytons, probably. He can fight fire with fire. We came home to clear his name, for Christ's sake, and now you've both ruined it. All because you *had* to listen to that lying prick."

My hands go up in the air and blood hits my temples. I can't do this anymore. I'm heading for the closest door, ignoring mom's breakdown, her wails echoing through the whole house.

"Kara!" Matt yells after me. I don't stop, refusing to look at him when I'm out on the driveway, calling a co-worker for a ride.

I'm heading back to my condo, and then I'm going straight to the sheriff's office. He'll probably lock me up on orders from Reg's family, or have me committed to a psyche ward, but I don't care.

It's not going down this way. I won't let it end like this.

Matt grabs me by the shoulder. I spin so fast I drop my phone. My palm doesn't stop, heading straight for his face. I hit him at least three times as hard as I can before my brain starts working again, and I stumble back, hating every blinding second of this.

My brother's hand reaches up, touching the burn on his cheek. No, he doesn't deserve this, he's just trying to help.

"I'm sorry, I'm sorry, I'm sorry," I whimper, folding my arms around myself, turning my back.

"Sis…I deserved it. Didn't listen. I got taken for a ride

by that piece of shit when I really shouldn't have, just like mom." He shuffles up behind me, standing so he blocks the wind nipping at my back. "I owe you an apology. Everything you said sounded crazy. I never thought in a million years dad would lie to me, lie to all of us, and mom would back him up."

"Yeah, well…now you get how I feel. But you'll never understand it, not if you try till Holden's half-grown." I look down, kicking a stray rock across the pavement. It helps me fight the urge to burst into tears. "You put him away, Matt. You didn't mean to, but you did. You, mom, and Reg's fucking lies."

"I don't need to understand," he says, laying a hand on my shoulder. "Before everything went to shit, I cared about Ryan. He was my best friend. Still might be, knowing what really went down, or near enough. We're going to get him out of there."

I refuse to look at him until he nudges my arm, turning me around. After everything that's happened, it seems impossible that I'd ever get a friend in this fight.

"This isn't your fight. Mom and dad weren't exaggerating about the danger we're putting ourselves in, even if they were wrong with how they handled it. I can't let them come down on you and Holden. Let me do this, alone."

"Sis, you're looking at me and seeing your big brother. Guess it's too easy to forget I've been overseas for four years, dealing with brutes who make the Draytons look like a damned joke. You need me, however much you don't want to hear it." Both his hands are on my shoulders now, squeezing, forcing me to keep looking at him when I want nothing else except to turn away and run. "The Sheriff's compromised. His first instinct's going to be protect the Draytons. He'll push you out of his office and send you down to some flunky, who'll throw your statement in a drawer where it'll just gather dust. They can't do that with a decorated Marine."

I hate it, but I know he's right.

When I pull myself away, we head for his truck. I send him the same file from my phone, the one with the only evidence we have to set Ryan free. Then we're rolling onto the highway, too anxious to turn the radio on, never saying anything our eyes can't when we share a glance at every light.

We have to get him out of there. There's no telling what Reg will try to do with his family's connections. His family will want a spectacle in the local press, portraying them as victims, but Reg won't wait forever, knowing who he is and what he meant to me.

He doesn't take risks. If he doesn't know the truth about what happened with Nelson, he'll make sure it's only his family's version that ever goes on record.

I don't know what they're capable of. I remember Patricia's anger, the way she'd get whenever someone disappointed her.

These people don't play around. There are no morals. They'll do their damnedest to arrange an accident, or something worse, every hour Ryan spends locked up.

I'm thankful he's come to his senses, and he's helping me. But I can't ignore the ice creeping up my spine, the chill that keeps telling me it's too late.

* * * *

I take a seat in the waiting room at the town's tiny police station, as soon as the sheriff's secretary gives my brother an audience. It doesn't take long to hear the two men bellowing at each other behind the closed door.

The secretary looks up when I stand, walk over, and press my ear against Sheriff Dixon's door. But she doesn't stop me, just walks over herself after several seconds pass, listening with me.

"You've lost your mind, Lilydale, with all due respect. I'm not sticking the FBI in the ass with a flimsy lead like this." The sheriff's gravelly voice seeps through the wood, resonating in my ears.

"Flimsy? That what you call a list of pervs screwing around with girls they ought to have no business touching? What about the one who's been busted, doing time in a Federal pen?"

"I don't know anything about that," the sheriff says, shooting down my brother's accusations. He's treating him like the crazy man. Like he's just told him he shook Elvis' hand on the moon. "Look, you know what the Drayton family means to this town. These are serious accusations. I know what Mr. Caspian means to us, too, and what he used to mean to you and yours. You'll have to do better than showing me a list of names if you want me to dig into old

Nelson, and turn the worst suspect this town's ever had loose."

"Then I'll have to do the impossible," Matt growls. There's a dull thud. I imagine his hands hitting the sheriff's desk, leaning over him. "You've sold out. Failed to protect everybody in this town like you're supposed to, all because you're afraid to go after those fucking assholes."

"Get out of my face," Dixon snarls. "We're done here."

"You're not a bad man – at least, I want to believe you're not. Christ, man, get past the fear. Do the right thing. I've brought you proof. You could have this list of names in the lead investigator's hand tonight, blow open a slavery ring, and go down as the town's greatest hero in a generation when they're busted."

"Please. Fame isn't on my agenda. You're good at what you do, Matt, and I appreciate your service to our country." The sheriff pauses, trying to regain his calm. "But you're a fool if you think busting the Draytons won't leave this town reeling. They pull their business, we've got nothing."

"Did you forget you're about to cook a self-made man who's built a billion dollar business?"

"That's hardly relevant to the scope of the suspect's crime," Dixon snaps. "I'm sorry, I can't help you. If you think so little of this office that you believe we're here to serve one family, instead of Split Harbor, you're welcome to go to the FBI yourself."

"Bullshit. We both know the Draytons have got their hands in the Feds, too. Our only shot at breaking their backs starts here." My brother pauses, holding in his anger.

I watch his silhouette turn in the frosted glass, heading for the door. The secretary scampers away to her desk behind me. "It's your call, Sheriff, and you know it. If you make the right one, I'll be waiting outside with my sister for awhile."

Dixon never replies. Matt comes storming out a second later, shooting me a surprised look when he sees me standing next to the door.

"I know, it didn't go well," I tell him. "What are we going to do now?"

"Wait. We're going to hang out here until midnight, or until we see the sheriff leave. Whatever happens first. He's thinking things over. Deciding what kind of man he is tonight, one way or another."

Great, *more* waiting.

Meanwhile, I think about Ryan, holed up somewhere in the back of this building where they have the tiny cells. He's alone, wondering if his worst nightmare is finally coming true.

I can't lose him again. Touching my ring finger, I let the minutes flow by anxiously, remembering my promise.

When I said I'd marry him again, I meant it, down to my soul. This doesn't change that.

If I have to visit him behind bars, wearing his ring, and be a prison wife, I will. I'll wait my entire life to see him free. I'll keep fighting the bastards as long and hard as I have to.

Nothing's destroying our love a second time.

He's cleared his name with me, retaken my heart, and claimed me again. I'm afraid, but I'm determined.

As long as I hang onto that, I'll always have my husband.

XII: Just Breathe (Ryan)

It's amazing how time hemorrhages away in this little cell. I haven't been so numb or detached from the world since the night Nelson died, and Bart sent me away, protecting me the only way he could.

I'm the only prisoner here tonight. Split Harbor rarely ever has more than the odd drunken fist fight or a man wanted on petty crimes passing through town. There are only eight, maybe ten cells. I'm by myself back here, stuffed into a box that hasn't been updated since the 1930s.

Seeing how this is the town's first murder case in more than fifty years, I worry I'm about to become it's most famous inmate. Until they put me through a kangaroo court and shuffle me off to the nearest Federal penitentiary, anyway.

This can't be happening again.

Oh, but it is.

I'm losing her. Ruining her life for a second time because I'm leaving against my will. I'm being torn away, again, only this time I can't come back. Even my big brain isn't likely to hatch a jailbreak scheme.

I stand up, stretch, and walk to the edge of the cell. My hands grip the bars. Staring through the gaps, I let my head fall, wondering how big a mistake it was to come back here at all.

No. Don't you dare, I tell myself.

Whatever happens, it wasn't wrong. I couldn't have lived another day with my success, my billions, without letting her know the truth. It's her kiss on my mind for God only knows how long, hating the fact that I'll never have those lips again as long as I'm stuffed away behind bars. It doesn't matter because I cherish the memory.

I'm remembering last night, our very last in Seattle, when I hear footsteps. The sheriff coming toward me isn't a surprise, but I have to blink to check my vision when I see the other man at his side.

"Back up a bit," Sheriff Dixon says.

My old best friend stands next to him with his arms folded across his huge chest. Soon as I move, we watch the old Sheriff produce a set of keys, jam one in my lock, and undo the door with a deafening *crack.*

"What's this? What's going on?" I ask, keeping my distance.

"New evidence. There's no reason to hold you while it's pending investigation," the old sheriff says reluctantly. He turns to Matt. "I want both of you to find him. Only way we stop the Draytons from shooting down this case before it gets off the ground is if they're sent a message, loud and clear. They can't interfere, and it's our job to make sure they understand."

I don't get what's going on. Before I can even ask, the

old officer heads down the hall, leaving us alone with my door half open.

Matt waits for me to step outside. "I was wrong about you, Ryan. Wrong about my sis, too, thinking you'd driven her crazy all these years, thinking you were innocent. She showed me the dirt you had on Reg and Nelson. Mom backed up your story. She knew, all these years, and didn't say a fucking thing."

He sounds like he can't believe it. I know can't, and it's like the floor crumbling beneath me, one more twist in the longest, meanest winding road of my life.

Words won't do for what I've got to say. I throw my arms around him, giving the boy I grew up with a brotherly hug. "Forget it. We don't need to dwell on anybody's past mistakes. What did the sheriff mean when he said we need to send a message?"

Matt looks at me and smiles. "It's open season on the next asshole in line to screw this town over. Let's go have a little heart-to-heart talk with Kara's ex. Way more courtesy than he deserves after the sonofabitch threatened her."

My hands are already fists before we're outside, heading for his truck. Only thing I can think about is how I wish I'd done more than just tie him up with his mistress at that hotel in Marquette.

Too bad. Tonight, it's better late, than never.

* * * *

He's working late at the office tonight. Working, for real, the lone figure we see through the dim lit window on the third floor of Drayton Financial.

Matt gives me a look as he parks the car. "You ready?"

"Lead the way, Corporal. We'll corner him and figure out the rest from there. Just save some for me," I say, brandishing the brass knuckles he's loaned me. "I have plenty to give."

Matt nods, jumps out, and I'm following close behind him. It's a good thing I've stuck to my gym routine religiously. I wouldn't have a chance at keeping up with the quick, built marine any other way.

We're relieved there's nobody at the front desk. It's too late. We won't need to use the story we'd prepped, and we can save all our words for the bastard who deserves them most.

The Drayton office suffers from the same flaw everywhere in this town has – the doors are unlocked. I make a mental note to change corporate policy at Punch so we never have a crazy issue like two men bursting in after hours, eager to knock sense into a CFO.

He never sees us coming until it's too late. Matt steps aside, standing next to the wall, his hand on the pistol at his side in case Reg tries anything crazy. He gives me the honor of kicking the door open. My foot flies into it like a missile.

Who knew Venetian leather was so good at being a battering ram?

"What the hell?!" Reg jumps up, looking around in a panic, his lean, wiry body twitching when he sees me coming. His arms go up, and he screams when he sees I'm not alone. "Oh, God. I put you away!"

"You put yourself on suicide watch, shithead," I snarl.

In a second, he's cornered. Grabbing him by the collar, I whip him around, slamming him into the wall with a satisfying *boom.*

He's whimpering. He thinks we're going to kill him. For now, I'm more than happy to let him believe it, too.

Of course, I'm not a killer, whatever happened with his sick great uncle years ago. Despite the damage Reg has done, I want to believe he doesn't share the same wretched tastes as his older relative, even if he's inherited Nelson's arrogance.

"Walk with me," I say, pushing him toward Matt. My buddy takes his other arm, and we lead him out like a puppet, down the elevator to the parking lot.

"You scream, you tell anyone what's going down here tonight, you're done. I'll see the inside of a cell before I let you get away with what you did to my sister and my best friend," Matt tells him, motioning to the gun in its holster.

The asshole stays quiet the whole way out to the truck. Before we lead him to it, we bring him to his car, where he stops and looks at us with questions in his eyes. "Why here?"

"Open your trunk," I say, stuffing his hand into his pocket for him, searching for his keys.

He doesn't understand, but he will soon. Reluctantly, he reaches for the fob and taps the button to unlock it. I pop it open and start rummaging through. There isn't much inside, so it doesn't take long to find the bag with the shoebox.

My gut feeling was right. I tear off the lid and see a fresh new pair of candy blue high heels inside.

"For Amy?"

"Yes," he hisses, clenching his jaw. "I don't see why that's relevant."

"Shut up," Matt barks, turning him around, pushing him toward the truck. We hang onto him so he can't bolt, and I clutch the shoebox underneath my arm.

His icy silence persists as he's wedged between us in the truck, all the way out to the forest, undeveloped land just a few miles from the Armitage lighthouse. He doesn't start weeping until we're parked on the gravel road, noticing how isolated it is out here. Matt gets out, waiting for me to do the same, and drag him off his seat. I remember to carry the shoes under my arm again.

"I'm sorry, I'm sorry," he whines.

"Sorry you got caught?" I look this loathsome piece of shit up and down. It's hard to believe anything he says, even when he's shaking.

This time, his silence is deafening. Matt helps me drag him out, and we take him into the forest. We all walk half a mile before we find the perfect clearing.

"Please don't kill me, guys. I had to protect my family. I was just defending myself after what you did, Ryan. Jesus, you can have her! I never loved the little bitch, just wanted a trophy wife."

Matt beats me to the first punch. He hits him in the face so hard Reg rocks back, staggering back into my arms. I grip the prick tight, forcefully turning his head so he's looking at the Marine.

My eyes go to the brass knuckles on my hand. Christ, I

need to get them off. If I start hitting him now, I'm not going to stop, and then I'll really be a murderer.

"You call her that again, next time it'll be lead going in your skull," he says. "She loved you once, asshole. Fell for your lies. You come near my sis again, and I swear, I'll kill you."

He's quiet. Good.

The total lack of response says it's my turn. I push him down in the dirt and decaying leaves, falling on top of him, picking his head up by the neck so he can listen, and listen good. I let him feel the heavy, cold brass lining my fingers before I pull it off, pressing it harder into his cheek.

"You, Reginald, are done. We gave the FBI the truth about your sick dead uncle. It's going to take every weak, miserable fiber in your body to fight your instinct to squawk once the trial begins. We're going to nail your family to the fucking wall, and the entire town's going to know about it. Your parents are going to lose a lot of money. You'll be lucky if you can ever show your face around here again, without the good people turning their backs, or maybe worse."

"Look, if it's a settlement you're looking for –"

"No." My fist crashes into the back of his head, knocking him face first into the dirt. "I want justice, asshole. Peace. I want your fucked up family to pay for it's crimes because if Nelson did what he did with innocent girls, there's a lot more corruption for the FBI to find, and chances are you've benefited from it. I know he got them here with his charities, the same fucking reason I wound up in this town to begin with."

"I'm…I'm not Uncle Nelson. Whatever he's done, it isn't me," he says, venom running into his voice. "God, what's wrong with you? All *this* over her? I didn't do anything. I never meant to hurt her. She would've had a comfortable life. Nice justice you've got. Attacking a man over his family's sins."

Matt and I share a look. In any other situation, seeing the huge marine roll his eyes would be hilarious, but not here.

Neither of us are interested in an ethics lesson from this cheating, miserable prick.

"Did I say you could speak?" I ask, rubbing his face into the ground, messing up his hair as much as I can. "Did I ask for your fucking moralizing, when you thought nothing of cheating, manipulation, tearing me away from her? When you and your folks probably *knew* what Nelson did, and let this town think he didn't deserve what happened?"

Matt steps behind me, and I'm glad he does. I'm afraid he'll have to hold me back from murdering the trash whose face I'm ramming into the ground again and again. Good thing I pulled off the knuckles.

His choking stops me. He's coughing and sputtering, his nose full of dirt and leaves.

Snarling, I roll him over, straddle him, and reach for the shoebox. "You're right about one thing, and only one – you're not on trial here for Nelson's crimes. But I'm damned sure not going to let you get in the way, retaliate, and try to cover his tracks any more."

His eyes go huge when he sees me pulling out the heels.

His face is scratched, his lip bloody, several new bruises promising to overwhelm the makeup on his jaw he put there for sympathy, to make me look like a crazier, more violent beast than I really am when the woman I love is under siege.

Unfortunately for him, he doesn't have to exaggerate much.

"No, no...I don't understand. Those shoes...what're you doing?!"

"Insurance, jackass," Matt says, pulling out the protective stuffing inside them. He crouches behind me and gets to work on ripping off Reg's shoes, down to his bare feet.

I nod. "You're going to wear the shoes for a change, ass. We'll take pictures, and you won't move a muscle. Because if you decide to do something stupid again after we warned you not to, if you or your folks stick their noses into the investigation, the case, or come gunning for me, Kara, or any of the Lilydales ever again, I'll make sure these pictures hound you like a dog. You're so uptight about appearances, yeah? You won't have a reputation when every employer, every investment firm, every fucking politician you want to bribe knows what you look like in blue."

He screams and thrashes while Matt stuffs his feet into the slim shoes, several sizes too small. It takes five minutes to get it straight, and by then I'm sure his toes feel like they're about to snap.

Smiling, I look down at his work. Matt smiles, gives me a thumbs up, and we both reach for our phones.

The reprobate has gotten the message. His eyes stay

closed and he doesn't move a muscle the whole time we circle around him, snapping pics from every angle. I end with a snapshot of his face, just as his eyes pop open, scared and beaten.

Matt gives me a knowing look. We're done here. It's time to go home, and wait for further word from the sheriff or the FBI investigators who'll surely be calling me soon.

"Wait, wait. Where are you going?" Reg calls after us, his words like mush in his beat up mouth. "You can't just leave me like this?!"

We've only taken a few steps along the path we came when I stop, turn around, and look at the worm twisting on the ground. "Like hell we can't. Your phone's in your shoebox. Use it to call your gold digger mistress."

His eyes bug out. I smile. "Enjoy her while she lasts. I've seen enough chicks in the corporate world to know she's only putting up with your bedroom antics because you're keeping the heels and fancy dinners coming. Soon as they're gone – and they will be, once the FBI digs through family history – she'll run so fast she kicks dust in your face. After everything your family did to me and Kara, several years alone will do you some good. Maybe you can clear your head, figure out your shit before it's too late."

It's not hard to hear him struggling to get up in those heels clenched to his feet like vises. We just keep going, get in the truck, and leave beneath the moonlight.

We're heading back to the police station, where Kara's probably still sleeping. Matt left her there in the waiting room to get me in the back, after the sheriff made his choice.

She's blissfully unaware I was being released to give her ex the kick in the balls he deserves.

I don't give him a second thought. Only thing that matters is having her in my arms tonight, back in my bed, a smile on her face because she knows, beyond all doubt, that everything is *finally* going to be okay.

* * * *

"Ryan? Don't tell me – I'm dreaming?" She rubs her eyes before she'll believe it's me.

I could wait, let it sink in.

No, screw it. I haul her up off the seat, sweeping her into my arms.

There's nothing worth saying that these kisses can't for the next five minutes. Matt stands behind us, a smile on his face. I'm grinning like a damned fool the whole way through it, my lips conquering hers, knowing the universe is righting itself, one little piece at a time.

"They had you locked up," she says when I let her catch her breath. "I don't understand. How?"

"An old friend helped me out," I tell her, motioning to the gentle giant as he walks over. "Sheriff Dixon deserves some credit for doing the right thing, too."

"We've got to get busy protecting ourselves," she says, slipping out of my arms, grabbing her purse on the chair. "You know they'll come after us. The Draytons are in a fight for their lives, and they know who's responsible for what's coming."

"Babe, wait." I grab her by the wrist. Bringing her hand

to my face, I lay my lips on it, planting a reassuring kiss. "Reg is done. Matt and I made sure he's not interfering with anything again."

She gives us a desperate look, one after the other. "God. Tell me you didn't…you know."

There's nobody around, but she's smart enough to lower her voice, realizing we're still standing in a police station.

"He'll live, and he won't press charges," Matt says, throwing a brotherly arm around her shoulder. "All you need to know, sis. I'm not wasting another minute on his corrupt ass. Let's go home."

"We'll talk to the FBI in the morning, I'm sure. Is it too late to open up Grounded?"

She blinks, not understanding where I'm going. "I'm the manager. It's never too late…why?"

"Because the bars in this town close too early on a Sunday to let me buy my friend a proper drink," I look at Matt and he smiles. "Coffee will have to do for now, plus a few slices of that awesome cherry pie. I want you to bring your mom and the kid, if he's around. I can't wait anymore. We're sitting down like a family and smoothing things over tonight. As the man you're going to marry, I won't let anything come between us and our wedding."

"Shit." Matt pauses, then slaps me on the back so hard my knees lock. "I'd say you're moving too fast, but you were always the one for her, Ryan. We've waited five years too long to make it happen."

We're both smiling, but it's nothing compared to the angelic grin on her face. My eyes eat her up a little bit at a time. As heartwarming as this is, and as pleased as I am to see her happy, I can't stop the lewd thoughts pulling at me from the inside out.

"Call your mom, guys. I want to sit down tonight. All of us."

I want to take care of the last thing between me laying down the woman I love for a few hard hours in the sheets.

They both reach for their phones. I stand against the wall, ready to put one big happy family back together after an eternity apart. I'm ready for the nice.

The naughty's coming straight after.

There's nothing like the hours I spent in prison, thinking I'd never have her lips or her legs around me again, to make my dick stand on end.

This night isn't over until we find a bed, even if it blurs into morning. I'm going be inside her, celebrating our love, our promises, our future.

* * * *

"Amazing to see you again, Mrs. Lilydale." I take her hands as soon as she steps through the door.

Her eyes light up like I've returned from the dead. I'm not sure who's got the tighter grip.

"Ryan!" she throws her arms around me. "I'm sorry, son. I did you wrong."

"You kept a promise," I whisper, as soon as she pulls away to face me, tears brimming in her eyes. "I kept mine. The Drayton's won't be bothering us anymore, and I'm going to marry your daughter. Only thing I've ever wanted."

I release her. Kara comes over and helps her shaken mom to the table, where there's a fresh cherry pie and a giant steel thermos of coffee. I take a seat next to her, reaching for her hand underneath the table.

We talk past sunrise. There's a lot of catching up to do.

I hear all about Matt's exploits in Afghanistan, how hard the Lilydales fought to hang on since Bart died, how bad a blow it was when the divorce hit, and how Matt's ex still keeps the kid most weekends out of spite.

That last one makes me take a slow, smooth sip of coffee that burns my throat. When we've wrapped up loose ends, I'm going to get him the best lawyer in the state to wring more time with his son from the cheating bitch.

By dawn, Kara starts to doze. She's cuddled up next to me, a smile on her face, when Matt stands up, rubbing his eyes. "Time to get some sleep. It's my last week on leave before I'm on active duty again."

"You earned it, man. Couldn't have done any of this without you." I put out my fist. He bumps his on mine.

Just like old times. I came here for Kara, but I've gotten my best friend back too. "Whenever you're ready to retire from the service, call me. I'll do whatever it takes to help you set up something new. If it's in the cards for Bart's Auto coming back, deal me in."

"Nah, Ryan. I can't take your money, even if I think you're fit to join the family."

"Then let me help apply for a loan, or get you a deal on a place," I say. "Don't answer me now. Just think about it. When the time comes, you'll tell me. Worry about the big picture, and I'll do the details."

He nods respectfully, a small, understanding smile on his face. That's the last I thing I see before he turns his back and marches out the door. Mrs. Lilydale sits across the table smiling, sipping her coffee. She's tired, but the reunion keeps her awake, one we all thought we'd never see.

I look at my girl carefully, making sure she's asleep on my shoulder, before I lean in and ask the question I've been dying to pop since she stepped through the door. "There's something I need. Do you know what happened to Kara's old ring – the first one I gave her when we got engaged all those years ago?"

Smiling, she nods. "Locked away in my drawer. Your locket's there too. She couldn't stand the sight of them after she thought you weren't coming home. I kept them safe…just in case."

I reach for my wallet, pulling out a business card that has my personal address for the new office in town. "Please, when you get a chance, I'd love it mailed here. I've already got her a fancy new ring, but it isn't enough. I want her to have the ring I always meant her to wear, too. As far as I'm concerned, the last five years apart didn't happen. I'm using everything I can to remind her we were always meant to be, Mrs. Lilydale."

"It's time you started calling me Bets if you're going to be my son-in-law." The warm smile pulling at her lips brightens her face, smoothing away the accumulated sadness in wrinkles. "You'll have it by tomorrow, Ryan. Bart would've been so happy to see how wrong he was, you know."

I think about him when she grabs my hand. It's like I can feel the old man's ghost, big and approving, standing over all of us as he watches the impossible happen.

"I know, Bets. Hell, I'm honoring his memory by making this girl the happiest woman in the world, every single day we've got left on this earth." I lean down and kiss Kara's forehead.

It wakes her softly. Perfect timing because it's past six o'clock now, and the morning crew is coming in through the back of the cafe.

Soon, we're saying goodbye to her mom, and heading for my car. I'll have to keep looking over my shoulder in case Reg is stupid enough to ignore his final warning, but it's not slowing me down.

I'll have the girl in my arms claimed, wed, and worshipped by the time the winter thaws.

For the first time in my life, the wealth and success finally means something. The millions upon millions in my accounts are more than just bare numbers on a screen. I'm going to spend every damned dime giving her the moon, and then doing the same for her folks.

Good looks and money always bring power. It's worthless if it doesn't make her skin hot and happy to the touch every second her hand's in mine. Driving to our hotel, I try to comprehend how fucking lucky I am, having a second chance with the most beautiful bride in the world.

No matter how many times I roll it over in my mind, I still can't get it. But I'm damned sure not going to forget.

Ever.

* * * *

Seven Months Later

Church bells ring all the way down the coast. Several barges down the Superior shore blow their horns. A hundred thousand people in half a dozen towns know the hour has arrived.

Nobody except our gaggle of guests hears the most explosive, heartfelt rendition of *Here Comes the Bride.* That's for us, our friends, and our family, but it seems like the entire universe knows what's happening, down to the fire in our hearts.

Mine becomes an inferno the second I see her heading down the makeshift path strewn with flowers. That creamy, skin tight wedding dress clings to her like an angel's gown, making her a white shadow against the Armitage lighthouse's dark grey brick in the background.

I have to take my eyes off her, and face the priest, just to keep my dick from ripping through trousers in front of half the town.

God, what a woman.

Hell, what a town.

What a wedding.

It's hard to believe the changes over the last six months. This décor, music, and atmosphere are more than anything I imagined. It's all coming together perfectly. Easy when you own the place where you're getting married.

The Draytons abandoned the historical fund and half

the other charities in town as soon as they were busted. A hundred years of wealth and haughty reputations spiraled down the drain after the FBI proved Nelson's crimes. The Feds stripped away the assets he'd gotten from the sex trade, easily about ninety percent of their wealth, or so the papers said.

They even lost the lighthouse. It's mine now.

When it isn't open to the town, like today, I know it's the best wedding present I could've given us.

The music keeps going, and she's getting closer. I fix my eyes on hers, watching that beautiful veil ripple behind her golden hair. Behind her, there's Bets, little Holden bouncing on his grandma's lap. My mother-in-law reaches up and wipes a tear, just as Kara reaches the altar.

I step up, taking the last of the veil that's covering her face, drawing it back behind her head. When she sees me, blush fills her cheeks, and I have to fight twice as hard to control the raging erection in my pants.

It takes the song forever to end. Neither of us mind, content to relish the moment. I take both her hands in mine. Squeezing, rubbing, promising a thousand kinds of naughty and nice. She looks into my eyes and mouths one word.

"Soon."

A jolt runs through my spine. Can't come fast enough, hauling her into bed, stripping off the delicate white layers covering her beautiful body like the icing on our cake.

I'm never going to let these hands go. They're going to be in mine while we're taking our vows. They'll be tangled in my fingers while we're walking to the limo, heading for the reception. Later, they'll be clenched like they're going to break when I have her, pinning her little hands above her head while I take her good and hard.

Fuck later. I want it *now.*

Luckily, I want to make us official even more. We turn to the priest as the music dies down, and he smiles, the same warm glow on his face we've seen during the rehearsals.

"Dearly beloved," he begins. "We're gathered here today to unite two hearts once lost in holy matrimony, Ryan Caspian, and Kara Lilydale."

My eyes flit to the side. Matt stands there in military dress, my best man and best friend. He gives me a subtle smile and flashes a thumbs up.

I know the boys and girls from the office are cheering me, too. Leonard, Becky, and so many more who got rich on the way up, making Punch Corp a world leader in new technologies.

They helped me achieve that dream. It's been a stepping stone to this one, but now I have to do the rest alone. Wouldn't have it any other way.

"Ryan," the priest says, turning to me. "Do you take this woman to be your lawfully wedded wife…"

For better and for worse.
In sickness and in health.
To have and to hold.
Till death do you part?

Each phrase hits like lightning. The full, outrageous enormity of what I'm about to do stabs through my ribs, so sudden I have to lift her hand to my lips, and plant a kiss on her precious skin.

I love this woman. I'll never doubt it.

Through hell, through heaven, through five years of loss, through six glorious months back together, and all the years we had as kids. I'll love her to the end of time. I know it more than I've known anything in my life.

I can't keep them waiting. My hands lock tight on hers, pulling her closer, and for just a second, I'm lost in her jade green eyes.

"Obviously, it's a 'yes.' Kara, I love who you were, who you are, and who you're bound to become. Love that you're gong to be by my side the entire time, having my kids, and being the best girl any man stuck on this rock could ever wish for. Didn't think it was possible to love you more, Kara-bou, but I do today. I love that you're mine forever, and you're going to remember it every time you're flashing those rings."

That's right. Rings. Plural.

She's wearing *both* wedding rings. Our past, present, and future are reconciled on her hand.

Her face twitches. I reach up and gently clasp her chin, wiping away the tears that come down. We're lucky the priest speaks slow, prepping for her part, because she's in no condition to say anything for the next sixty seconds.

"Do you, Kara, take this man to be your lawfully wedded husband…"

To love and to cherish.
To worship and adore.

Today and all your days.

The crowd coos softly when I pull her into my arms. It's all I can do to steady her as she's shaking, overwhelmed with the same wave that hit me a minute ago.

Five years of pain go up in flames. We did it.

Against the odds, against the assholes, against the world, we won. There's no love like the one worth fighting for. Today brings us so much closer to winning the battle for good.

I give her a look, rubbing my thumb softly along her cheek. *Don't rush. Whenever you're ready.*

Her eyes open. She looks at the priest, before turning her eyes my way again. Next to me, Matt sniffs. I think the big marine is holding in his own emotional storm.

"Love you, Ryan, and I'm proud to be your wife. I never thought I'd be standing here today, marrying the one, the right one, the only one who's ever believed in me and didn't give up. So many things tried to get in the way, tried to take you away from me, but they didn't. I believe it's fate, and there's nothing like it to make me believe you're the only man I'll ever call my husband. Too many people have loved and lost. We won, and it's a once-in-a-lifetime win for our hearts."

There's my girl. I'm smiling at her eloquence, the sweetness in her voice. Mostly, I'm actually able to control the need to haul her into bed right now because those eyes on mine are about more than just sex.

So much more. I clasp her hands, waiting for the priest to say the final words.

He speaks legalities. Then what everybody gathered has been waiting for.

"Please, kiss the bride."

Like he even has to ask. Like I wouldn't turn the world over on its ass just to get her, pull her into my arms, and push my lips down on hers.

Everything explodes the instant we kiss. She's swept up in my embrace amid the cheers, the laughter, the tears. She's crying, letting loose everything she's held inside while we kiss, but it doesn't interfere with her tongue.

It's hot on mine. Desperate. Wanting.

I take her mouth, letting my hands roam across her body. Tonight, as soon as the big day's finished, I'm going to fuck my wife like she's never had it before. And if she's going to give me the wedding gift I think she is, I'm going to be sore for the next week.

* * * *

We're trying to eat our cake, stopping every minute for about a hundred people clinking their glasses, wanting us to kiss for them yet again. We indulge them, but it's really for ourselves. They can't see my hand on her thigh, clenching through the thin white fabric, ready to shred her pretty gown the second we're alone.

Smiling, I pick up my fork, and feed another bite into her mouth. Can't take my eyes off those lips. They're pink and perfect and ready to be wrapped around my cock.

Streams of people come by to give us their well wishes. We hear the chatter all around us, too, the latest town gossip.

Turns out Drayton Financial botched a couple hundred annuities for the town's wealthiest citizens. They've been slammed with so many lawsuits they'll probably never recover, and that's nothing compared to the restitution fund the FBI set up to claw back money made off Nelson's victims.

Nobody's seen Reg since the night we left him in the woods. I had a private investigator trail him a couple months ago. The man tracked him to Chicago, where he's wasting the last of his family fortune on high end escorts and thousand dollar heels, drinking himself into a sorry stupor most nights.

I'd feel sorry for him if he hadn't crushed my girl. I'm grateful I get to rebuild her, love her like he didn't. God help me, I'm still a little jealous, every second the miserable prick is alive and breathing.

I don't let Kara mention him, nor does she bother.

"I haven't seen them this happy in years," she says, leaning into me, motioning to Bets, Matt, and Holden several tables down.

I throw my arm around her and nod. "The family's fixed. Only a matter of time before your brother decides to leave the service and settle down. Hope he finds a better woman, someday."

"Me too," she muses, sucking her bottom lip. "That could've been me, Ryan. I might've made his mistake, marrying the wrong one. If the timing was different, or I'd turned you in the first time you showed up on my doorstep…I could've lost everything. And if I'd screwed up, gotten a kid into this mess…God."

"You didn't," I growl, laying a hand on her cheek. "Only kid coming out of you is going to be beautiful, and happy babe. We're going to make the happiest little things on earth."

She reaches for my hand, clenching it tight, giving me a look that makes my dick jerk. "Are you sure you're ready for this?"

Her voice is just a whisper. I lick my lips, staring through the crowd, wondering when we can slink off without anybody noticing our absence.

"Kara, baby, I've been waiting my entire life," I say. "We made our mistakes, screwing around with the wrong people, thinking we were dead to each other. That's all over. We're married now, and you'd better believe I want to build a family like yesterday."

"I hope we can be good parents. Daddy died so young, and you had it rough, moving through all those orphanages."

"Just tells us we know what family means." I rub her thigh beneath the table, waiting until she does the slow turn, her big green eyes burning. "We don't half-ass, Karabou. After everything we've been through, we can't. I love you with all my heart, and our son or daughter's going to share it all, because they're part of us. Maybe our best parts. Real question is, are *you* ready to get the hell out of here?"

She smiles, pushing her fingers into mine. We kiss one more time before I help her up, making our way through the crowd one more time. She's more ready to go than I am, her skin glowing with the warmth that tells me she's dripping wet. Her lips open in a silent moan every time my hand reaches her back, winds its way down, and flies off just above the top of her ass.

"Is our boat ready?" I ask the limo driver, as soon as we slide into the back.

"Absolutely, sir. The captain reported in about an hour ago, and told me to let you know there's even a fresh bottle of Dom chilling on ice in your private quarters. They're waiting for you to board."

"Great." That's all I say before the car jerks down the winding road leading away from the lighthouse.

It's only a quick drive to the marina. Good thing, too, because I can't keep my hands to myself.

Kara doesn't stop me. She puts her little hands over mine when it goes between her legs, pressing the dress dangerously close to her pussy.

She's about to be mine for the thousandth time with me in her, and the first time as my lovely wife.

I'm ready to fuck so hard our yacht almost capsizes. Every inch pulses, throbs, screams to be inside her, from my swollen balls to my pierced tip. It aches to mark her from the inside out.

We're ready for marriage, ready for a family, ready to make our love mix blood.

"I love you," she whimpers, trying to stop my hand from stroking her through the bridal layers. "God, I can't wait."

Neither can I. She's breathless, blushing, going beet red and hot to the touch with primal need. When I push her hand away and rub slowly between her legs, I feel the dual rings clinging to her fingers. Something about having her wearing my symbol makes me want to rip through her dress, pull down my pants, and fuck her right here in the back seat.

But it's our honeymoon, and she deserves better. I'm putting million of dollars to work this week to make her swoon, and give us the best send off into the future money can buy.

It's a small price to pay for happiness, for love, for the bright dreams I nursed in the dark all those miserable years.

We've worked like dogs to get here. Tonight, we're working on our family, and I'm going to shoot every hot drop of come I have into her.

* * * *

"Please let the crew know if there's anything you need, Mr. Brooks" The Captain escorts us to our room personally once we're on the ship.

"It's Caspian," I remind him with a smile. "That's the old name. I know it'll take time for the real one to sink in, and I'll keep correcting the world until it does. There's nobody I'd rather be than Ryan, wed to the lovely Mrs. Caspian."

Kara nuzzles her face into my shoulder, drunk on my words, or a little too much wine back at the reception. Doesn't matter to me, as long as she's feeling good.

"Ah, of course. My apologies. I've followed the tabloids, of course, but old habits die hard. Have a wonderful night, and please let us know if you need anything," he says, putting his hands up in apology before he heads down the hall.

He's not the only one making the adjustment. It's taken everybody around the office months to start calling me Ryan, or Mister Caspian, ever since I set the record straight.

I'm a new man, leaving Tanner to die in that other world, the lonely, miserable one I've left behind for good.

Names are just words. But mine's the only one I want hanging on her lips tonight, tomorrow, and every night after.

"Let's see the bed where I'm going to have my wife for the first time," I tell her, pushing my keycard against the scanner lock. The door pops open.

Before we cross through, I lift her up, carrying her over the threshold. No, this yacht isn't our home, but it's going to be the first place we're living as man and wife for the next week as we cruise the Great Lakes. It's also where I'm planting my seed deep. My balls tighten, burning a little hotter at the thought.

She laughs as I carry her into our spacious room, and throw her down on the silver sheets. The bottle of Dom sits next to the bed on ice, as promised. I'm not interested in having a drop unless it involves slurping it off her naked body just now.

"Careful," she pleads, feeling the eager force in my hands when I start tugging on her dress.

Lucky for her, I'm a disciplined man. I take my time, careful not to tear a single scrap of her dress as I lift it away, piece by ivory piece, stripping her down to the bare, beautiful skin I've been craving on mine since the second I saw her coming toward the altar.

"Don't know how you wore them all evening," I tell her, sensing the wetness in her panties when my fingers go between her legs. "You're soaked, Kara. You've been craving my cock for hours. Admit it."

"Mmm, guilty," she purrs, wrapping her arms around my neck.

She grabs at my tie, lifting it out of my jacket. Grabbing her wrists, I spin her around and pull her down on the bed, making her straddle me.

Her bra cup comes down easily when I push the right side. Wise choice, considering I've fulfilled all the requests I've had this evening to please be gentle with the clothing. My mouth finds her hard little nipple, takes it between my teeth, and sucks.

Kara grinds her pussy into my bulge. Her feral moan singes my ears, and soon I'm snarling, tearing her bra away by the strap. I throw the lingerie over her shoulder to the floor, pulling her ass onto me while my mouth goes to work, alternating each breast.

My tongue flicks each bud, softening them, already eager to move to her clit. If it isn't as hard and swollen as the ends of these tits, it's going to be soon.

She oozes into lust with a breathless moan, panting every time her hips lurch into mine. I resist the urge to buck back. There's a wildcat moving on top of me, and I'm damned sure not going to risk going off anywhere inside her, throwing my seed into her womb.

This isn't just honeymoon fucking tonight. We're here to breed, and knowing I can give her my kid causes my pierced dick to leak like mad down my shaft.

"Ryan, yes!" her hand covers mine when it goes between her legs, tugging at her panties.

"Stand up," I say, lifting her off me. "Take the edge of the bed, and bite the sheet, love. They're going to hear you scream through these thin walls when you come on my mouth if you don't."

The filthy thought causes her back to arch when she obeys. I'm smiling, standing behind her, dropping to my knees. Fuck, I want them knowing. I want the entire ship to hear the frantic monkey sex we're going to be having all night, and I think she knows it.

I don't give a damn who hears us, sees us, or strokes themselves off, wishing they could fuck their wife half as hard I take mine. We've suppressed our love long enough, and tonight's our night to put it on parade.

My fingers hook her panties in the center. I'm waiting. Refusing to jerk them down until her legs start shaking.

Only takes my lips falling down above her ass for about three seconds before it starts.

There she is. My panting, begging, needful little wife. Beautiful and helpless, trembling for every inch of me.

She buries her face in the bed, suppressing a scream, when her panties hit her ankles. My face moves into her before I've even got them off. The hot, wet bundle remains in my hands while I'm growling, pushing my tongue into her, tasting the pussy that's going to be clenching, sucking, and coming on my cock all night.

There's no words for this sweetness. My tongue strokes

long and hard, teasing her clit when she starts to arch. Her feet leave her panties behind with slow, halting steps.

My hands clasp her ass, and my elbows hug her thighs, keeping her legs open for me. I eat my fill, and fuck, she tastes amazing.

My tongue lashes her clit every time she moans for me, quickening when the moans become screams.

Her shrill vibrations cut through the bed. The room sways gently around us, a sign the ship is out on the water. We're going out to sea, just as she's coming.

Growling, I fuck my tongue into her delectable cunt again and again. Her pussy convulses a few seconds later, tempting me to bring her off.

Naturally, I do.

I lick, suck, and grind my face between her legs. Her hips buck, twitching as her body fights for control. I don't stop until she's given everything up.

It takes forever before the trembling in her legs dies down. Then I'm on my feet, caressing her spine, kissing my way up her back. She collapses on the bed, sucking in oxygen, while I undress. It's a mercy when I free my cock from the trousers holding it in all evening.

It's needier than it's ever been in my life.

When I'm naked, I grab her by the waist and turn her around. She gasps, seeing how hard I am, past ready to fuck her into nirvana and back.

Her fingers go around my cock. It jerks in her hand when the warm gold rings press into it. I take her chin in my hand, tilt her up, and pull back before she can kiss me.

"You really want it, don't you, baby girl?"

"I want *your* baby, Ryan. Please." Her eyes shine big and bright, green gems twinkling with wicked truth.

"Yeah?" I push her hand off, grabbing my cock in my fist. Pre-come trails out as I move it over her, depositing it on her belly, just above the spot where her strip of hair begins. "Then take every fucking drop I put in you, love. First of many I'm going to put in that soft little belly. First of many nights you'll be savoring this dick as Mrs. Caspian, my knock out, gorgeous, horny wife."

She bites her lip. I can't hold back when I see the tension in her face, the insane *need* in every square inch of her skin.

I pull my cock back, tugging her legs around me. Then I'm sinking in, angling my way to the edge of her womb, making her gasp when the head of my cock presses as far as it can go.

Discipline is the only reason I've earned my money and won her hand in marriage. Too bad even I have limits.

I can't hold back as soon as I'm in her hot, wet center. My hips roll on, instinct taking over, the need to claim her, fuck her, and knock her up pounding in my temples.

It's in my veins and in my sweat. Grunting, I quicken my strokes, feeling her clenching around me in a matter of minutes.

"Ryan! Oh, God."

Oh, fuck me. I almost lose it when she explodes on my cock a second later, clenching the sheets so she doesn't fall off, stabbing her heels into my muscular ass. My cue to fuck her harder.

Now, I drive into her, running on pure lust. I fuck straight through her first O and into the next. The second time, she's grinding her clit into me each time I thrust deep, stopping long enough to make her burn so good.

"Please," she whines between her teeth.

I slow my strokes just long enough to palm her face, bring my lips to hers, and taste the insatiable need in her kiss.

She wants this as bad as I do. I know it, down to my balls, and they churn like they're full of lava the instant I pull away.

"You'll get it when you come for me again," I tell her.

Her eyes are wide, telling me she can't possibly do it again. She doesn't know I've got one more surprise.

When my strokes speed up, I reach between us, pressing my ring finger into her clit. There's a lot a man can do when he owns a technology company. My platinum wedding band looks no different than any other wealthy man's on the outside. Inside, I've had a sophisticated circuit installed, designed to make this ring scream when it reaches the right temperature.

It vibrates on her clit. Her legs tighten around me when she realizes what's happening, and I watch her head snap back, making me catch a fistful of those golden locks.

Her lips form a ring. She wants to scream, cry my name, or just beg me again. I make out the most important word, the same one flashing in her eyes when she looks at me again, right before her lids go down and they roll into her head.

Please.

"Come for me, baby. Take every fucking drop from my balls." I'm growling, ramming myself balls deep, letting the fire coursing up my spine hit my brain a second later.

We're sharing fireworks.

Coming together.

Coming fierce.

Coming so fucking hard it makes the dense sea rocking our ship seem like a breeze.

I lose myself in her. My balls spit fire, and the same flames consume me. There's yesterday, tomorrow, and the next decade all at once.

My seed flows thick. Furious ropes spit from my cock and blaze into her. Kara's pussy massages every inch of me, making me growl while I'm spilling it all.

It's cool in our room, but we're both red and dripping sweat when I remember how to think. My lips go down on hers while we cool down, tasting what's mine. There's room to be tender after I've ravished her like an animal.

She's so warm, skin burning beneath my hands. When I pull out, I walk across the room, grabbing the champagne and two glasses. I also take a handful of ice.

"Suck," I tell her, popping an ice cube into her mouth. She takes it like a good girl, turning it over with her tongue, tempting me to kiss her and fuck her all over again.

No, I need to pace myself. It'll be dawn before I'm done with her, before my balls are dry. And then we'll be coming above deck to enjoy ourselves at the first port tomorrow, before we head back here for another night tangled together.

That's how it's going to be every night until I know my seed takes. We're smiling, sipping our champagne, my free hand against her thigh, ready to pull her legs open for me again as soon as we're ready.

"Is this honeymoon everything you imagined?" she asks, mischief dancing in her eyes.

I smile, knowing it's the same thing she asked me after our first time, so long ago. But she's not that virgin girl anymore.

When I look at her, I don't just see my beautiful wife. I see all the Karas I've known, every one I've fallen in love with.

There's the kid who slid in the oil the first day we met, her face as innocent then as it is now. There's the woman I first asked to marry me, young and radiant, ready for a life together. There's the darker, sadder, unhappy girl I found when I came home, the one it's taken months to wipe away.

Then there's my bride. Mature, beautiful, and finally happy. My woman, future mother of my children, and eternally, irrevocably mine.

Whole again. Every single part of her. My hand drifts down to her hip, feeling the tattoo that used to be a broken heart.

"I'm glad you got this touched up in time for the wedding," I tell her, kissing her shoulder.

She beams. "My heart's not broken anymore, so I kinda had to. You never answered my question."

I'm laughing. She can't be serious, wondering if I'm so far over this honeymoon, I'm halfway to Jupiter. Isn't it obvious?

"Babe, it's more, and I think you know it," I say, wrapping my arms around her. "We couldn't have appreciated this as much as we do if we hadn't paid the price to get here."

Her smile softens. She's quiet for a moment, thinking to herself, rolling my words around in her head.

When I brush my lips across hers, she looks at me, the smile I want to devour taking over her face. "It's strange that you're right. I never would've imagined anything good coming out of those years – but here we are. Where would I be without your perspective?"

"Married to some jackass I'd have to kill to get you back," I tell her, moving my hands down, pulling her on top of me. "I'll blow every speck of fame and fortune I've accumulated all these years to keep you, Kara-bou. Don't ever doubt it."

Her lips merge to mine again, just as she sinks down on my cock, tall and hungry. "You're lucky I'm a bargain, then, and we get to live your crazy billionaire lifestyle without you running dry."

"No, babe. You're priceless," I growl, moving my hips, loving how her nails stab into my shoulder. "If you don't believe that now, you will. Love you more every day since I asked you to marry me again, and that's a damned fine return on investment."

Several strokes in, she's too lost in pleasure to quip back. I take her lips again with a smile, knowing I've got her where I want her, the only place we ever ought to be.

XIII: Hard Won (Kara)

Eighteen Months Later

It's starting to feel normal.

Coming home to our beautiful castle on the shore after a long day at Grounded, only rivaled by our lovely corporate condo in Seattle. I take over for our nanny and put dinner on, usually having an hour or two for our little boy and me, before Ryan comes walking through the door.

When I huddle on the sofa with our son, Joseph, I marvel at the beautiful boy we've created.

He's calm, strong willed, and has his father's eyes. He'll have a sibling in another year, one more beautiful link in the long chain of our love.

These evenings alone, I think about the past a lot. I remember what he said on our honeymoon – *you're priceless.*

But it's wrong, even if it makes me smile. It's our love that's truly special, irreplacable, a love like I've never had and never will have with another man.

When you meet the one, you know. You'll fight to bring him home when he lays out his heart, miss him when he's gone, and embrace every second chance.

I'm nodding off with our baby boy in my arms when I hear the door open. I don't look up until he's standing behind me, laying his hand on my shoulder, his intoxicating scent filling the space between us.

"Welcome home."

"Where's my kiss?" He brushes his lips against my neck, a reminder that words are cheap every time we get to have another evening together.

Smiling, I turn my face up, and we kiss. He runs strong fingers through my hair, tugging loose strands down my back, running his stubble against my neck when he pulls away.

He still excites me in a way that should be impossible.

Hell, impossible is what all of this should be.

Ryan Caspian has taught me about faith in his love. It happens whenever I start doubting him, whenever I wonder if this lifestyle will last forever, or if he can really keep spreading happiness to our whole family, and our town.

"You're a little late," I tell him, noticing the time.

"Your brother called before I left the office. He wanted to set up the installation next week, and I told him I'd check it out personally after it's done."

"You're crazy if you think anybody can afford to bring a driverless car into his new garage," I say, letting my tongue tease him between my teeth.

"No, not now. But in five, ten years?" he says, pulling my hair again. His fingers always make me yearn for more. "I'm planning for the long-term, Kara-bou. Just like I do with everything. And your brother's graciously decided to set up his business with the first prototypes designed to service the new models."

"Sure, Nostradamus." I stand up, turning our little boy to face his dad. Ryan leans down and kisses his forehead. "It makes me sad to think there probably won't be a part-time job in Lilydale Garage someday. It'll all be robots in fifteen years."

"Babe, he'll do anything he wants, and so will the rest of our children. Love is enough for any future, robots and all," he says, moving in, resting his forehead against mine.

He's there so long I can't help but smile. "I guess. Love, and money, is surely enough."

"Well, there's always plenty of that."

He isn't kidding. His company has exploded the last couple years. It's easily worth another billion, maybe more. I don't obsessively follow the articles anymore, like I used to, when I was settling into my role as a billionaire's wife.

I know how to act in public at his corporate events in Seattle and throughout the U.P. It scared me at first, but I learned to adapt. Every dinner feels more natural, and my smile is real every time I lift my glass for a toast.

Thankfully, amid all the changes, some things stay the same.

In Split Harbor, I'm still just Kara. Not Mrs. Caspian, married to a celebrity. I'm the girl who serves up the best coffee and cherry pie on this slice of Superior shore.

"What'll it be tonight?" I ask. I love that he lets me cook for him, even though we could easily hire a caterer for every meal.

"How about that new Mediterranean recipe you've been wanting to try? We haven't had lamb since Easter." He smiles, taking our baby boy from my arms. Joseph bounces up and down until he cracks a smile and giggles. "We're as rich as most Greek billionaires. Might as well eat like them, too."

I pour him a glass of wine and get to work. He chills on the couch with our little boy, relaxing for ten minutes, before he puts our baby in the play pen and joins me at the counter.

He's humming along with the radio while we chop vegetables. It takes me a few minutes to recognize the song, but when I do, I'm joining him.

It's a miracle I can hum anything through my smile, which couldn't possibly get any wider.

It's *Stairway to Heaven*. The Zeppelin tune that always used to play over the radio in daddy's garage, the same song I remember hearing the day I fell face down in the oil slick, tumbling into the love of my life.

It's taken years to reach this love, this happiness. Time for thousands of songs, just as many tears, and two marriage proposals. Sometimes, like now, it hits me all at once in a giant wave that makes my head spin.

I have to focus, moving the knife on the cutting board, flashing him a smile when I get up to grab something from the refrigerator. His rich blue eyes remind me there's one thing embedded in my mind and in my heart.

I'd marry him again.

I'd do it a thousand times over.

Through tears, through grins, through countless winding years, I love my Ryan. Loved him when he was just the orphan kid working in my father's garage, and when he came home a billionaire, going from heartbreaker to hero before my eyes. I'll love him when he's seventy, everything on his face going silver and pale except those gorgeous blue eyes.

Every day I have on this earth, I'm his alone. I'll still be smiling, wiping away tears, next year when I'm holding our next born or renewing our vows.

Second chances are real. Every hour since embracing mine, I'm reminded how lucky I am.

Thanks!

Want more Nicole Snow? Sign up for my newsletter to hear about new releases, subscriber only goodies, and other fun stuff!

JOIN THE NICOLE SNOW NEWSLETTER! - http://eepurl.com/HwFW1

Thank you so much for buying this book. I hope my romances will brighten your mornings and darken your evenings with total pleasure. Sensuality makes everything more vivid, doesn't it?

If you liked this book, please consider leaving a review and checking out my other erotic romance tales.

Got a comment on my work? Email me at nicolesnowerotica@gmail.com. I love hearing from my fans!

Kisses,
Nicole Snow

More Intense Romance by Nicole Snow

FIGHT FOR HER HEART

BIG BAD DARE: TATTOOS AND SUBMISSION

MERCILESS LOVE: A DARK ROMANCE

LOVE SCARS: BAD BOY'S BRIDE

RECKLESSLY HIS: A BAD BOY MAFIA ROMANCE

STEPBROTHER CHARMING:
A BILLIONAIRE BAD BOY ROMANCE

STEPBROTHER UNSEALED:
A BAD BOY MILITARY ROMANCE

PRINCE WITH BENEFITS:
A BILLIONAIRE ROYAL ROMANCE

Outlaw Love/Prairie Devils MC Books

OUTLAW KIND OF LOVE

NOMAD KIND OF LOVE

SAVAGE KIND OF LOVE

WICKED KIND OF LOVE

BITTER KIND OF LOVE

Grizzlies MC Books

OUTLAW'S KISS

OUTLAW'S OBSESSION

OUTLAW'S BRIDE

OUTLAW'S VOW

Deadly Pistols MC Books

NEVER LOVE AN OUTLAW

NEVER KISS AN OUTLAW

NEVER HAVE AN OUTLAW'S BABY

NEVER WED AN OUTLAW

SEXY SAMPLES:
PRINCE WITH BENEFITS

I: Tripped Up (Erin)

"Look, I know American reporters, and their little interns. I've worked with plenty. You think you can get away with anything as soon as the cameras roll, but let me remind you again. We have rules. No flash, no interruptions, and absolutely *no* unauthorized social media. His Highness keeps a very strict media presence, and it's my privilege to enforce it."

How I stopped myself from rolling my eyes at this pompous, self-absorbed bitch, I'll never know.

Serena Hastings flips her long blonde hair back, giving me the stink eye one last time, before she moves through the gaggle of media and finally takes her seat.

Eyeballing the stage, I'm wondering if I made a huge mistake taking my summer off campus to come to Saint Moore.

It's my father's crowning career achievement, though. An interview with Prince Silas Erik Bearington the Third.

It isn't hard to understand dad's excitement. It's taken his whole life to get here, and I'm just along for the ride. A very hellish, testing-my-patience-every-damned-day kind of ride.

From the brutal jet lag flying from LA across the

Atlantic, to the correspondence dinners where I have to be on my best behavior to avoid embarrassing him, to the constant entourage around the palace who think they're sent by God…sweet Jesus.

Now, I'm sitting here in these stupid heels that are *way* too tight, wishing for a miracle. What comes next dwarfs *everything.*

Don't worry, dad said. He told me he'd show me how it's done. I wanted to follow in his footsteps, didn't I?

When the lighting adjusts and a hot, narrow beam shines on my face, pulling sweat from my pores, I really have to wonder what the hell I've gotten myself into.

Of course, dad isn't even sweating before his interview with Prince Playboy himself begins. Yes, *that* Prince.

The twenty-something, six foot and then some giant who's scandalized several continents. The Prince who's brought the tabloids and dirty blogs more gossip than a hundred celebrity wardrobe malfunctions.

He, who my friends used to swoon over during late night truth-or-dare sessions in our freshmen year dorm, putting him at the top of most eligible celeb bachelors they'd love to have between the sheets. A man I've never been able to stand, much less crush on. A living argument against any country having kings and Queens in modern times, when all they're likely to get out of it are media scoundrels.

Prince Charming, Prince Skirt Chaser, Prince Hung, and a thousand other names.

The Prince, the bastard, the legend.

Silas.

"One minute, Mister Warwick!" the camera man shouts to my father as he climbs up onto the stage, taking one of the two empty chairs beneath the halo.

The other, with the gold and burgundy back, is reserved for the devil himself. I wonder if he's going to walk into this interview late, and throw my dad one more complication.

That would be just like him, wouldn't it? It's not like he takes this Prince thing seriously. It's just the world's biggest license to be a dick, to drink and fuck himself stupid every chance he gets. That's what the blogs have told me, anyway.

None of it fazes dad, ever the professional. He sits up there in his finest suit, his silver hair slicked back, the same prim smile on his lips that I've seen him use in a hundred interviews growing up.

Game time. It's the look that makes me wonder if I'm really cut out to follow in his footsteps. He's wearing the calm, measured, controlled mask I've tried to don before, and failed every time.

I don't have to wonder long because there's new commotion surging through the room. The door off to the side opens, and in walks four strong men in designer suits, the Bearington family crest pinned to their lapels in royal purple and gold. It's a double-headed eagle holding a crown.

A taller, younger, stronger man steps out between them. They part like water, making way for His Highness.

My heart skips a beat. It's him. For real.

Prince Silas, arriving in all his smug, unwavering, damnably sexy glory.

Okay, so maybe the SOB really is what they say in the looks department. If I had any doubt, it's blown to pieces, now that he's quickly stepping toward the stage, taking the five stairs up in two big strides.

My father stands respectfully, extending a hand. The Prince takes it, towering over him by nearly a whole foot, and dad isn't a short guy.

"Charmed, Mister Warwick." The Prince has that foreign, not-quite-English accent everybody in the kingdom does, except his is somehow thicker, more refined.

"It's my honor, Your Highness. I've been looking forward to this for a long time," dad says, nodding.

"Twenty seconds!" Another cameraman roars out, flinching for a second in the hopes that his interruption hasn't upset the Prince.

Based on what I've read, I don't think that's even possible. Nothing upsets him. He basks in every scandal and fresh jab the media takes at him like they're triumphs.

They both take their seats across from each other. I can't believe they look so casual, like it's the most natural thing in the world, when there's so much on the line.

If dad pulls this off, he's going to be seen by billions over the next week. Serena, bitch that she is, has reminded us since day one that the Royal Press Corps is looking for a new American correspondent. And with rumors swirling about how much longer Queen Marina will continue to rule before passing the crown to her grandson, my father could be front and center at the Bearington's wild court for a very long time to come.

As for the Prince, it's his time to shine with something besides his dick. It's no secret the world's been holding its breath, waiting for him to shape up, and act like a statesman for one of the wealthiest countries in the world. A future King.

Saint Moore is virtually the last monarchy in Europe where the ruler is more than just a figurehead. For fifty years, Queen Marina has rallied her country to good causes and swayed more than a few votes in their parliament, even if she's been very respectful of democracy.

As for Prince Hung – who knows? He's taken his pleasure demonstrating all the things he'll do with modern day concubines throwing themselves at him. Not politics.

"Five…four…three…two…one…"

Cameras roll. Dad looks into the closest one confidently, and begins to speak.

"Welcome to this special edition of the Warwick Report, ladies and gentleman. Today, I'm coming to you from the Kingdom of Saint Moore, where I'm sitting down with a man who needs no introduction." He pauses, three seconds, just long enough to let everybody tuning in remember the insanity that surrounds everything Silas. "Prince Silas Erik Bearington, heir to the island's throne, one of the most powerful, scandalized, and adventurous men in the world."

"Tom, you flatter me too much," Silas says, that wicked smirk above his chiseled jaw pointing up like pitchfork ends. "Let's get it on, shall we?"

"Absolutely, Your Highness," dad says. If he's rattled at all by the Prince's need to control the conversation, he doesn't show it. "You're recently back in the kingdom after completing your duty in the Royal Marines, serving in Afghanistan. Tell me, sir, how has that experience changed you? I think everyone was surprised to hear about a Bearington Prince flying into an active combat zone. Thankfully, on our side, this time."

The Prince smiles. Smug as ever, but a little darkly.

"Yes, we always did like to play both sides, up until the Second World War. It's been good for me, Tom. Reminds me why I'm really here, next in line to the crown, how fortunate I am to be born into this royal lineage. There's pride in serving a man's kingdom, and beyond. I'd never imagined Afghanistan until I stepped foot there. Some truly awful circumstances, just beyond our borders. Life and death. War. Poverty. Terrorism. A lot more exciting than who's wearing last year's style at the next big charity ball, I'm sure you can imagine. Also, a much bigger challenge for me, and I *love* those."

"Oh, yes," dad says, returning the Prince's smile. "They called you a hero in the press after Kandahar. Said you single-handedly thwarted a terrorist attack on an allied base, saving your own troops and dozens more from several different countries, including the United States. What really happened?"

"Please. The media embellishes everything." Silas shakes his head, waving it all away, pushing his stern hand through the air. The perfectly tailored gray suit he's wearing fits him like a glove, exposing more of that powerful body each time he moves, even subtly. "I gave the orders, sure, as soon as I saw them creeping up on our base. Still took everyone in uniform that day to stop the attack, to swarm out and hit them at the right moment, before the suicide bomber could plow through the main gate and do God knows what."

Dad straightens in his seat. I can tell by the look on his face that things are about to get serious. The tension in the palace room thickens, and even the ornate ceilings soaring into the air can't hold it.

God, I wish I'd picked different shoes. These heels are totally *strangling* me now.

"That's a very modest account for those who know you, Your Highness," dad says. "Some might say unnaturally modest. More like the kind of attitude a future King should have, rather than the playboy Prince."

"Look, Tom, we all know what's bound to happen one day. Truth is, any talk about it now is shoveling Her Majesty in her grave while she's still very much alive and kicking ass." Prince Silas pauses, the dimples in his cheeks deepening. He knows he's about to blow his carefully crafted tact.

Several people behind me suppress snickers. A woman coughs. I'm trying to pay attention to the interview, read dad's body language, to see how he's going to handle things if they take a nasty turn.

But damn, I can't take my eyes off Silas' face. Those deep blue eyes of his betray nothing, perfect royal compliments to his dark black hair, and a day's worth of shadowy stubble on his chin that probably makes every woman in the room wonder what it feels like against their skin.

Myself included. *Shamefully.*

"Certainly, Your Highness. We all hope Queen Marina will be around for another hundred years, but you and I both know what's realistic." Dad pauses, the confident smile on his face disappearing.

He swallows something hard in his throat. "Frankly, you have people in your own kingdom saying you may be the last Prince, and your grandmother could well be its final Queen. They want a referendum once she's gone. That could mean trouble in a time when royals are an endangered species all over Europe, and indeed, the world. Let me just come out and ask – are you trying to *save* the monarchy?"

"Really, Tom? You think my bloodline needs saving from a joke protest movement like Republic First?" Silas' dark blue eyes storm angry, full of disbelief. "The Bearingtons have ruled this island for over a thousand years. We'll do it again for a thousand more, when we can all drive across bridges to Scotland and Iceland. We've kept our people safe in war and guided them into the modern age with wealth, class, and good sense. I know that might be difficult for someone like you to understand, when your own government has barely been around for three hundred years."

Dad's chest swells as he quietly inhales a big breath. He sinks back in his chair, his hands tightly folded in his lap, staring at the Prince.

Oh, God. What's going on? He isn't...offended? No, too unprofessional.

But I've never seen him shaken in an interview like this.

I can't believe it's happening because he's face-to-face with this Royal Prick.

Prince Silas senses it, too. The tension in his face softens, and he looks at my father, cocking his head ever-so-slightly. "Tom, you're just asking the tough questions, and I appreciate it. That's why I agreed to this interview personally. Let's move on, shall we? You've got plenty of ammo left, I'm sure. Ask me about the latest supermodel I'm bedding, or the hot new custom sports car I've added to my stable. I just broke in one of those things yesterday. We both know how history and politics gets damned boring."

Silas has a huge grin on his face. I can't tell if he's joking, trying to ease the tension, or if he's just in a mad rush to deflect more questions about the kingdom's future.

Dad doesn't give up that easily, even when his subject is getting pissed. I wonder if he'll press on with the same questions, or circle back to them later, after he's probed the bastard Prince a little more.

For the first time in my life, I'm not sure who'll crack first.

He doesn't do either. Instead, he grabs the sides of his chair, his hands visibly shaking.

Jesus. Something's wrong.

Stiffening in my seat, I watch him lean forward, reaching for something that isn't there. The shadows shift around him, changing the bright light.

For the first time, I notice he's completely drenched in sweat, the collar around his jacket stained wet.

Time to panic. Several murmurs run through the crowd.

The Prince stands up at the same time I do, and he sees me, several rows behind the other journalists. Our eyes lock for one intense second. We share our confusion, dismay, and utter shock before dad rolls out of his chair and goes crashing down on the podium.

Everybody jumps out of their seat, searching for a better view, chattering away. Cameras snap, hyenas feasting on daddy's suffering. Several swarms of guards flood the stage, surrounding my father and the Prince, one carrying a small white box with a red cross on its side.

I can't see what's happening. My heart races, and I try to push forward, shuffling through the purple rope separating the media from the interview stage.

The kingdom's official cameras have got to be off by now. Even if they aren't, it's too late to worry about embarrassing myself or my dad any further, when he's up there seizing up, sick or dying or maybe both.

I don't bother with the tiny staircase. I move right past it before anybody can notice and haul me away. My hands clench the edge of the podium, and I pull myself up, cursing the skirt I'm wearing for tangling up when my leg finally gets enough leverage.

Somehow, I manage it, without getting yanked away by the guard. My eyes turn to dad and the little crowd hunched around him, barking orders back and forth in that rich, regal accent that's becoming chalkboard on my ears.

"Hurry, boys, hoist him up! Get this man the hell out of here. I want an ambulance out front in the next sixty seconds."

No, I can't just stare. I have to move.

One step forward, and my fucking heel catches on the stage's edge, throwing me backward. It's a long enough fall to do some damage if I slip, so I throw my weight forward.

I don't know what's worse. The fact that my dad is having a stroke or a heart attack right in front of me, or that these stupid, *stupid* shoes are twisting my ankle, sending me crashing to the floor next to him.

There's no time to brace for impact. Next thing I know, I'm falling, face first into the podium's hard black surface. I wonder if I'll get to share a room at the hospital with dad when I break something.

But I don't hit the surface. Something catches me, yanks me back, saving me from hitting the floor.

Make that two big somethings.

Hands. Thick, strong, determined, and locked around me.

Blinking back the dizzying confusion, I open my eyes. Prince Silas' dark blue irises widen when they see my face.

Like my heart wasn't already beating a hundred miles an hour. I'm lost for words.

Any words.

He's holding me in his arms like we've just done the last move in a fiery dance. His fingers press into my skin, tense and surprised, but completely unshaken. In control.

What the hell does a woman say when she's literally been swept off her feet by one of the most powerful, handsome, and arrogant men in the world? A man I'd scoffed at every time he showed up in the tabloids or in clickbait on the web?

The Prince, the heir to the throne, who's probably laid the female population of a small country. The Prince, with those ridiculously deep, beautiful blue eyes that are always saying *fuck me.*

And right now, they're trained on me.

Me, Erin Warwick. Intern. Nobody. Damsel in distress.

She, with the worst heels in the world. Him, with the icy, dominating eyes a woman could lose herself in forever.

"That's my father!" I stammer, trying to explain, hoping I'm not about to get tasered and thrown to the floor when the royal guards catch up to me.

"Don't move, love," he says, never breaking eye contact. "Everything's going to be fine."

Easy for you to say, I want to tell him. But I can't find the words.

Everything starts spinning again. This time, it's got nothing to do with the crappy shoes. I'm on the verge of blacking out.

"Stay with me," Prince Silas growls, his fingers pressing harder in my skin.

Dad groans, several feet away, reminding me why I'm up here, mysteriously thrown into a Prince's arms by my own clumsiness in these God forsaken heels. They're starting to move him.

Wait, damn it – dad! I have to follow him. I have to –

I never get a chance to do anything. The guards I've been expecting surround us, but the Prince holds one hand up, telling them to stand down. His hands tighten on me one last time.

One on my shoulder. One against my lower back, holding me up, helping me back on my feet.

"See that she has a ride to the Royal hospital, and wherever she'd like to go after that," Silas snaps, looking away from me at last.

I'm barely able to stand on my own without collapsing again. Thankfully, I don't have to support my own weight for long.

"Right this way, madame."

Several guards tug sternly, but gently on my arms, leading me down the stairs, right behind the entourage that's ferrying dad away.

Just a few minutes later, I'm outside the palace, led down the hundred marble steps, and into one of the sleek black sedans below. A man sits next to me in the back. The driver stomps the gas as soon as my seat belt is on, without saying a word.

I'm grateful for the silence. I hate it, too, because it lets me think. Exactly what I can't afford to do just yet.

I won't let myself comprehend what a complete disaster this is until I know dad's going to be okay.

* * * *

A couple hours go by just waiting. Then, I'm in his room, staring at my father laying feebly in bed. It's a tiny, clean, white chamber. Sterile looking. Maybe just a little more stylish than the bland, depressing places I'd find back home in LA.

Nobody ever said the kingdom didn't have a great

medical system. Its reforms and upgrades were personally encouraged by Her Majesty, whose reign has always turned a lot of attention to her subjects' health and wellness.

That's what the Wikipedia article says, anyway, something I lazily gloss over while I wait for dad to wake up.

His hand feels so cold in mine. Whatever they've given him, he's out like a light.

It's early morning the next day, and I haven't slept a wink. We're both waiting for the initial test results to come in.

They've checked his heart, done several x-rays, and determined there's no need for immediate surgery. I'm not sure if that's good news, or a sign there's something worse lurking in his system. Something much harder to fix.

Morning light drifts over us, somber as it is bright. I'm starting to drift off myself, when dad finally groans. He sits up while my grip tightens on his hand, easing him awake.

"Christ. Feels like I got hit by a damned freight train. How long was I out, Erin?"

I shrug. "All night. It's early morning now."

Dad reaches up, running a shaky hand across his face. About a second later, his eyes stretch huge, and suddenly his fingers tangle around mine.

"The interview – shit!" He pauses, like it takes the full horror several seconds to set in. "I blew it, didn't I? Jesus Christ."

"Don't think about that now, daddy!" I lean in, stroking his fingers, kissing him softly on the forehead. "You need to get some more rest. There'll be plenty of time to sort out what happened later with the palace, I'm sure."

I hate having to lie to him.

He knows damn well nobody gets second chances in this business after a meltdown like that.

Maybe the Warwick name will salvage his career, carrying him to new prospects. But as far as I'm concerned, we probably won't hear a word from the royals, except when they're going to send us on our merry way with impersonal wishes for good health.

"Fuck." Dad slumps back in his bed, pulling his hand from mine. The IV in his arm stretches as he rubs his eyes.

My heart sinks like a stone. He isn't really…crying…is he?

Oh, God.

"Dad, no," I say gently, wondering if there's any combination of words to ease the dagger cutting through him. "Work doesn't matter. You have to get well. That's the only thing worth worrying about right now. Whatever else is on your mind, forget it. Don't let it take over. Turn it off. You're a smart man. You'll bounce back from this…all of it. You've got more experience and connections than anybody else in this business. The world won't end just because you need a little time off, I promise. Dad, I –"

"Erin…" he cuts in, a defeated expression turning his face gray. "Shut up."

I do.

Hell, I don't know what else to do. I've never seen him like this.

His rudeness hurts, but I try not to let it get to me. Standing up, I walk toward the window, staring out into the early sunrise.

The hospital overlooks a ragged shore, where the wind sends foamy waves crashing against the rocks. My hands become fists at my sides, and the only thing that keeps running through my mind is that I have to forgive him.

He isn't in his right mind.

He's hurting.

We don't even know what's wrong.

I won't let myself cry – not even when I hear him gently snoring again after a couple minutes pass.

Holding in tears is worse than anger. They sting my eyes, my soul, make me question everything about why I'm standing in this foreign hospital after watching my father's career self-destruct, waiting to find out how much longer we need to stay here before we jet back to the States, completely humiliated.

There's a TV in the corner. It's been muted since the moment I stepped in, and now the early morning programs are starting. I see two prim reporters at their desks, smiling, going through the latest news on the continent.

Another bailout coming in the Eurozone. Something about nuclear security in Belgium, and then a thirty second segment on military drills near the Russian border.

Then another headline. The one that twists the knot in my belly and the rock in my throat at once without mercy.

BOMBSHELL INTERVIEW! PRINCE GOES FROM HOT WATER TO HERO!

Turning nervously to make sure dad's still asleep, I look up at the screen, that anger in my eyes beginning to pour out in hot, salty streams down my cheeks.

I see it all again.

The painful look on dad's face before he rolled out of his chair, collapsing in front of the Prince.

The swarm of security and paramedics. Panic. Commotion.

A flash of myself jumping onto the stage, my hair a mess, lunging to save myself from toppling off the ledge. I'm less than a foot from planting the ground face first when Prince Silas grabs me, jerks me up, straight into his arms.

Jesus, it looks even more picture perfect seeing it in the third person, like something from a movie. They didn't bother capturing anything after that, the long, awkward stare between us, how I gazed into his deep blue eyes.

The footage cuts off. I storm over to the TV, lean up on my tippy toes, careful not to let these overly tight heels screw me over again. I punch the off button, without bothering to give the other dramas and kids shows from Saint Moore and Europe a chance to take the edge off.

I'm pissed. Hurt. Worried.

Scared.

There's another chair in the corner, and that's where I park my unsettled ass for what seems like the next hour. I wish to God I hadn't flipped on that stupid program.

I should be thinking about dad, brushing off his outburst.

Instead, I'm thinking about the Prince. The first and last

time I'll ever be close to him. The way he held me – firm, but gentle. Almost like a decent man should.

Sure, the media was eating up the drama, recasting it as a heroic spectacle.

I wasn't fooled. Even utter bastards can be gentleman in the right time, right place.

Hell, I wouldn't be surprised if Silas drove off the second we were gone, straight to his little mistresses. Maybe that flashy club for royalty and multimillionaires he owns, the one I've read about on the trashy blogs, hosting parties for the most eligible supermodels in Europe.

His own private hunting grounds for sex.

My hand reaches for my phone. I'm about to pull it up, and read more gossip about Prince Not-So-Charming for reasons I don't even understand, when the door pops open. The noise wakes dad, and he groans, sitting up in bed while the visitor enters.

A tall man in a white coat with salt and pepper hair steps in. "Ah, you must be Miss Warwick, I presume. So glad you're here so I can update you both on the news. I'm Doctor Jameson."

The physician rounds the bed, standing next to dad, and begins pulling something from a manila folder. I'm studying his face. It isn't hard to notice the complete lack of any pleasantries or warmth.

He's serious business. And serious is never good when it comes to medicine.

"Mister Warwick, there's no easy way to say this, so I'm just going to come out with it. We've found a shadow near your pancreas in scans."

My ears start ringing, and his voice fades out. *A shadow? A shadow?! What the hell does that mean?*

"Shadow?" My dad repeats, just as confused as me.

The doctor holds up three x-rays on a sheet, and begins going through them, pointing at the areas in question.

"Yes, an unusual growth, of sorts. Not benign. We'll know for certain once your labs come back. Regardless, it's something we'll need to deal with shortly." The doctor pauses, straightens his spectacles, before he goes on. "Regrettably, it's near a nerve cluster that's likely to cause intense nausea and a shock to the system that stresses the heart. That's why you had the attack yesterday. The good news is, it's fully operable. I'm recommending surgery soon, once you decide whether you'd like to have it done here in Saint Moore, or back home."

"Home," dad says, without a second's hesitation. "Don't want to spend a second longer on this damned island than I really need to."

Doctor Jameson's face tightens. Dad gives him a sour look and mutters an apology.

"It's okay. He's been under a lot of stress," I say weakly, looking at the physician.

"Yes, yes, I understand. Well, the two of you ought to talk things over and try your very best to remain calm. We'll have more news for you this evening. Assuming this isn't anything to *really* be concerned about beyond the surgery, we can have it done in under a week, wherever you choose. The Warwick Report can be back on the air in no time at all."

"No, I'm taking time off," dad snaps, his eyes going dark. "Whatever the outlook here."

I want to reach out, squeeze his shoulder, but I know him too well. He's always been so high strung, the sort of man who has zero tolerance for failure.

"And if there's more to worry about?" I ask, fighting to ignore the sickly feeling building deep in my stomach.

"We'll deal with that scenario when it's on the table." He collects the x-rays and shoves them back in his folder. "I have some other business to attend to. Rest assured, Miss Warwick, your father is getting the very best care here. Not just because it's our duty, but because His Highness himself has requested extra attention to detail."

"The Prince?" I squeak, doing a double take. "Why?"

"I don't know. He didn't divulge any further details, madame. He's requested nothing but the best to handle your father's case by name. Since I'm at the top of this field available at the royal medical center, well, here I am. Suffice it to say, His Highness cares very greatly about all his guests, and he's deeply sorry for the trouble your father ran into the other day."

"Trouble my ass." Dad snorts, tips his nose up, and rolls over, facing away from both of us. "He can't possibly be more sorry than I am. Believe me."

"If you'll excuse me…" Doctor Jameson looks at the door awkwardly.

I nod, and he's gone without another word.

As soon as he's out, I take the chair next to the bed. Dad never turns around to face me, drifting off yet again after a few minutes.

I don't know if I should be grateful he's getting his rest, or worried about his dark attitude.

Just now, my own exhaustion catches up to me. Turning in the chair, I tuck my head against the back, and close my eyes.

Prince Silas Bearington, and the fact that he might know me by name, is the last thing on my mind.

* * * *

I don't have a clue how long I'm asleep. It seems like evening by the time I'm awakened by a light tap on the shoulder.

Looking up, I see Doctor Jameson standing over me, his face more grim than before. "Miss Warwick, could I speak to you outside for a moment, please?"

"Of course," I say, looking down at dad, still fast asleep in his nest of tubes and bedding.

I follow him out and watch as he closes the door gently behind us. We're alone in the long corridor, where it's eerily quiet. I take one look at his face and know I'm about to get bombed.

"What is it? What's wrong?" My heart moves ten times faster than my lips, pure adrenaline in every pulse.

"Your father's growth is cancerous, Miss Warwick. A rare, aggressive cancer. Very difficult to eradicate in this area. Something I've never seen." He pauses, as if he needs to stoke his bedside manner, to prevent cold scientific fascination from taking over. "I'm very sorry."

That's it then. Cancer.

What was that word he used again? *Aggressive?*

I'm devastated.

Or else, I should be. The weird thing is, I just feel numb, standing there underneath the bright white lights overhead while the doctor waits for some kind of reaction.

"How does this change things?" I ask softly.

"He'll need additional treatment, of course. If it were up to me, I'd recommend a full round of chemotherapy immediately after surgery, a regimen we call…"

I'm listening, but all the terminology washes over me. So does the pain, the disappointment, the sad realization our nightmare isn't over. I thought the worst was behind us when dad collapsed during his interview, and I fell into the royal bad boy's arms.

No, it's only beginning. I couldn't be more wrong.

"Let me assure you once again, Miss Warwick, your father is more than welcome to make full use of our facilities and expertise. We have plenty of experience working with American insurance. But just between you and me…" He pauses, looking around, and leans in when he's sure nobody else is around. "I told you this is rare. We have our own research wing, yes, and we're doing well, all things considered. However…we can't make miracles happen. If it were me, I'd go abroad. Opt for something more experimental. Only the best of the best."

Experimental? Abroad? Obviously, he's used to dealing with billionaire royals who never think twice about their finances. Even more obvious he doesn't have as much experience working with insurance as he let on.

Despite his success, daddy isn't a rich man.

He's done well as a journalist, sure. He's comfortable. But his last divorce took him to the cleaners not so long ago.

He barely has the money for globe trekking and time off if he wants to keep his condo. Let alone for things like experimental treatments abroad.

"I don't know if we can afford it," I say, trying to stop the anger from creeping into my voice.

Doctor Jameson cocks his head, quickly scratching his nose. He looks at me like I've lost my mind.

I still can't believe it. How a perfectly normal trip, the highlight of dad's career, has turned into *this*.

"Well, you certainly don't have to decide now, Miss Warwick," the doctor says reassuringly. "You have time – a little time – before any difficult decisions need to be made. Know that they *do* need to be decided in a timely manner, though. As soon as you're able, if I'm frank. The quicker you move against this sort of the thing, the better his chances."

God. The people on this island all seem to have a way with being 'frank.' They're too honest, everybody from Prince Playboy to his subjects, and always in that haughty not-quite-English accent that makes me want to slap them across the face.

You can't get angry, I tell myself. *For dad's sake.*

"I understand," I lie, right before a new worry takes over. "Should I tell him the news?"

"No, no, that's my responsibility," he says, surprise flashing in his eyes. "We'll let him rest awhile longer. I'll make the rounds later today, and inform him when he's awake. Better to get the shock out of the way so both of you can begin running through your options in earnest. I'll bring you more details about the experimental option, if you'd like. Now, if you'll excuse me..."

You have no idea. I'd love to excuse you, Doctor Dick, and this whole stupid, pompous island.

I'd love to excuse my father's cancer, his heartbreak, and these brutal heels still attached to my feet.

Raw emotion paralyzes me while he disappears down the hallway, leaving me alone.

Slumping against the wall, I try to hang onto the anger, the frustration. It's the only thing that's stopping me from breaking down into an ugly crying fit right here.

That's twice as hard to hold back when I realize just how achingly alone I'm about to be. More lonely than I've ever been in my entire life once dad starts to go through treatment.

Not to mention if it doesn't work. If, God forbid...

No, I won't let myself think the rest.

I won't let myself cry.

I definitely won't let the scream I'm holding in out, even though it's tearing me to pieces.

Several people walk past, nurses holding charts, slinging medical jargon back and forth. It's just another day for them, and why shouldn't it be?

They belong in this twisted fairytale kingdom where even the Prince is bad when he isn't playing hero for the cameras.

I want to go home. I want to help dad get well. And then, I never want to hear about Saint Moore or any of the royal assholes running this place ever again.

They've brought nothing but terrible luck into our lives.

When I finally force myself to move, retreating to his room, my right foot is so numb it almost drags across the floor. My heel catches, and I barely stop myself from tripping yet again.

I have to be more careful. I definitely need to pick some better shoes.

There's no Prince waiting for me if I stumble again. And there damned sure isn't a glass slipper at the end of all this suffering. There's no reward, no magic, except my father's survival.

I'll do anything to make sure he's got a fighting chance.

GET *PRINCE WITH BENEFITS* AT YOUR FAVORITE RETAILER!

Printed in Great Britain
by Amazon